REQUIEM FOR THE RIPPER

THE STUDY IN RED TRILOGY BOOK 3

BRIAN L PORTER

Copyright (C) 2020 Brian L Porter

Layout design and Copyright (C) 2020 by Next Chapter

Published 2020 by Gumshoe – A Next Chapter Imprint

Edited by Debbie Poole

Cover art by Cover Mint

This book is a work of fiction. Names, characters, places, and incidents are the product of the author's imagination or are used fictitiously. Any resemblance to actual events, locales, or persons, living or dead, is purely coincidental.

All rights reserved. No part of this book may be reproduced or transmitted in any form or by any means, electronic or mechanical, including photocopying, recording, or by any information storage and retrieval system, without the author's permission.

'Requiem for The Ripper' is dedicated to the memory of Enid Ann Porter, (1914 – 2004). Her belief in me and my work never wavered even though she never lived to see the first book in publication, and to Juliet, who provides the help and support without which none of my books would ever be completed.

And to Sasha xxxx

ACKNOWLEDGEMENTS 2020

When the original publisher of my Jack the Ripper trilogy ceased trading in 2020, I feared that the books would sink without trace without a publisher behind them. However, I approached Miika Hannila, CEO of Next Chapter, who have published my work for the last eight years hoping he would be interested in publishing new editions of the three Ripper books, plus Pestilence, also previously published by my Canadian publisher. To my delight, Miika was more than happy to offer to publish new updated versions of the books, which will bring all my books under the umbrella of a single publisher. Next Chapter's art department has been responsible for the terrific new cover designs for the four books which I'm delighted with, so I owe a big thank you to Miika and the team at Next Chapter.

I have to thank my researcher and proof reader Debbie Poole who as always, does her best to keep my work precise and accurate.

As always, my dear wife Juliet has played her part as she

does for every book in providing me with her support and advice as the new edition took shape.

It wouldn't be fair to omit the original acknowledgements from the first publication of the book as the people mentioned below all played a part in helping me bring my fictional trilogy to print.

ACKNOWLEDGMENTS 2010

Requiem for the Ripper is the final part of my fictional trilogy based on the gruesome Jack the Ripper murders, committed in the space of a few short weeks during the autumn of 1888 in Whitechapel, London. Over the years, much debate and research has taken place in an attempt to identify and name the man responsible for those killings. So far, no authoritative answer has been provided and the mystery of who Jack the Ripper's identity remains just that, a mystery.

My own research for this book and those that preceded it was helped along the way by a number of people without whose help the final book could not have appeared.

My thanks are therefore due to my fellow members of the Jack The Ripper Forums.com for their help and support, in particular to Howard Brown and Mike Covell, and also to the members of The Whitechapel Society 1888, who took the trouble to invite me to judge their first short story contest during 2009.

Science fiction author Carole Gill joined my group of critique readers, which includes publisher Graeme S Houston and my lovely wife Juliet, and my thanks go to all who have helped with their critique and comments during the writing of 'Requiem'. Without their continued support and occasional inspirational ideas, the finished article might not be quite so 'finished'.

Finally, to all who have read and enjoyed the first two books in the trilogy, I pass on my thanks, for giving me the will and the inspiration to go on and complete this final episode.

INTRODUCTION TO THE STUDY IN RED

Requiem for The Ripper is the third and final part of the trilogy of novels that began with *A Study in Red – The Secret Journal of Jack the Ripper*, which was followed by *Legacy of The Ripper*. For anyone unfamiliar with the first two books the following introductory pages give a brief outline of the first two books, and will I hope add to the reading pleasure of this, the third and final part of the trilogy.

A STUDY IN RED - THE SECRET JOURNAL OF JACK THE RIPPER

Following the death of his father, psychiatrist Robert Cavendish is bequeathed a set of papers and a strange age-yellowed journal. As he unpacks and begins to read the papers he is astounded to discover that he is holding the journal of the infamous Whitechapel Murderer who stalked the streets of the East End of London in the autumn of 1888. The pages are warm to the touch, and a force of great malevolence seems to guide Robert's journey through the mists of time as he is transported by the words upon the pages into the mind, and the world of the one and only Jack the Ripper! His mind begins to feel the pull of another time, another place, as images of the Ripper's crimes fill his thoughts and Robert is beset by waking nightmares of such sadistic and terrible bloodletting that he begins to doubt his sanity. As he delves further and further into the demented world of the killer Robert begins to sense that his family has been hiding a terrible secret for over a century, a secret that he knows will only be revealed when he completes the task of reading 'The Secret Journal of Jack the Ripper'.

An Excerpt

The London of the 1880s differed greatly from the city of today. Poverty and wealth existed side by side, the defining line between the two often marked only by the turning of a corner, from the well-lit suburban streets of the middle-classes and the wealthy, to the seedy, crime and rat infested slums, where poverty, homelessness, desperation and deprivation walked hand in hand with drunkenness, immorality, and crime most foul. In the teeming slums of the city by night the most commonly heard cry in the darkness was thought to be that of 'Murder!' So inured were the people who lived amongst such squalor and amidst the fever of criminal intimidation that it is said, in time, no-one took any notice of such cries.

It was into this swirling maelstrom of vice and human degradation, London's East End, that there appeared a malevolent force, a merciless killer who stalked the mean streets by night in search of his prey and gave the great metropolis that was London its first taste of the now increasingly common phenomenon, the serial killer! The streets of Whitechapel were to become the stalking ground of that mysterious and as yet still unidentified slayer known to history as 'Jack the Ripper!'

AN EXTRACT FROM THE JOURNAL

Blood, beautiful, thick, rich, red, venous blood.
    Its colour fills my eyes, its scent assaults my nostrils,
    Its taste hangs sweetly on my lips.
    Last night once more the voices called to me,

And I did venture forth, their bidding, their unholy quest to undertake.

Through mean, gas lit, fog shrouded streets, I wandered in the night, selected, struck, with flashing blade,

And oh, how the blood did run, pouring out upon the street, soaking through the cobbled cracks, spurting, like a fountain of pure red.

Viscera leaking from ripped red gut, my clothes assumed the smell of freshly butchered meat. The squalid, dark, street shadows beckoned, and under leaning darkened eaves, like a wraith I disappeared once more into the cheerless night,

The bloodlust of the voices again fulfilled, for a while...

They will call again, and I once more will prowl the streets upon the night,

The blood will flow like a river once again.

Beware all those who would stand against the call,

I shall not be stopped or taken, no, not I.

Sleep fair city, while you can, while the voices within are still,

I am resting, but my time shall come again. I shall rise in a glorious bloodfest,

I shall taste again the fear as the blade slices sharply through yielding flesh,

when the voices raise the clarion call, and my time shall come again.

So I say again, good citizens, sleep, for there will be a next time...

To my dearest nephew, Jack,

This testament, the journal, and all the papers that

accompany it are yours upon my death, as they became mine upon my father's death. Aunt Sarah, and I were never fortunate enough to have children of our own, so it is with a heavy heart that I write this note to accompany these pages. Had I any alternative, I would spare you the curse of our family's deepest secret, or perhaps I should say, secrets! Having read what you are about to read, I had neither the courage to destroy it, nor to reveal the secrets contained within these pages. I beg you, as my father begged me, to read the journal and the notes that go with it, and be guided by your conscience and your intelligence in deciding what course of action to take when you have done so. Whatever you decide to do, dear nephew, I beg you, do not judge those who have gone before you too harshly, for the curse of the journal you are about to read is as real as these words I now write to you.

Be safe, Jack, but be warned.

Your loving uncle,
Robert

LEGACY OF THE RIPPER

JACK THOMAS REID, nephew of Robert Cavendish who first appeared in A Study in Red - The Secret Journal of Jack the Ripper, languishes in the secure Ravenswood Psychiatric Hospital, sentenced to confinement 'at Her Majesty's Pleasure' for a series of apparent 'Jack the Ripper' copycat killings in the picturesque English coastal resort of Brighton. Jack's defence at his trial, that he is a descendant of Jack the Ripper and that the crimes were conducted by an unknown 'mystery man' and that Jack had been drugged and made to appear as the killer came to be regarded as so preposterous and unbelievable that his sentence was never in doubt. When one of the policemen who conducted the original investigation into the murders begins to doubt the truth of the case against Reid, Sergeant George Wright and Ripperologist Alice Nickels begin an investigation into his story. What they find is told through the voice of Doctor Ruth Truman, Jack's psychiatrist at Ravenswood, and through a series of events that take place as far afield as the beautiful island of Malta and in Warsaw, Poland. Slowly but surely and with the help of Wright's boss, Inspector Mike

Holland, the link between the events that shocked and terrorised Whitechapel over a century ago, and their link with the case of Jack Thomas Reid and the 'Legacy of Jack the Ripper' is revealed.

An Excerpt

My Name is Jack, A Statement by the Patient.

When did it start? That's what they all want to know. Doctor Ruth is always asking me:

"When did it start? What are your earliest recollections of these feelings?"

I keep telling her the same as I'm telling you all now. It's hard to put a time or a place on when it began, though I was young, incredibly young, maybe four or five years old when I first realised I was 'different' to other children of my age. Even then I knew that my life was mapped out ahead of me, that I had a destiny to fulfil. At such a tender age, of course, it was impossible for me to comprehend what that destiny was. Only much later did I realise that I was being guided by a hand far more powerful than mine, one whose intelligence and guile was such that I had no doubts, when the time came, of the course of action I must take.

I was different you see, different from all of those children who made my life a misery, the ones who called me names because I didn't want to join in their silly games or take part in stupid group activities after school. When I was very young, I didn't know that I held the power and the means within me to put an end to their taunting and name calling. Only when I reached the age of nine did I suddenly make a stand against those silly, laughing, taunting voices. That was the day when a group of children cornered me in the school playground, out of sight of the watchful teachers and playground assistants. Somehow, they'd heard about my regular visits to the child psychologist. My going in itself wasn't a secret of course. They all knew that I had to attend regular doctor's appointments, but, as happens from time to time, word spread around the school about the real reason for my appointments.

"Bloodsucker, Dracula, do you eat your meat raw, Jack Reid?" they shouted in a cacophony of screeching, childish screams.

"He's a vampire, he sucks the blood from living cats, that's what I've heard," screeched Andrew Denning, one of the ringleaders of the haranguing group.

"You're a weirdo, Reid, that's what you are," Camilla Hunt shouted in my face.

I'd had enough. As Denning came closer to scream in my face once again, I waited until he was within touching distance, and, quick as a flash, I grabbed my tormentor with both hands, one either side of his face, and pulled him close to me. He struggled as I bent my head to the side and the others screamed in panic, but no-one came to his aid as my teeth sunk deeply into his flesh, biting hard on the tender mass of sinews and muscle that made up his ear. That was when the loudest scream of all erupted, this time from Andrew Denning himself, as I pulled my head back from his, to reveal a large chunk of his ear still stuck between my teeth. Blood pumped from the side of the boy's head and the other children stood screaming, rooted to the spot in their fear and fascination. In seconds, the sound of an adult voice could be heard shouting,

"What's all this commotion? If you boys have been fighting I'll.... Oh my God! Jack! What have you done?"

Miss Plummer almost fainted on the spot, but, to her credit, she maintained her equilibrium enough to send two of the other children running for help. How she did it I can't remember, but she made me open my mouth long enough for her to retrieve the bitten remains of Andrew Denning's ear, which she quickly wrapped in a handkerchief she pulled from a pocket in the side of her skirt. The others were quickly dismissed, and Miss Plummer stayed with me and Andrew, who continued to scream until another teacher arrived and escorted him away. Soon afterwards a car disappeared through the school gates carrying the injured boy to the hospital. I learned afterwards that the doctors had sewn what they could of his ear back together, but in truth it would never look right again, and Andrew Denning I'm sure will never forget our encounter. I say that because I only heard these things second-hand. After that incident, the headmaster summoned my parents to the school and I was removed from that particular place of education and sent to what is laughingly called a 'special school', where children with 'special needs' are taught. I thought it odd at the time, that no-one really seemed to appreciate what my own peculiar *'special needs'* were.

It wasn't until much later that I would begin to realise just where my life was heading, and what I was destined to fulfil, just after my eighteenth birthday in fact, my 'coming of age' as they call it. That was when things really began to fall into place in my mind, and that is why you and all those who follow you, and Doctor Ruth especially, will never, ever forget me. I'm sorry, I've been remiss. Perhaps I should introduce myself before going any further. My name is Jack, Jack Thomas Reid, and this is the letter that began everything that transpired after that fateful day when I received my legacy from Uncle Robert.

As for the rest, I suggest you go and talk to Doctor Ruth. She's the *expert* after all.

AND NOW THE FINAL INSTALMENT BEGINS

Welcome to
'Requiem for The Ripper'

ONE
SKERRIES ROCK

Skerries Rock is, to most people who've heard of it, one of the most desolate and unwelcoming places in the whole of the British Isles. Lying just a mile off the coast of Cape Wrath, the most north-westerly point of the Scottish mainland, the island, which is rarely if ever shown on any maps is barely one and a half miles long and less than a half mile across at its widest point. Once home to a small band of hardy crofters who long ago abandoned their tiny homes and sought wealth, or at least a decent living on the mainland, it has long been my personal idyll, the place where if I could, I always promised myself I'd retire to one day, living in splendid isolation with nothing more than the seabirds and the sound of the constantly buffeting Atlantic winds for company.

I'd visited Skerries Rock as a child when my father had brought me to the place during a fishing trip. We'd hired a boat from the village of Balnakiel, where my ex-ship's captain father was well known, and where he holidayed often, enjoying the panoramic views and the relaxation afforded by the local golf course and staying in the village's only decent hotel. We landed on Skerries Rock on the third day of our fishing trip, accompanied by Hamish Foyle, and his son Angus who comprised the crew of the oddly named 'Whispering Lady'. I never found out why the boat carried its odd name, but at ten years of age such things were of little interest to me.

What did catch my attention however was the sheer beauty of the tiny island that my father had brought me to. Small as it may have been, it held a grandeur that penetrated my young mind and left a lasting impression upon me. On the cliffs that appeared to rise almost vertically from the sea on its eastern shore, I watched in awe as thousands (or so I estimated) of puffins with their brightly coloured beaks nestled together, gathered, as my father explained, for their annual mating season. Dolphins broke through the dark blue-green surface of the ocean as we approached the only practical landing point a mile east of the towering cliffs. Here a small wooden quay jutted out from a rocky beach. It stood in good repair, and Hamish Foyle explained that the crofters who once lived on the Rock had used this place for the receiving of supplies from the mainland, and also for putting to sea in their own small fishing boats, from which they'd cast their nets close to shore in an attempt to augment their supplies with a regular infusion of fresh fish. They'd possessed the sense to build the quay on the leeward side of the island where a degree of shelter from the towering Atlantic breakers existed. Anywhere else on the island would have made landing ashore a physical impossibility. When not in use, their small but highly seaworthy fishing vessels would be hauled by hand onto the shore, where they'd await their owners' next voyage out to sea.

Nowadays, Hamish told me, the island was privately owned and only rarely visited by birdwatchers and conservationists. The owner, a philanthropic millionaire, had decreed that the quay be kept in good repair so that those who wished to land and take advantage of the sights and sounds of the island could do so.

I think my father knew I'd be captivated by the place. He knew only too well that his son had a love for the natural world and for all the creatures that inhabit it, and the puffins and the myriad gulls, terns, skuas and petrels that swirled in the skies above us made the whole place seem alive. I felt as though I'd stumbled on to one of the last truly wild places on Earth, and perhaps I had.

The place left such an impression on my receptive young mind that memories of Skerries Rock filled my head so many times during my teenage years and I would beg my father to take me there whenever he visited Scotland. My mother, reconciled to the knowledge that her husband and son were about to embark on one of their treks to the north, would usually remain at home in our comfortable house in the port of Hull on the East Coast of Yorkshire, and I'd cheerfully wave goodbye to her and sadly, scarcely give her another thought as we headed towards the border, following the coast road along the east coast and them traversing the width of Scotland once Edinburgh trailed in the wake of our exhaust. I say sadly, because, shortly after I'd attained the age of sixteen, my mother fell victim to a cruel cancer and within six months of her contracting the dreaded disease, she'd passed away, and my father and I were left alone with our joint grief and horror at the ravages the illness had wrought in my poor mother.

So it transpired that years passed without another visit to Skerries Rock, years in which I attended university, gained a degree and slowly built a career for myself. I became successful in my chosen profession and became able to afford to ensconce myself in a house that overlooked the North Sea in the coastal resort of Scarborough, a brass plaque on the wall announcing my trade and my surgery hours, from where I carried out my work as a consultant psychologist. I carried out much of that work of course at the local hospital, and as time passed and my star rose, I became known to the police as something of an expert in the field of criminal psychology, not only in the local area but across the north of England and I was often called in to provide suspect profiling in cases where such expertise was required or desired.

As with many childhood dreams, my thoughts of Skerries Rock remained firmly embedded in my mind, though they grew fainter and less vivid with the passage of time. I would occasionally promise myself that I'd visit the place again one day, but after the death of my father, (another awful cancer, dammit), fifteen years after the loss of my mother, such ambitions assumed less of a priority in my life.

My success continued and then, at the age of fifty, while idly reading through a copy of The Times one day as I waited for lunch to be served in my favourite restaurant, my eyes were suddenly drawn to an advertisement on the property page.

The words *Skerries Rock* leaped out at me from the page as I read the advertisement offering my dream island for sale!

I could scarcely believe my eyes. The millionaire philanthropist who'd originally bought the place had died and the executors of his estate were selling Skerries Rock for a knock-down price. After all, they'd probably surmised, who the hell would want to own such a place, even less likely, who might want to live there? They probably saw the tiny island as an encumbrance to the estate and seemed to be determined to off-load it quickly, or so the asking price implied.

From that day forward the idea of owning Skerries Rock and having the opportunity to live my childhood dream became an obsession. I'd become financially sound, certainly I could afford the asking price, and I quickly came to the conclusion that I could also easily give up my general practice in

Scarborough and augment my income through consultancy work which could just as easily be conducted from a home on the island. After all, most of such work came via the internet and the telephone, and therein I realised the enormity of what I'd just suggested to myself. Skerries Rock possessed no mains electricity supply, nor gas or telephone links to the mainland. It would take some creative thinking and a fair amount of investment to install a private generator and arrange for a telephone line to be installed.

My mind had been made up however, and I knew I had to try. So, with a lot of help from my solicitor, I found myself able to place a ridiculously low bid for the island of my dreams that even I was surprised to find accepted by the executors of the estate. The generator cost less than I'd anticipated, and the telephone line wouldn't be a problem with the advances in modern technology. All I had to do was build a habitable home for myself and Skerries Rock could become my home. I hired a team of builders from Balnakiel, in fact, the only builders in Balnakiel, owned oddly enough by Angus Foyle, with whom I'd first set sight on the island. In less than six months he and his men had converted two of the old crofts into a single, warmly insulated and completely adequate dwelling for a single man such as me. Power came from the use of the newly acquired generator, the telephone and computer links were soon established and in far less time than I'd imagined I found myself unscrewing the brass plaque from the wall outside my Scarborough home. As I took it down from its place of prominence I read it one last time. Listing my name, David Hemswell, and my professional qualifications, that plaque seemed at that moment to stand for everything I'd worked so hard to achieve and was now poised to leave behind. I placed it almost reverently into one of the packing cases that would be used to transport my goods and chattels northwards and left the house on a warm Saturday afternoon in June, without looking back once as I drove towards my future.

In less than a year, I'd made myself feel totally at home in my new environment. As I'd expected, consultancy work came my way on a regular basis, and I found myself easily able to attend to most of it through the mediums of computer or telephone. Only twice did I deem it necessary to leave the island and conduct hands-on inquiries in connection with a couple of rather complicated cases that had been presented to me by the police. I'd spend time each day walking and observing the life that abounded on my own personal dream world. Little appeared to have changed since my childhood days. Puffins and gulls and all the other seabirds still used my island as their home, at least for the time they required to set foot on dry land. Entire pods of dolphins continued to make their presence known, occasionally leaping from the sea, riding the waves in playful abandon until they'd become bored with their game and disappear once more beneath the mantle of the Atlantic waves. The wind would howl, not fearfully, but as a lullaby that would gently send me to sleep each night, blissfully happy and contented with my place in the world. Skerries Rock had become my world at that point, and I felt as though nothing could ever bring discord or disharmony into my new life. I found myself living the idyllic life I'd dreamed of living since my childhood. I felt supremely happy, happier than I'd ever believed possible. With no wife, no family ties and no one to answer to except my own conscience, I now entered without doubt the happiest period of my life.

The only thing I hadn't factored in to my new life, my world of tranquillity and being at one with nature was the telephone call that I received one dark winter's night in January.

"Doctor Hemswell?" a stranger's voice inquired when I picked up the receiver.

"Yes, who's speaking, please?"

"You don't know me Doctor, but I've heard of you and your reputation. I got your number from Chief Inspector Gould of the Strathclyde Police. He said you were the best man to help with my, er, problem. I wondered if I might visit you and talk to you about a matter of the gravest importance."

"I'm sorry, but I don't even know your name yet, or what this matter of importance is. Could you please enlighten me before I agree to any sort of meeting? I don't usually receive visitors here you know. I am rather isolated."

"Yes, I know. You live on a private island off the coast of Cape Wrath. Chief Inspector Gould told me about it."

"Correct. Now, your story?"

"Oh, yes, I'm sorry. Allow me to introduce myself. My name is Forbes, William Forbes, and until recently I was a solicitor. That is, until something odd began to happen and I found myself becoming embroiled in something I didn't, and still don't understand."

"Mr. Forbes, you're not making a lot of sense," I said, in an attempt to force the caller to get to the point.

"Yes, I know, I apologise. Look, have you heard of Jack Reid, Doctor?"

"Yes of course, I think almost everyone has. He was accused of a series of copycat crimes that mirrored Jack the Ripper's Whitechapel murders, was convicted, then released from a secure hospital due to new evidence, then years later he was convicted of another series of murders. Is that the Jack Reid you mean?"

"Yes, that's him. Look, Doctor Hemswell, I know it sounds

preposterous, and you'll think I'm mad, but, well, Jack Reid was my client and he died a few weeks ago. Since then I've come into possession of a document that makes me believe things I don't want to believe, and I admit to being in fear for my life. Please, I don't want to say too much on the telephone. I'm begging you doctor, please let me come and see you and talk to you in person. Perhaps then you'll understand what I'm getting at."

The Jack Reid case had become notorious in the recent annals of crime. Only a fool or someone who'd been shut away on a desert island for years could have failed to possess at least a rudimentary knowledge of the so-called 'Ripper Copycat' killer who had stalked the streets of Brighton and finally, Whitechapel itself in his fiendish lust to recreate the murders of Jack the Ripper. Somehow, this man had become embroiled in the life and the case of Jack Reid and though he sounded agitated and afraid, his occupation at least merited granting him a little leeway.

"Listen Mr Forbes. You say you feel as though your life is in danger and yet you also tell me that Reid died a short time ago. I hadn't heard of his demise, but please, all things being equal, who do you believe you're in danger from?"

Just before the man replied a sudden howling gust of wind shook the house, and perhaps that same blast of chilled Atlantic air caused the generator to miss a beat and made the lights flicker briefly off, and then on again. His voice, when it came, delivered his reply in a deadpan, totally serious monotone.

"Who? Why, Jack the Ripper of course."

From that moment onwards, life at Skerries Rock would never be quite the same again. Without knowing if my new client were deranged or just deluded in some way, I gave him directions and agreed to meet with him two days hence. I'd rendezvous with him on the mainland in my own motor launch and ferry him to the island. I explained that I wasn't geared up for receiving guests, but he assured me he expected nothing from me except the opportunity to talk and to show me the document which he insisted had been the cause of so much of his current grief.

Finalising the conversation, I said my goodbyes to the mysterious Mr Forbes, and sat thoughtfully ruminating on our conversation for a minute. He'd said very little and given away even less and yet here I sat, ready to receive this stranger in to my home, a man who appeared to be under the delusion that his life was in danger from a serial killer who'd died over a hundred and twenty years ago.

The lights suddenly dimmed once more, the wind gathered in intensity and the windows of my home, despite being triple glazed to keep out the wind and the draughts, visibly appeared to shake in their frames. I made a mental note to check the fuel lines to my oil-fired generator in the light of the following morning and turned in for the night, though in truth, my mind felt more disturbed than I'd imagined at the strange phone call from Mr William Forbes, and sleep eluded me until the sheer weight of exhaustion forced my eyes to finally close at a little before three in the morning.

After a mere three hours sleep. I woke as usual at six a.m. only to find that the generator had failed during the night. I found myself without heat, light and power of any description. Forbes would be arriving the next day and it appeared I had much work to do. The wind had died, and the sea rolled in to the island in a gentle flat calm, unusual at any time of the year on Skerries Rock. As I worked on restoring power to my isolated home that day, even the sounds of the seabird's calls sounded muted, and an air of hesitant expectancy appeared to presage the arrival of William Forbes, solicitor, of London.

TWO
PREPARATIONS

REPAIRING the generator had proved a simple task, even for a ham-fisted townie like me. The power failure had resulted from nothing more sinister than a blocked fuel line, caused by a build-up air in one of the bends of the pipes that fed the diesel oil into the generator. The comprehensive instructions supplied by the makers enabled me to get the machine up and running again in just under an hour and I cleaned up and spent most of the remainder of that day preparing the spare bedroom for my expected guest.

 My converted croft houses comprised my own bedroom, the spare, a living room, library/office and a well-appointed kitchen, in addition to a couple of outbuildings, one of which I'd utilized as a garage for my all-terrain Range Rover, and the other as a general workroom for any necessary D.I.Y jobs that might be required from time to time, and where I also kept a large deep-freeze that held enough frozen food to last through an entire winter if necessary. I'd found it easy to forget that Skerries Rock, though lonely and isolated most of the time, stood in fact only a stone's throw from the mainland and any essential supplies and equipment I required could be obtained by boat in the space of a few hours. My motor launch was modern and fast and housed in readiness at all times in a boathouse I'd had specially built for it beside the landing quay. In truth, I had the best of both worlds. No intrusions by strangers unless invited, and reasonably close proximity to civilisation if I needed it.

The spare room stood sparsely furnished with a double bed, wardrobe, side table and a rather old-fashioned but eminently practical dressing table, with four drawers provided for the user. It took no time at all to make up the bed with fresh linen, and to run round the room with a duster, and to vacuum the carpets.

As I sat down to a late lunch, I reflected that there remained little more I could do with the room to make it any more habitable for my guest. It gleamed, clean, comfortable and as ready as it could be, so the rest of the afternoon would be devoted to a little research into the case he'd mentioned.

The internet provided most of what I needed to know to give me a brief background on the case. Jack Reid had been the nephew of a psychiatrist who had been involved in a road accident, one in which his own father died. After the accident he'd come into possession of some papers that appeared to have caused some disturbance of the mind, and Robert Cavendish died sometime later, convinced that he'd been haunted by the ghost of Jack the Ripper during the coma he'd lain in during his time in hospital. On reaching the age of maturity, young Jack Reid had also received a legacy, this time from his Uncle Robert, and his life had immediately entered a downward spiral. It seemed that Reid had led a disturbed childhood and whatever happened to him after the receipt of the bequest from his uncle; it certainly did nothing for his state of mind. He'd disappeared from home one night, apparently going in search of something or someone, though no-one knew who or what, or where he'd gone. He wasn't heard from again until his parents were informed by the police that he'd been arrested in Brighton, suspected of the murders of three women, all of whom had been slaughtered in the manner of Jack the Ripper.

Found guilty by reason of insanity at his trial, Reid had been incarcerated in the Ravenswood Secure Hospital, a facility built specifically to house the criminally insane. Somehow, a leading ripperologist had become involved in the case and she began to cast doubts on Reid's guilt. After the police re-opened the case following her intrusive intervention, they eventually found that Reid may not have been the killer after all and during an extensive retrial, it emerged that Reid had been the unwitting dupe of a person or persons unknown who'd framed him for the murders, and Reid had been released from Ravenswood soon afterwards, against the advice of his psychiatrist, a Doctor Ruth Truman.

All appeared to go well with Jack Reid for a while, until he left his job and disappeared from sight once more. He wasn't heard from again until the bodies of prostitutes began turning up in the Whitechapel area of London, as they had during the reign of the original Ripper. This time, Reid had been clever. He didn't try to use the original murder sites as defined in the original Ripper case, but simply picked his targets at random in the red-light district. He knew that if he stuck to the original area used by the Ripper he would easily be tracked down and that the police would simply set traps and lie in wait for him, so he simply picked up his victims on the street and led them into the nearest darkened alley or parking area and carried out his gruesome killings. Of course, during the time of the killings the police didn't know that Jack Reid was responsible, at least not for certain, but when the London Police received a contact from Inspector Holland in Brighton who had first arrested Reid in Brighton, they soon began to suspect that Jack Reid could be their man.

Three women had already died at the hands of the new Whitechapel Murderer before the police got lucky. Holland's information proved vital and the authorities distributed a photo of Reid to every police officer in the Capital. It was a member of the British Transport Police who eventually spotted Jack Reid innocently waiting for a tube train on the London Underground. Rather than tackle the suspected killer himself the officer radioed his headquarters with confirmation of his sighting and then followed Reid onto the train. When Reid left the train, the officer notified HQ again and then followed the suspect, keeping in radio contact with his supervisor at all times as a tactical firearms squad from the Metropolitan Police deployed quickly to the area.

As Jack Reid entered a small apartment building less than a mile from the scene of the last killing, he found himself surrounded by armed police officers and arrested on the spot. He readily admitted to his crimes and once again he used the excuse of being a descendant of Jack the Ripper and having been compelled by the soul of the long-dead killer to carry out the latest series of horrific killings and mutilations.

Following extensive psychiatric examinations, Jack Reid had been declared unfit to plead at trial, diagnosed as criminally insane and promptly incarcerated once again in Ravenswood. What had happened to him after that, I had no idea as I found myself strangely unable to find any further information on the internet, after the time of his admission to the secure hospital. He'd simply dropped off the public radar.

I knew I would have to wait for the arrival of my guest the

next day in order to discover more and to find out just what Jack Reid had done in the last years of his life in Ravenswood and how his actions, whatever they may have been, had resulted in such a dramatic impact on his solicitor. Obviously, Forbes appeared in fear of his life, or why else would he have contacted me and asked to visit me so urgently? At the same time I wondered how I, a psychologist, could possibly be the man to assist him in his quest, whatever that might be. As I laid my head on the pillow that night, with Forbes's imminent arrival just a few short hours away, I confess to feeling a sense of excitement, tinged with an expectation that something out of the ordinary was taking place.

Whatever that something may be, I would discover soon enough, and as the darkness enfolded me as I turned out the bedside lamp that night, I slept better than the previous night, and didn't stir until the hands on the clock read six a.m. once more.

Dawn brought with it a clear blue sky, a fresh but comfortable breeze and a hint of hazy sunshine. In short, a good day for Skerries Rock. After a good breakfast I dressed in my usual warm outer clothing and made my way to the quay. I soon had the launch's engine fired up and as the gentle swells carried their white wave crests towards the rocky shores of my island home I set off against the current to my pre-arranged pick up point in Balnakiel, where I knew William Forbes would be waiting for me.

As I pulled up to the dock in the village of Balnakiel sometime later, I could easily identify the man I'd travelled to meet as he stood watching my arrival. Although I'd never set eyes on William Forbes before, this man could be none other than my client. The fear and the hunted look in his eyes as I drew close enough to discern his face identified him to me as clearly as if he'd carried a placard with his name emblazoned upon it. Never had I seen such a look on the face of a living soul. For the first time since Forbes's telephone call, I realised the severity of his trouble and I perceived quickly that this may just prove to be no ordinary everyday case. This man appeared, by his very demeanour, terrified out of his wits!

THREE
WILLIAM FORBES

After tying up the launch, I stepped expertly from the boat onto the steps that led up the harbour wall to the walkway above where William Forbes waited anxiously for our first meeting. In seconds I found myself face to face with my soon-to-be house guest. The man exchanged a firm handshake with me, somewhat at odds with his hunted or perhaps I should say *haunted* appearance. I experienced little doubt in my mind that, rightly or wrongly, William Forbes held a genuine and serious belief that someone or something was out to do him harm. His stood hunched against the mild breeze, his shoulders stooped as though he were hiding from some unknown and unseen enemy. He wore a camel-coloured overcoat, an old-fashioned trilby hat and well-polished brown brogues, and under his left arm he clutched a battered brown leather document case, slightly at odds with the obvious quality of his attire. If he possessed hair, there couldn't be much of it as none showed from beneath the sides or back of his hat. His eyes appeared to scan the horizon as he looked not so much at me, but through me as we exchanged polite greetings.

"I'm so very pleased you agreed to see me, Dr Hemswell."

"Please, call me David," I replied. "If we're to share my home for a day or two I think we should dispense with the formalities, don't you?"

"Thank you, yes, I agree of course. David it shall be then. But, please, Doctor, er, I mean David, can we be on our way as soon as possible? I really don't like being out here like this. We seem so exposed."

"Listen, we're in a tiny village on the very tip of the British Isles. This place is exposed by the very nature of its existence, but that doesn't mean it isn't a safe place to be. I know everyone in this village Mr Forbes. They are my friends and my neighbours, despite the distance to my own home. None of these folk would do me, or anyone staying with me, the slightest harm, believe me. I hope I can call you William by the way."

He nodded.

"Very well," I went on. "I need to pick up a few things at the local store, then we can return to the boat and be on our way. Will that be okay with you?"

"Yes, of course, I'm sorry," said Forbes, his eyes once again scanning the surrounding area for whatever threat, real or imagined, that he perceived in his mind.

"It won't take long," I assured him.

Forbes nodded again, words appearing hard to come by. Without another word he simply fell into step with me as I made my way up from the tiny harbour to the small village high street where the grandiosely named Potter's Emporium stood, imperiously overlooking the dock area and the small boats that bobbed gently at anchor. The Emporium stood sandwiched between the tiny post office/chemist shop, and McMurdo's Ships Chandlers. I'd always wondered how a ship's chandler could make a decent living in Balnakiel with the entire fleet of fishing boats owned by the locals amounting to no more than a dozen small inshore boats, and couple of small pleasure cruisers that gave tourists trips round the bay and the isles in the summer months, but somehow, old McMurdo had survived in business for many a year gone by, and probably would for many more to come. Sandy McMurdo had even had the funds available to purchase Potter's Emporium when old man Potter died the previous year, and had now become one of the wealthiest men in the village though one would never have known it from his permanent frown which greeted the pair of us as Forbes and I entered the emporium which was in reality nothing more than a general store and mini-supermarket, selling mostly canned foods and pre-packaged meats, delivered each week from the nearest town, in addition to the varied dry goods and haberdashery required by the locals in an isolated location such as Balnakiel.

"Well, if it isn't Doctor Hemswell, and friend, I'm supposing?" said old McMurdo as we crossed the wooden floor boards that smelled of polish and linseed oil, ending up across the high counter from the old man.

"Yes indeed, Mr McMurdo," I responded. "I need a few things to see me through the next few days. Extra food and so on for my guest."

"Aye, as I thought," said the old man. "And this will be...?" He looked directly at Forbes.

"As you say, a friend, Mr McMurdo," I replied, not wanting to give away my guest's name for fear of displeasing him, or of fuelling unwanted gossip in the village.

The local tom-toms could easily build a mountain from a molehill from the merest piece of loose information, and I had the feeling that William Forbes would appreciate the privacy of anonymity during his stay with me.

"Aye, well, you just help yourself to what ye need and we'll tot it up and add it to your regular monthly bill, if that's agreeable to ye," said the shop owner.

"That'll do fine," I said as I began trawling through the shelves of the store, picking up the extras I felt would be needed with a guest in the house, extra toilet rolls, toothpaste, a few tins of salmon, beans and such like. Within ten minutes I'd filled two large cardboard boxes and old McMurdo had added a princely forty pounds, give or take a few pence, to my account at the emporium.

Before we left, I asked Forbes if he'd made arrangements for his car. It would be left unattended during his stay with me.

"I left my own car at home. I used a hired car to drive up here. It's a blue Mondeo parked in the little car park near the harbour," he informed me.

"We'll pick up your bags and I'll arrange for someone to look after it while you're on the island."

"I hadn't thought of that," he replied.

Sandy McMurdo was also the owner of the only garage in Balnakiel and I quickly made arrangements for him to pick up the car and keep it garaged on his premises until 'my friend' returned to collect it. We quickly walked back to the car, drove it back to the village and left the keys with McMurdo, who promptly locked up his emporium and ushered us along the road to his own car and kindly gave the two of us, and Forbes's luggage, a lift back to the harbour, where my launch awaited us, gently bobbing on the end of its tether.

"I appreciate what you did back there, not telling the shopkeeper my name," Forbes said as we loaded the boxes into the launch back at the harbour.

"Don't mention it," I replied. "I just thought it best not to give the locals too much title-tattle to talk about. There's little enough happens in Balnakiel as it is and any hint of a newcomer with a strange story to tell might soon get blown up out of all proportion."

"What d'you mean, strange story?" asked my visitor.

"Well, you did tell me that you thought Jack the Ripper is after you, didn't you? That's a little strange to say the least. After all, this is the twenty-first century. Jack the Ripper died over a century ago so there's little chance of him prowling the streets looking for you is there?"

"You just don't know, or understand," Forbes said as we exited the harbour and picked up a rolling swell as we hit the open sea beyond the breakwater. "There are things in this world that defy logic, David, really there are, as you'll find very soon."

"Yes, well, let's save your story until we reach Skerries Rock, shall we? I'd rather talk in the peace of my house than out here on a rolling sea with a gale brewing."

"How long till we get there?"

"With a following wind, about an hour, or just over."

With that, Forbes fell silent and simply gazed out to sea, his eyes continuing to scan the four points of the compass as though he expected a battleship with all guns blazing to suddenly appear over the horizon and open fire on our tiny craft. I remained content to continue our short voyage in silence, concentrating instead on following a sure course and hugging the coast as much as possible in order to prevent my guest from experiencing too much in the way of those rolling seas I'd already mentioned. I certainly didn't know if he possessed his sea legs or not, but at least I could do my best to help him avoid any seasickness and thus save myself a cleaning job if he'd thrown up in my neat motor launch.

Looking to the sky I could see a mass of dark rain-laden storm clouds fast blowing in from the north and I opened the throttles to the stops in an effort to beat the weather to Skerries Rock. Even though we were close to shore I wanted to avoid the pitching and yawing and thunderous waves that would accompany the arriving storm.

Forbes remained silent for the rest of the trip, his mind seemingly miles from our current location. He barely seemed to register the ever-increasing swells and the heavy pitching of the boat as we ran before the storm, until, finally, I swung the launch round in towards the shore of Skerries Rock and he finally broke his silence.

"It's beautiful," he exclaimed as he took in the awesome grandeur of the land as it rose from the shore towards the centre of the island. I hadn't even realised his mind had made contact with the view as we'd approached my home.

"It looks even better when the sun shines," I replied, trying to keep the conversation light as I struggled to bring the boat in to the quay despite the efforts of a cross-current that appeared determined to push us further out to sea. I was too experienced at docking my launch however and five minutes later, with the launch safely stowed in the boat-house, we stood on dry land and I led Forbes up the steep path that led to my croft, my home, my retreat from the outside world. He clutched his briefcase as he walked. I nobly carried his overnight bags. I suddenly realised that William Forbes would be not only my first house guest since moving to Skerries Rock, he might also have brought with him something of the outside world that I'd rather not be here with me, something that I might find hard to put aside once I became aware of whatever had brought the man hundreds of miles from London to see me.

We entered my home some ten minutes later, and I allowed

my guest to enter ahead of me. As I closed the door behind us, I watched Forbes as he appeared to visibly sag. The man sighed and his shoulders drooped a little more. When he turned to face me however, some of the fear that been evident earlier appeared to have vacated his expression. Perhaps my home represented some kind of sanctuary for him, an escape from whatever terrors lurked within his mind.

No sooner had that momentary relaxation registered, a resounding clap of thunder sounded from what seemed to be a position right above, presaging the coming storm.

Forbes jumped, nerves getting the better of him and in an instant the fear had returned. As a bolt of brilliant lightning rent the sky and lit up the room through the sturdy windows of my home, William Forbes shrank still further into himself. I watched, fascinated, as the well-built solicitor, a man whose entire life should have been built around logic, order and the law, and who I'd have imagined to be one of the least likely to panic at the forces and sounds of nature, backed away from the window, until, his eyes once more displaying the fear of one hunted by terrors unknown, his back came to rest against the wall beside the fireplace.

His body shook and his mouth opened in fear. His lips moved but not a sound came from them. Though he remained in the room with me I felt as though William Forbes were no longer with me, but had retreated to some dark place, locked away in his own private world of fear and dread.

"Mr. Forbes...William," I implored, trying to break through whatever barrier had risen in his mind.

I received no reply, just the sound of the wind as it swirled round the house:

the thunder roared again, and another sheet of lightning rent the sky. William Forbes shook, as though the storm's force might be directed solely at him, and he were under attack by unseen forces and for the first time, I contemplated the absurd notion that

    perhaps, just perhaps, he was...

FOUR
A PIECE OF YELLOWED PAPER

I'D TRIED but found it impossible to break Forbes out of his panic attack, for that constituted my diagnosis of his state of mind.

"Mr. Forbes, William!" I'd implored and beseeched him to snap out of it, tried to reassure him out of his terror of the storm. I switched on all the lights in the room in an effort to calm him, all to no avail. Whatever demons had invaded the man's mind, they held a far stronger hold over his psychological equilibrium than anything my own feeble entreaties could break through.

I made the decision to try and allow him to break free from his fears in his own time and I simply walked to him and took him by the arm, gently guiding him to the nearest armchair. He allowed me to lead him, still shaking, to the comfort of my own fireside chair, and I eased him into a sitting position as his eyes continued to dart around the room in search of…what? I couldn't tell and I had the distinct impression that my guest, if he'd had the opportunity, would have run from the house in his terror, and possibly careened across the landscape of Skerries Rock until he pitched into the ocean, becoming a victim not just of the power of the sea, but of the irrational fears (as I thought) that had temporarily deranged his mind. At least, I hoped it would prove to be a temporary state. The possibility that I'd allowed a madman to enter my home and made up my spare room for him to occupy had begun to grow in my mind.

As the warmth of the room began to reach into his body, and the lights burned without flickering, (I'd done a good job of repairing the generator), and the storm slowly abated in its intensity, so William Forbes began to visibly relax a little. Though still rooted to his place in my most comfortable chair, his hands no longer gripped the arms of the chair as though his life depended upon it, and his chest stopped heaving with the intensity of his rapid breathing. I'd heard that allowing the victim of a panic attack to breathe into a paper bag could help, and at last he appeared sufficiently lucid for me to try and get him to do so, utilising one of the bags containing a number of my purchases from the emporium. The brown paper bag seemed to help and within five minutes the previously panic-stricken solicitor had calmed down sufficiently for me to attempt conversation with him once more. He at last removed his hat and coat, revealing an almost bald head, with just a few wisps of light brown hair clinging to his scalp, and a dark brown jacket and a pair of designer jeans.

"I'm sorry," he eventually volunteered as I knelt on the floor in front of him, and I eased the bag from his hand, and laid it on the floor beside the chair.

"Listen, these storms are part and parcel of my life here on the island. They're quite normal and do no harm at all. You really mustn't let them have such a fearful effect on you. There's no-one else on the island, just you and me. No-one is going to harm you while you're here."

"How can you be sure of that?" he asked. "You haven't heard what I have to tell you yet. When you have you may just change your mind."

"Then, my dear chap, you must tell me your tale, and let me be the judge of whatever evidence you wish to place before me. Before you do, I have a question, however."

"Yes?" He appeared surprised that I should wish to ask him anything, rather than just listen to what he had to say.

"Why me? There are any number of psychologists out there. Why choose one who lives in such a remote and inaccessible place? We've never met before, and I'd simply like to know how you heard of me and why I became your choice in all of this, whatever this is."

"Dr Hemswell, I needed someone who I could trust and who wouldn't dismiss my so-called rantings, as I'm sure you think they are, out of hand. Andy Gould is an old friend of my family. We used to live in Leith, and that's where I first met him, years ago when he was just an inspector. When these terrible things began to happen, and I needed someone to confide in I approached him and told him the whole story. He too thought I was crazy, I'm sure of it, but he at least heard me out and then called a friend of his at Scotland Yard. That friend suggested your name as he informed Andy that you had handled a number of similar cases in the past."

"In what way, similar?"

"Well, you apparently helped the police in the Tremaine case some years ago and also in the case of the Halliwell family curse."

The cases he referred to were both instances where a hint of the supernatural or at least delusions of the supernatural, had influenced not only an individual, as in the Tremaine case, but an entire family, as had occurred within the Halliwell family. Martin Tremaine had killed two people, convinced that he'd fallen under the control of the spirit of Sweeney Todd, the so-called demon barber of Fleet Street. Both victims had their throats cut and Tremaine then cut up the bodies in the cellar of his home. Before he could take his scheme any further, he'd found himself apprehended when a neighbour reported strange smells coming from the ventilator above the cellar and the police were swift to arrest the perpetrator. Psychiatric examinations of the accused failed to agree on a diagnosis. He remained unshakeable in his belief that Sweeney Todd had visited him in a dream and had infiltrated his mind to the extent that he no longer had control of his actions. People in authority were actually beginning to believe that he had indeed been the subject of some kind of demonic possession and at that point the police asked me to meet with Tremaine and talk to him, assess his story and his state of mind.

In the end Martin Tremaine admitted that his Sweeney Todd story had been nothing more than a blind. The two victims had both been victims of the killer's road rage. The first had simply cut him up at a road junction, the second had overtaken him on the road out of town and Tremaine had felt aggrieved at being passed by a smaller, older car. He'd followed both of them to their ultimate destinations, and then rendered each man unconscious before taking them to his home in his car, before butchering and dismembering them. He'd come up with the Sweeney Todd defence after watching a movie about the demon barber on late-night TV.

The Halliwells had been different. The family owned a substantial home in the country and on the death of seventy-year-old Timothy Halliwell, the estate passed to his eldest son, Mitchell. Mitchell announced to his two brothers and three sisters that he intended to renovate the crumbling old mansion and convert it into a thoroughly modern resort hotel, complete with nine-hole golf course and health spa. The younger brother of the family, Randolph, stood out as the only one who appeared upset by the decision, and made a number of threats against Mitchell, saying that the home should remain a home and not become a tourist attraction. Mitchell argued that the sheer size of the house made it too large and cold to remain a family home in the current financial climate and anyway, the decision was his alone to make. The other siblings had all been financially catered for in their father's will. The house, he reiterated, had now become his to dispose of as he saw fit.

As soon as work commenced on the conversion of the house however, things began to happen. One of Mitchell's sisters, Grace, died when the brakes failed on her car and she ran off the road into a river. The poor woman drowned, trapped in the car.

Next, middle brother Simon burned to death in a mysterious fire at his home in the country. The fire brigade investigation revealed that the fire had started in the garage attached to the house, and though the fire investigators suspected arson, the case couldn't be proved. As rumours began of a curse that had afflicted the family, and that the conversion of the house to a hotel and spa had promoted the deathly visitations on the family, the police naturally suspected Randolph, due to his previous obstinacy and opposition to the new plans for the family home. That was when the police called me in and asked me to speak to the remaining family members, to see if I could ascertain whether Randolph's state of mind rendered him capable of the acts of murder.

Before I could speak to anyone, Marilyn, the youngest sister died of food poisoning. Foul play was again suspected but couldn't be proved, as she'd been alone at the time she ate the fatal meal that precipitated her death. That left only Mitchell,

Randolph and the middle sister, Chloe to be interviewed. Contrary to the police's suspicions I found Randolph to be a level-headed, well balanced individual, petulant as a younger brother might be at losing what he saw as the family's ancestral home, but I believed him no more capable of cold blooded murder than I would be. Not so with sister Chloe, however. That lady would eventually be proved to be a calculating and evil woman who would stop at nothing, not to just gain control of the house, but of the entire family fortune. Mitchell and Randolph, she later admitted, were on her list to be eliminated in the near future by the so-called family curse. She of course, would then return the house to its original purpose, thus escaping the curse and living happily ever after.

So, those were the cases that had brought me into the frame for William Forbes's current dilemma. He obviously felt that his own predicament had some supernatural or other-worldly connection and my assistance to the police in the past had thrust me into the limelight as far as he was concerned. I made a mental note to have a word with Chief Inspector Gould of the Strathclyde Police at some point in the future. Thank you wouldn't be the words I used. Somehow I had the distinct feeling that working with Mr William Forbes would be one of the most difficult cases I'd embarked upon in many a year.

For the time being I decided that the time had come for my guest to be a little more forthcoming. The time had arrived for him to tell me a lot more than he'd so far confided.

"Okay, William. I've helped the police in one or two cases in the past, but that doesn't make me an expert in the paranormal or in the supernatural. Just how do you think I can help you? You really need to tell me much more than you have so far. You've mentioned Jack Reid, and Jack the Ripper, who for some reason you think has reached out across the years to persecute you, sorry, to want to kill you, but you've given me no hint as to why you believe this to be true."

"Look, I'm sorry. I know I've been reticent and even economical with what I've told you so far, but I'm sure you'll realise why when I tell you the full story."

"Let's hope so shall we?" I asked, and, without waiting for an answer, I continued, "I'm going to put the kettle on, make us both a cup of good strong tea, you like tea don't you?"

He nodded.

"Good, then when we're settled down in here once more, you can tell me your story. I warn you now, William. I can be quite sceptical, so you may have to do a lot to convince me that what you tell me has any credibility."

"That's fine with me," Forbes replied. "I came for your help, and for your guidance. I'm prepared to answer any questions you may have, after of course, you hear me out first."

"Sounds fair enough to me, William. Now, let's get that tea shall we?"

Ten minutes later the pair of us were back in my sitting room, armed with freshly brewed tea and a plate of digestive biscuits. Forbes appeared to have lost much of the fear and trepidation that had marked his arrival at my home and I thought that perhaps the mere act of being isolated away from the throng of civilisation here on Skerries Rock might be working its therapeutic effect on him much as it had always done so for me. Outside, the storm had abated, the wind had dropped to nothing more than a stiff sea breeze, and a light drizzle bounced gently off the window panes.

Seeing my guest in a more relaxed mood, I smiled at him and found myself surprised when Forbes actually smiled back at me. It was the first time I'd seen him smile and in doing so the years fell away from his face. I suddenly realised that, far from being an aging and possibly retired solicitor, William

Forbes was probably far younger than he looked, younger than me for a start.

"How old are you, William, if you don't mind me asking?"

"I'm forty-four," he replied. "I know, I know, I look older, but then, when you hear what I have to tell you, you'll perhaps understand why."

"I'm sorry for asking. But you looked so much younger when you smiled just now, nearer your real age I might add."

"I haven't always looked this old," he went on. "Up until a few months ago I had a good head of hair and was part of a thriving firm in London. That all changed, thanks to that devil incarnate, Jack Thomas Reid."

"Then, my friend, I think you'd better begin your tale"

William Forbes looked me in the eye, hesitating for a moment before speaking.

"What I have to tell you is so extraordinary, so terrifying in the reality of what's happened to me, that I implore you not to say anything during my narrative, at least, not unless you feel you really have to. I don't want to lose my train of thought and miss anything out."

"Very well, William. I shan't interrupt, unless I need you to clarify something or I have an important question, agreed?"

"Good enough," he said, and the man leaned back in his chair.

"Can I ask you one question also before I begin?" he suddenly asked.

"Of course."

"David, Doctor Hemswell, please tell me if you think it's possible for the soul of a man, an evil man, to live on beyond his death, carried through the years in the words scrawled upon a decrepit piece of aged, yellowed paper?"

I stared at the man in incredulous disbelief. Could he really believe in what he'd just asked me?

"I know it sounds preposterous," he went on, "but wait until I show you this." Forbes quickly twizzled the combination locks on his briefcase, reached inside the opened lid, and then withdrew a plastic sleeve which contained a yellowed sheet of paper, nothing more.

With that, and as he reached out to pass me the plastic sleeve, his strange and compelling narrative began...

FIVE
THE STORY BEGINS

"Whatever you do, please don't take the paper out of the sleeve, at least, not yet," Forbes pleaded as I looked at the single sheet of certainly elderly looking and well-yellowed paper that lay under the protective wrapping of the plastic sleeve.

"Do you want me to read it?"

"Yes, but not right away. Keep it with you until you think the time is appropriate."

"Sounds a bit melodramatic to me," I ventured.

"I know, but please, humour me, Doctor, just for now. Let me start at the beginning and when the moment arrives I'll tell you to read the page. It probably won't really make much sense in the context of what I'm about to tell you if you read it too soon."

"So, why give it to me now?"

"To be honest, I just feel a lot better knowing it's in your possession rather than mine," said Forbes, deadly serious.

"Okay, then, perhaps you'd better begin," I urged.

"Right. Here goes then, and please, don't judge what you're hearing until I reach the end of my rather strange tale."

"Don't worry William. I agreed not to interrupt unless it's to ask a question or for clarification of something. I'll stick to that."

With that William Forbes began his narrative. I admit to having no real clue as to what he was about to reveal to me, and as the wind outside the house continued to whistle gently around my island home, and the log fire crackled in the grate, my visitor at last appeared to relax as he spoke. Perhaps the opportunity to relate his story to someone had already begun having a therapeutic effect on him.

"Perhaps I should give you some background to the case before I dive right into what I have to tell you," he said. I remained silent, aware that he would probably tell me much that I already knew from my own research into the Jack Reid case. William Forbes, however, intended to go back in time much further, back to the nineteenth century, to the reign of Queen Victoria, and the terrible crimes of Jack the Ripper himself.

"I first met Jack Reid during his second period of incarceration at the Ravenswood Special Hospital. As with the first time, the doctor assigned to his case turned out to be Doctor Ruth Truman, a very competent and highly qualified psychiatrist who of course had held out against the release of Reid following his first trial and imprisonment. She believed that although there existed sufficient evidence to clear Reid of the Brighton murders, he remained a potential threat to society due to his extremely disturbed state of mind. The Appeal Court judges chose to ignore her advice of course and released Reid into the community with the subsequent tragic and bloody series of murders in London resulting from their decision. I've often wondered if those judges ever lost any sleep after learning of Reid's horrendous killing spree in Whitechapel which of course, they could have prevented by allowing him to remain under treatment at Ravenswood as Doctor Truman had begged.

Anyway, it transpired during that second spell in Ravenswood that Jack Reid decided he wanted to appoint a new solicitor to act for him. I wasn't hired to try and secure his release, you must understand, or act for him in any way at all with regard to his conviction. Oh no, Jack Reid wanted someone to whom he could tell his story and have it notarised and recorded for posterity. You see, Doctor Hemswell, er, sorry, I mean David, Jack Reid could be, on the surface at least, a personable and charming man. There was no hint of the monster that lurked behind the surface, not when one met and spoke with him under relatively 'normal' circumstances. Being held in a top-security mental institution might not be most people's idea of a normal environment but by the time I met him, Reid had been there long enough for him to refer to the place as 'home'. He apparently felt that the old Cavendish family firm of solicitors in Guildford were 'too close' to the case for him to be able to make a clean breast of things and he'd picked the firm I worked for from the Yellow Pages. I say 'worked for' in the past tense because the strain of all that's happened recently led to me resigning my position with Randall and Merryweather some weeks ago.

Anyway, you must forgive me for digressing. Now, where was I? Ah yes, Reid contacted the firm through the hospital authorities. They have a 'patient's advocate' who handles such things as I later discovered. I'd worked for Randall and Merryweather for over ten years and was one of the senior solicitors at the firm, so when they received the call from such a potentially high profile client, Charles Randall asked me to take on the case, a task I accepted immediately. After all, it appeared to be nothing more than a routine matter of listening to the client and compiling a dossier of notes to be transcribed into a format acceptable to Mr Reid, and then storing them in a place of his choice until we were instructed further as to what to do with them.

Had I known then what I know now, I would have turned Mr Randall down there and then when he offered me the case. As things turned out however, some three days after accepting, I drove down to Ravenswood on a bright, rather warm, sunny morning with no hint in my mind of the horrors that lay in wait for me.

Doctor Truman met me at the reception desk after I'd managed to make my way through the various security checks that exist at Ravenswood. It's a damn hard place to get into, I can testify to that. I can understand why no-one's ever escaped from the place. She took me into her office and told me in no uncertain terms that I would be dealing with an extremely dangerous man, and that under no circumstances should I be taken in by his mild and co-operative demeanour. Jack Reid was a convicted cold-blooded killer, she reminded me, and even though his compulsion to kill came as a result of a psychological illness, it didn't take away the fact that he remained a risk to anyone who came into contact with him. When I made the point that all of his victims had been women, each one an East End prostitute, Ruth Truman answered me with a slightly chilling, "So far, Mr Forbes, so far."

So, suitably warned, I found myself being led along a corridor to a consulting room where Jack Reid would apparently be waiting for me. Ruth Truman opened a door two thirds of the way along the brightly lit corridor and ushered me into a room that took me by surprise. It appeared not so much a traditional doctor's consulting room, but rather it resembled a comfortable sitting room, with large armchairs, strewn with big, plumped up cushions, and an extra wide sofa that could easily accommodate four persons. Positioned in front of a barred window that admitted the bright rays of the morning sun was the only item of furniture that gave away the purpose of the room, a desk on which stood a computer keyboard and monitor, and a push button alarm on the corner of the desk should the physician require assistance in a hurry.

"Jack, your new solicitor, Mr Forbes is here to see you, as you requested," Ruth Truman spoke as we entered the room.

On hearing her voice a figure rose from one of the high-backed chairs that stood with its back facing the door, thus having it made it impossible for me to see that the chair contained an occupant. The slight, yet somehow imposing figure of Jack Reid rose from the chair soundlessly, turning as he did so to allow me my first look at the infamous Ripper copycat, and of course, affording him his initial view of his new legal representative.

I'd only seen head and shoulders shots of Jack Reid previously and meeting him in the flesh was to say the least, rather unnerving. Young looking, he stood rather taller than me, and his hair had thinned considerably during his stay at Ravenswood, when compared with the photographs I'd seen of him in his younger days. He stood erect, and his face, at first a mask of apparent indifference, suddenly broke into a most disarming smile, and Reid held his hand out to me in greeting. I cast a nervous glance at Doctor Truman, who nodded to me and I thus took the proffered hand and accepted the handshake of Jack Reid. As I expected, he had a firm and confident handshake and as he took my hand in his, he spoke his first words to me.

"Welcome, Mr Forbes. I've been reliably informed by the patient advocate that you are the finest solicitor on the payroll at Randall and Merryweather. I hope you'll find working with me an agreeable experience."

"I'm sure I will, Mr Reid."

"Please, you must call me Jack. Everyone else here does, don't they Doctor Truman?"

"Yes of course, Jack. We do, but Mr Forbes has only just met you and may feel it a little improper to be using your first name so soon. After all, he is here in a professional capacity, isn't he?"

"Ah, but we have much to do together. What I have to relate to you, Mr Forbes, will take more than one or two meetings, I'm sure. As I said, please call me Jack. That is my name, after all."

"Very well, Jack it is," I replied

"I'm afraid, Mr Forbes, that Doctor Truman here doesn't quite trust me and has suggested that she remain with us during our talks. I'm not sure if that's acceptable to you. It certainly isn't the way I'd like to do things. Surely, whatever we discuss should remain private between you and me under client-attorney privilege, or whatever it's called."

I wasn't sure how to reply. If Reid's psychiatrist felt uneasy leaving him alone in the room with me, who was I to argue? After all, I may be his solicitor, but that didn't mean I had to place myself at risk in any way.

"Well, I'm not sure if ..."

"Listen, Doctor Ruth," Reid suddenly exclaimed, his whole facial expression becoming animated. "I know that you have video cameras positioned surreptitiously in the room. Don't deny it. We all know you watch us constantly even if we can't always see where the cameras are located. Why don't you just watch Mr Forbes and me on one of those and leave us to talk in peace. After all, what I wish to convey to my solicitor is of a confidential nature. I don't want you or anyone else overhearing what I have to say."

It was plain to see that Reid had planned this all along. It was obvious that the doctor had already told him she'd be sitting in on his meeting with me, but now, he'd managed to manipulate the situation, and indeed the doctor into a position where she could hardly refuse. After all, murderer he may be, but he was still entitled to the privilege of confidentiality when speaking with his solicitor.

"Would you be happy enough to go along with that, Mr Forbes?" Ruth Truman asked.

"Of course," I replied. "I'm sure Mr Reid, er, Jack that is, has no malevolent thoughts about me. After all, I'm here at his request aren't I?"

"Well, said, Mr Forbes," said Reid, apparently pleased at my support of his position.

"Very well," Doctor Truman conceded. "I won't be far away, if you need me, either of you. If you do feel you need assistance Mr Forbes, please press the button on the right-hand side of the desk. It will bring someone immediately."

"Oh, come now, Doctor Ruth, what on earth do you think I'm going to do? Mr Forbes is my new friend. I intend to spend a lot of time in his company in the coming weeks. I'm hardly likely to jeopardise that am I? I need him, and his skills, in order to put my affairs in order. I'm allowed that, at least, aren't I?"

Beams of golden sunlight shone in streams through the barred windows of the room as Ruth Truman rose and took her leave of us a minute or so later. As the door to the consulting room closed behind her I found myself alone with Jack Reid, serial killer and possibly a deranged psychopath for the first time. Did I feel afraid, you might ask? You can bet I did, despite my forced aura of outward calm. I couldn't be sure exactly what this man wanted to tell me or what he expected from me in the coming weeks, but the warmth of the day and the brilliance of the sunbeams that played around the room as I waited for him to begin couldn't take away the sudden chill that gripped my heart and my mind as he settled back in his chair, and I in mine, notebook and micro tape recorder in hand.

Without further preamble, Jack Reid began to slowly relate his story, one which would take me back a hundred years and more before slowly bringing me back to the present. I'd embarked on a time machine of terror, though, as he launched into his strange and at times terrifying tale, I wasn't truly aware of just what I'd let myself in for. That would only become evident later, much later, and by then it would be too late for me to do anything to prevent the terrible events that were simply waiting patiently to reveal themselves.

For now though, the voice of Jack Reid spoke softly and almost hypnotically as it transported me back through the mists of time, back to when, according to him, his story really had its birth, to a time when terror had been not just a word used loosely by the popular press, but a real feeling that gripped the hearts and the minds of a people who lived in a microcosmic world within a world, the denizens of the nineteenth century East End of London, and in particular, the streets of the areas of Whitechapel and Spitalfields. This then, would be the world of Jack the Ripper, a world that Reid was about to introduce me to, though precisely how, or why, I would have to wait to discover."

Forbes hesitated. I smiled in encouragement and for a few seconds I could have sworn that though he sat in the same room with me in my home on Skerries Rock, his mind had drifted far, far away, to another time and another place as his eyes glazed over and he appeared to be in close communion with someone or something I couldn't identify. As quickly as he'd entered that fugue state he appeared to snap out of it, his mind, his thoughts, returning to his body and the present time. I waited, but for a short time the only sound in my sitting room was the rhythmic, sonorous ticking of the grandfather clock that stood to the rear of my chair. Forbes sat silently until, with a sigh and a shrug of his shoulders he readied himself for whatever he was about to reveal.

SIX
THE BIRTH OF A MONSTER?

WHAT I'M ABOUT to relate is the story as told to me by William Forbes. These are his words, as recorded on my own voice recorder, so I make no apologies for any seeming irregularities or exaggerations in the tale.

"This machine can hold two hours of conversation. Will it take any longer?" I enquired, as he prepared himself for his narrative.

"Much longer, I'm afraid," he responded. "We may need a couple of days, with rest periods accounted for too."

"In that case, I'll let you know when the tape's running out. You must give me time to change the tape and check the batteries. If your tale is so extraordinary, I don't want to miss a word of it."

He nodded his agreement. I could see he was anxious to unburden himself.

"You may be surprised that I'm not referring to any notes when I tell you this incredible tale," he began, "though there are notes in my briefcase, I can assure you I don't need them. I've lived with this for so long now that every word of Jack

Reid's story is engraved and embedded deeply in my mind, as though the words were my own. Believe me, Doctor Hemswell, I will tell the story exactly as it should be told."

"You must tell it to me in your own way, William. Please, go on."

He nodded and clasped his hands as though he were about to pray, but of course, what followed was anything but a religious homily, rather a tale of terror and utter degradation told to him by a notorious and very, very clever psychopath.

"And so," Forbes now went on, "My story, or at least the Jack Reid story really begins some twenty-five to thirty years before the streets of Whitechapel ran with the blood of the victims of Jack the Ripper. What I'm about to recount to you is for the most part established fact, but with regards to the Cavendish family history I had to rely on the words of Jack Reid himself. Most of what he'd learned had come from reading the so-called 'Secret Journal of Jack the Ripper' which he assured me had been handed down from generation to generation within his family.

During the latter half of the nineteenth century, in eighteen fifty-six, so I'm told, an eminent doctor, a psychiatrist to be exact, fell in love with the wife of another man. Obviously, such occurrences are commonplace in our modern world, but to have admitted to such an affair in the days of Queen Victoria would have been to invite scorn and approbation from all who knew both the doctor and the lady. So it was that Doctor Burton Cleveland Cavendish and his paramour kept their affair and their love for each other a closely guarded secret. The lady's husband, a colleague of Cavendish's, would surely have cast his wife out had he known of the affair, and the ensuing scandal would have ruined Cavendish's career without doubt. As fast as it had begun, the affair appeared to end when the woman begged Cavendish to leave the small country town where he'd visited her and her husband and return to London, never to see her again, for fear of the repercussions should they be discovered to have indulged in their adulterous liaison.

Reluctantly, but understanding the motives for her request and sharing her dread at the potential results of disclosure, Cavendish left his lover behind, returned to London and threw himself back into his work, his own wife never suspecting his infidelity. It appears that Cavendish genuinely loved his spouse, despite having tarried with the 'other woman' and he set about making life happy for the two of them, though he always clung to the bitter-sweet memories of his short and passionate dalliance.

Sometime later, he received a communication by letter from his former lover who informed him that she'd fallen pregnant. She begged him however, never to return to the little country town where she resided with her husband who professed himself overjoyed at the thought of a child of his own. Only she and Cavendish would ever know the truth, but she implored him, for the sake of the child, to never make any attempt at contact, as to do so might jeopardise not only her marriage, and Cavendish's too, but would also result in their child being declared a bastard, which would bring about his automatic disinheritance by her husband, who would bring the child up as his own. Burton Cavendish therefore relinquished not only his love for the woman, but for the child he thought he'd never know.

Cavendish's career blossomed in the following years and he rose to a position of some eminence within his profession. His wife and son had no inkling of the brief encounter that had seen him father a child he had all but forgotten when, some thirty-two years later, a knock on his door brought a stranger into his life, one who would have a terrible bearing on the future of not only Cavendish, but on the annals of crime in not only England, but throughout the world. The man who stood before Cavendish bore, as his credentials, a letter of introduction written by his late mother, identifying him as the son that Cavendish had fathered so many years previously. It appeared that the woman had fallen ill, been confined to a lunatic asylum, and had died, so along with her husband, the only father the young man had ever known also dead some years previously, Cavendish found himself as the only living relative of the stranger who presented himself at his door. He had no doubts as to the young man's story, as apparently he bore a striking resemblance to his mother, right down to the fact that his eyes, as Cavendish put it in his notes, *'were those of his mother, without a doubt. He shared the same, dark, gypsy-like looks and exhibited the identical lilt in his voice that meant he could be the son of no other woman.'*

The great psychiatrist was crestfallen to hear of the death of his one-time lover, and even more saddened to hear of the circumstances of her illness and subsequent death. The young man appeared to have been well-educated, spoke with a polished accent and testified that he bore Cavendish no ill-will and merely wished to become better acquainted with his natural father, having come to terms with his mother's dying revelation of his true birthright.

So, Burton Cavendish set about trying to make amends for his years of absence from his son's life. He helped him to gain certain social acceptance, introduced him to a number of gentlemen's clubs, and tried to help in furthering the young man's chosen career. Only later did Cavendish discover that his illegitimate son bore the same defective gene that had seen his unfortunate mother descend into madness and despair. Even then the psychiatrist did all he could to try to alleviate and treat the younger man's symptoms. He prescribed laudanum to help with the incessant headaches that beset the man and tried to counsel and advise him even though he could and perhaps should have seen that his efforts were in vain. At no time did Cavendish consider placing the young man in an asylum, where the psychiatric care of the day would leave much to be desired by today's standards. He preferred to give his illegitimate son the benefit of the doubt even when his symptoms began to grow more violent and pronounced, even when the younger man confessed to him during one of his bouts of intense melancholia, that he was in fact the man who all of London sought and reviled, the man the police were unable to lay their hands on, despite a massive and previously unprecedented manhunt. Bedevilled by syphilis and its accompanying madness, the young man became further and further detached from reality and descended into the bowels of society where his new blood lust could be satiated. Still, Cavendish stood by him, and refused to believe what lay before his eyes.

So it was that Burton Cleveland Cavendish, disbelieving the man's confession and dismissing it as the result of his dementia caused by the illness that Cavendish diagnosed as having befallen him, found himself as the father-figure and unofficial physician to a man who the rest of the world would eventually come to know first of all as The Whitechapel Murderer, though within a short space of time that name would change to the more famous (or should that be infamous?) one by which he remains known today.

By the strangest and perhaps most unfortunate set of circumstances, one of Victorian London's most eminent psychiatrists found himself to be the father, though he refused to believe it for a long time, of none other than *Jack the Ripper*. It would be many weeks after the killings began that Cavendish finally began to believe that the unfortunate young man he'd fathered all those years before had degenerated into the most hated and hunted man in the kingdom. Of course, in those weeks, so much would happen and so much blood would flow that the Victorian Press had no compunctions about dubbing those weeks as quite simply 'The Autumn of Terror.'

It would be remiss of me not to give a brief resume of what took place in those few brief, but bloody weeks as the streets of Whitechapel ran with the blood of the Ripper's victims and the population of the East End of London became gripped with a fear such as had never been seen or felt before."

At that point, Forbes sighed, and stretched as though suddenly overtaken by a great tiredness.

"I'm sorry, David," he said wearily. "I didn't realise how exhausted I am. It's tiring me just to talk and tell you the story. Maybe the long journey and the stress I've been living under is catching up with me. Would it be possible to have some coffee perhaps? It might serve to rejuvenate me a little."

"Of course," I replied, rising from my chair and heading for the kitchen. "Stay there and try to relax. I won't be long."

"Thank you," Forbes spoke wearily. "I'm sorry, I don't want to delay things, but I can hardly keep my eyes open."

"No need to apologise, we're in no real hurry. Now that you're here, it's okay to relax and tell me whatever you have to in your own time."

I spoke encouragingly, though I admit to being a little frustrated at Forbes having interrupted the telling of his story so soon. No matter, we weren't going anywhere, and it would only take me a few minutes to prepare a refreshing and hopefully revitalising pot of coffee for the two of us.

I worked fast, hindered only by the time it took for the kettle to boil. As I waited, I pondered on Forbes's introduction to the story. If what he'd related to me so far proved true, then Jack Reid had given him the only recorded account of the birth of Jack the Ripper, though of course, he'd appended no name to the bastard offspring of Burton Cavendish thus far. I hoped that would come soon as Forbes delved deeper into his story. I knew that what he was telling me might prove to be nothing more than the ravings of a psychotically deranged madman, and yet, there remained the tantalising possibility that this could be the one and only definitive biographical account of the life of that most heinous of Victorian serial killers, Jack the Ripper himself.

Returning to my sitting room a mere ten minutes later, eager for Forbes to resume his narrative, I was disappointed to find my guest slumped in the armchair, where I'd left him. He was snoring loudly, one arm draped over the arm of the chair, the other supporting his head as he used it as a makeshift pillow against the other chair arm. The tiredness he'd felt earlier had obviously been more exhausting than he'd realised and had taken its toll on his consciousness. I felt he needed to rest and refresh his body and mind, so, though disappointed at the early interruption to his strange tale, I relaxed into my own chair and poured myself a mug of hot coffee. I pulled up a footstool from beside the chair and put my feet up. I glanced toward the window. The light outside was growing dim as the twilight darkness of evening raced the incoming high tide to be first to arrive at my island home.

The rain had thankfully long-since relented and passed us by and after finishing my coffee I stood at my open front door for a few minutes, enjoying the calm and peaceful serenity that had descended upon Skerries Rock. The sound of the

Atlantic rollers breaking against the rocky coastline of the island reached me, and brought with it a feeling of permanence, as though my island was an indestructible fortress that had withstood such tides for many a century and would continue to do so for many more to come.

Evening came quickly on Skerries Rock, and as the darkness slowly overwhelmed the fading twilight, I closed the door and returned to my chair by the fireside. Forbes continued to snore, and I forced myself to rein in my own frustration. As much as I wanted to hear the rest of his story, he so obviously needed to sleep. Putting my feet up once again I felt my own eyes growing heavy. Surely if my guest could enjoy a much-needed sleep, a short nap couldn't hurt me either, could it?

The scream that brought me back to the land of wakefulness a short time later made a mockery of my innocent thoughts of restorative sleep!

SEVEN
THE CRIMES OF JACK THE RIPPER

"William! Mr. Forbes! For God's sake snap out of it. It's okay, you're safe. You're with me, David Hemswell, remember?"

The terrible sound that Forbes had unleashed and which had woken me from my all too brief slumber continued unabated as I leaped from my chair and gripped the hysterical man by the shoulders, doing my best to calm him down and bring him back to reality, for it was plainly evident to me that he'd entered some dark, nether world where his own personal demons were playing havoc with his mind. His eyes, though open, appeared to be looking at something that I, in my own, safe, sane, and ordered world, could only guess at. The terror that lurked within his mind had taken full hold, and Forbes appeared lost to reality, at least for the time being. Had I been possessed of neighbours in close proximity to my home, they would have been fully justified in calling the police under the assumption that a horrific murder was taking place within my walls. There are times when solitude and isolation can be a blessing. This was indeed one of them.

I tried again: "William. Please, listen to me. Nothing is

going to happen to you. You're perfectly safe and secure. You're on Skerries Rock, not in London. No-one can harm you here."

The man's terror showed no sign of abating as his body began to shake uncontrollably and he continued to stare at something I possessed no comprehension of. I thought that perhaps he was in the throes of a psychotic seizure, such was the intensity of the spasms which now rocked his body, and I began to fear for the man's sanity. Had I done the right thing in allowing him to come to my home? If indeed the man was deranged in some way it would take a great effort for me to summon the specialist help he would require. The nearest hospital that might be in a position to help him stood on the mainland, in the village of Durness, the most north-westerly village in Scotland. I doubted that they would possess a psychiatric unit however and envisaged a long and perhaps disturbing journey ahead for the man if he were to require specialist treatment. Durness itself is a bleak and lonely enclave of civilisation, with the remaining area of the North West of the country being off-limits to ordinary folk such as me due to the presence of the nearby military base.

As I pondered on the options for a medical evacuation of William Forbes, the man's seizure began to dissipate. The glazed and fixed look in his eyes began to soften and the muscle spasms that wracked his body began to subside. Slowly, very slowly, physical normality returned to my guest, and I looked at my watch, surprised to discover that barely two minutes had passed since his screams had wrenched me from my brief sleep. It felt as if I'd battled with his terror for more than an hour. Such is the power of the mind to confuse and distract any one of us from reality!

I continued to kneel before the man as a modicum of mental equilibrium returned to his troubled mind. At last, the fear appeared to depart from his eyes, and he looked around, as though unsure of exactly where he was. As his eyes locked on to mine, realisation dawned on him and his entire body visibly relaxed. William Forbes had returned from whatever dark place had held him captive. Now I needed to discover just where or what that place might be and how it connected with the story he was attempting to relate to me.

As his breathing returned to a near normal rhythm, I at last ventured the simple question, "Feeling better?"

"Yes, thank you. I'm so deeply sorry you had to see all that. I've hardly slept for so long, because I try so hard to stay awake. As soon as I fall asleep, it begins, slowly at first and then the intensity grows and grows, and I get dragged deeper and deeper in to the filthy degraded world of that vile evil monster!"

You mean Jack Reid?" I asked.

"No, David, not Jack Reid, I'm talking about Jack the Ripper!"

"But how, William? How on earth do you expect me to believe that somehow you're being used by or haunted by the ghost, the spirit, call it what you will, of Jack the Ripper?"

"That's what I tried to tell you," he said, breathlessly. "It's that damned paper." He pointed at the plastic sleeve containing the page he'd entrusted to me.

"Somehow, and don't ask me how, but it seems to carry all the malevolent evil that existed in the black heart of the Ripper. When I've told you my tale, perhaps you'll understand. At least, I pray to God you will, for if you don't and you say you can't help me, I don't know what I shall do."

In my own heart, I wanted to tell him not to be so irrational and that a piece of paper couldn't possibly be responsible for what was happening to him. I honestly believed that William Forbes was experiencing some form of psychological breakdown, and for that reason, decided to keep quiet for now and try to get him to reveal everything in the course of his story.

"Then perhaps you should continue to enlighten me, William, but before you do, please tell me what you saw in your dream that so disturbed you."

"Oh, my God, I can't possibly tell you what I saw. The mere thought of it is simply so horrendous, so absolutely disgustingly terrible that you would never believe me."

"Try me."

"All of the horrors of the Ripper's crimes are revealed to me in those dreams, David. Not only the blood and the gore and the awful mutilations, but I see the spirits, if that's what they are, of the women he murdered, being tortured and tormented in a perpetual and blood-soaked carousel of terror. Where they are I have no idea, but they are like unearthly wraiths, formless and yet solid enough to grip my heart, my soul, and my mind, to take a hold of the very fabric of my being and they try to drag me into their horrific world, for what purpose, I have no idea. You have to help me David, really, please you must!"

"William, calm down, please. I've already told you that I'll listen to your story and if it is in any way possible for me to help you after hearing what you have to say, then you may rest assured that I shall do so. Now, what you tell me is indeed a horrifying and terrifying thing to dream of, a nightmare of very great proportions, but it is still just a dream. You mustn't allow it to affect you so much."

"I know you don't believe me," he went on, "but maybe you will when I finish telling you my story."

"Then I implore you, William. Please continue your intriguing story."

With that, William Forbes once again began to speak in that characteristic soft and melodic voice of his, and I found myself once again being transported back in time to the streets of Victorian Whitechapel, to the world of the infamous, and as yet unidentified, Jack the Ripper.

"In order for you to fully understand the true horror of the terrible story I've found myself wrapped up in, I really do have to make sure you know just how all of this came to pass. I assume you know something of the Whitechapel Murders of 1888?"

"I know of Jack the Ripper, and I know he went on a murderous spree on the streets of Whitechapel, killing prostitutes, and I even know some of their names, Mary Kelly and Catherine Eddowes for example. I'm not fully conversant with all that took place, but I do know that the police never apprehended or charged anyone with the crimes. There've been numerous theories as to his identity over the years, even some who've tried to implicate royalty, or who have hinted at a Masonic conspiracy, but that's about the full store of my knowledge on the subject."

"Okay, David, please listen very carefully. I've learned these events so exactly, the fact that I can recite them back to you without notes is scary enough as it is. When I tell you that I've actually 'seen' some of these events in my mind, it will give you an idea just how terrible a mess I've become caught up in."

I said nothing in reply to Forbes's outlandish claim to have seen the events of 1888 'in his mind'. I merely listened as he took up his tale once more.

"The crimes of Jack the Ripper took place against the backdrop of filth and degradation that pervaded the Whitechapel and Spitalfields areas of Victorian London. In what became known as 'The Autumn of Terror' the world's first officially acknowledged 'serial killer' stalked his prey and carried out his hideous campaign of murder and mutilation amidst the streets and alleyways of a veritable rabbit-warren of streets that reeked of human effluent, mirroring the poverty and deprivation that stared out at the rank thoroughfares from the windows of squalid, bleak buildings that housed the employed, the unemployed and the unemployable of the city's vast underclass of the poor. Even regular employment provided no guarantee of a healthy or a long life on those mean streets, with the work available to the denizens of Whitechapel usually being that of the manual labourer, back-breaking work with long hours, poor pay and no assurance of job security. Often, such work, perhaps in the markets of London or at the vast docks that served the Capital city of the British Empire, via the comings and goings of the great ocean-going ships that carried goods to and from the capital was of the casual, transient kind, a day here or there if the worker was lucky. Every single day huge queues would build up wherever the prospect of earning a few shillings, or often no more than a handful of pennies presented itself.

Women's prospects were even worse. Education was certainly not universally available to girls, particularly those of the working classes, and marriage often proved the only means of escape from total destitution. Such marriages in themselves would often lead to the eventual descent of many a young (and often not-so-young) woman into the ancient art of prostitution. Sometimes, it would be the only way for a woman to supplement the meagre earnings of a poorly paid husband, or, often tragically, the only way for a widow, (and there many), to keep body and soul together after the loss of a husband's earnings. You may be surprised to learn that the majority of the victims of Jack the Ripper were at one time married women, mothers, and with the exception of the final victim, Mary Jane Kelly, all were what today would be termed 'mature' women.

So, the streets of Whitechapel literally teemed with those least able to cry for help in a society that cared little or nothing for the very people whose efforts powered the great city's factories and dockyards, or who worked in the great houses of the rich, returning home each night to the squalor and deprivation of their so-called 'homes' in the East End of London. Many of those homes were nothing more than a single, rented room which might house a family of perhaps seven or eight persons, living in filth and with no sanitary provision. Even the dubious 'luxury' of having such a place to call home was denied to thousands more, who spent their lives on the excrement-strewn streets and who would try to raise a few pence a day to rent a bed in one of the many foul smelling, overcrowded doss houses that had sprung up in the area to cater for this pitiful underclass of the poor.

Little wonder, David, that disease and crime was rife, given the appalling conditions in which those poor souls attempted to eke out their miserable existence.

Somewhat perversely overlooked from almost every angle by the spire of Christ Church, Spitalfields, Jack the Ripper's killing ground covered only a small geographical area and spanned only a few weeks in time, yet his reign of terror would reach out to touch the hearts and minds of almost everyone within the vast metropolis of London and far beyond, as the notoriety of his crimes became known throughout the country and afar. There were those who would later attempt to attribute other, later killings to the Whitechapel murderer, but most scholars are of the opinion that the murders of Jack the Ripper ended with that of Mary Kelly on the 9th November 1888.

There was some speculation and disagreement at one time as to who was indeed the Ripper's first victim, with many wishing to blame the killing of Martha Tabram on some other, unknown assailant. It's now generally believed and accepted however, that Tabram was the Ripper's first victim, and so we will take the date of her murder, 31st August 1888 as the beginning of the Ripper's terrible killing spree, ending with the butchery of the unfortunate Mary Kelly on 9th November, a mere ten weeks from start to finish.

The murders of Martha Tabram and Mary Ann Nicholls took place on the 7th and the 31st of August, respectively. Following the death of Nicholls, a mere eight days passed before the killer struck again, this time with even greater severity. Annie Chapman's injuries showed the gathering intensity of the killer's bloodlust and sent shivers down the spine of every right-thinking citizen as they were revealed in detail both at the inquest into her death and in the pages of the popular press. At that time, the name 'Jack the Ripper' hadn't yet been coined for the murderer. The name only began to be applied to the killer after the receipt of a letter, mailed to the Central News Agency on 27th September, and reproduced in the morning newspaper *The Daily News* on 1st October, the day after the so-called 'Double Event' to which I shall refer in a moment. Often regarded as a hoax by modern Ripperologists, the 'Dear Boss' letter nonetheless identified the killer by the name with which he will always be remembered, being signed "Yours Truly, Jack the Ripper."

I have memorised that fearful text, which was full of apparently random spelling and grammatical errors and read as follows, though I've also written it out for you as the killer wrote it.

Forbes passed me a piece of paper that he'd drawn from his pocket and I read it as he continued:

25 Sept 1888

Dear Boss

I keep on hearing the police have caught me but they wont fix me just yet. I have laughed when they look so clever and talk about being on the right track. That joke about Leather Apron gave me real fits. I am down on whores and I shant quit ripping them till I do get buckled. Grand work the last job was. I gave the lady no time to squeal. How can they catch me now. I love my work and want to start again. You will soon here of me with my funny little games. I saved some of the proper red stuff in a ginger beer bottle over the last job to write with but it went thick like glue and I cant use it. Red ink is fit enough I hope haha. The next job I do I shall clip the ladys ears off and send to the police officers just for jolly wouldn't you. Keep this letter back till I do a bit more work, then give it out straight. My knife's nice and sharp I want to get to work right away if I get the chance. Good luck.

Yours truly
Jack the Ripper

With those few words, a new terror was born, and a name given to the faceless assailant who appeared free to roam and kill at will. The people of London and the rest of the world would forever associate the crimes of that autumn with the man who, though never captured, identified or brought to justice will always be known as Jack the Ripper.

That terror, the fear of the ordinary citizen and the anger at the police force's seeming inability to apprehend the killer grew to massive proportions when, twenty two days after the murder of Annie Chapman, the night before the letter was delivered to the press agency, the as yet un-named Whitechapel murderer claimed not one, but *two* victims in one night.

Swedish born Elizabeth Stride, (nee Gustavsdotter), aged forty-five, became the third victim of the ripper, her body being discovered in Dutfield's Yard by Louis Diemschutz, a street seller of cheap jewellery, as he drove his horse and cart into the yard at around 1 a.m. Her body had not been subjected to the mutilations present in the bodies of Tabram or Chapman, but Diemschutz testified that he believed he may have disturbed the killer before he was able to carry out such mutilations and so perhaps fuelled the killer's need to find another victim upon whom he could satisfy his evil lust that night.

That second victim of the night and the fifth victim in Jack's reign of terror was forty-six-year-old Catharine Eddowes, a native of the city of Wolverhampton, who had long since descended into a life of prostitution on the streets of the capital. Her savagely mutilated body was discovered by a police constable, Edward Watkins, at around 1.15 a.m. in the southwest corner of Mitre Square. Watkins saw and heard no-one as he entered the square and Eddowes proved to be the most brutally mutilated victim of the killer thus far, perhaps a victim of his fury at being interrupted in his 'work' upon the body of poor Elizabeth Stride a short time earlier.

The post-mortem examination of her remains was carried out by Dr Frederick Gordon Brown and his report provided disturbing reading to say the least. Catharine Eddowes throat had been cut, "to the extent of about six or seven inches." The big muscle across the throat had been completely divided on the left side. The large vessels on the left side of the neck were severed. Her larynx had been severed below the vocal chord and all the deep structures of the throat were severed to the bone. The cause of death was haemorrhage from the carotid artery and Brown estimated that death would have been immediate, and that the mutilations were carried out post-mortem.

On examining the deceased's abdomen he found that the front walls had been opened from the breast bone to the pubes. The liver had been stabbed and slit through by a sharp object. Her intestines had been drawn out and placed over the right shoulder, with one section having been cut away completely and placed beside the poor woman's body. The face had been heavily mutilated, with the nose almost being cut away, one ear virtually severed, mutilating cuts about the face resulting in flaps of skin being formed around much of the face. The womb had been cut through horizontally, and the woman's left kidney had been carefully and precisely removed from the body. These were but some of the injuries listed in Brown's post-mortem report and serve to show the escalation in severity of the Ripper's attacks and I ask you, who on earth could do such things to another human being?

The police investigation continued, hampered slightly by the fact that Eddowes' body had been discovered within the boundaries of the City of London, thus coming under the jurisdiction of the City of London Police Force as opposed to the Metropolitan Police who had been in sole charge of the case up until that time. A public clamour soon broke out, with demands that the police take action and discover and bring the murderer to heel. There were demands for the resignation of the Commissioner of Police, and vigilante committees were formed and took to the streets at night in the hope of catching the killer.

Despite the police flooding the streets with uniformed and plain clothes officers, not one shred of viable evidence was ever found that might have led to an identification of the man responsible for the terrible crimes that were being perpetrated, seemingly at will upon the citizens of Whitechapel.

Within days however the killer had an almost universally known name, as the 'Dear Boss' letter appeared in the press and the name of *Jack the Ripper* was being shouted from every street corner by the newspaper sellers and the fear that had gripped the East End of London grew with every passing day that brought no results in the police investigation.

October passed without another killing on the streets of Whitechapel, and though the public continued to demand action from the police in tracking down the killer, the public outcry that had greeted the first four murders began to dissipate. Perhaps, some thought, Jack the Ripper had gone, left the country, or simply ceased his evil ways and that the terror had passed. They couldn't have been more wrong. Jack the Ripper's most heinous crime was yet to come, an act of barbarism and butchery so terrible that grown men, hardened police officers used to seeing the most hideous sights that man could inflict upon his fellows, actually broke down and cried when confronted with the scene that met their eyes on the morning of 9th November 1888.

In a room in Millers Court, off Dorset Street in Whitechapel, the body of Mary Jane Kelly was discovered by Thomas Bowyer as he attempted to collect the rent she owed on her room. Aged around twenty-five, Mary Kelly proved to be the youngest victim of the Ripper and the mutilations carried out upon her body were so terrible and so vile that little was left of the woman that could be positively identified.

Her breasts had been cut off, the right arm slightly abducted from the body and rested on the mattress. The whole of the surface of the abdomen had been removed and thighs had been removed and the abdominal cavity emptied of the viscera. The tissues of the neck had been severed all the way round, down to the bone. The viscera were discovered in various places around the body. The uterus, kidneys and one breast were found under the head, the other breast placed by the right foot. The liver was between the feet, the intestines by the right side and the spleen by the right side of the body. The flaps of skin that had been removed from the abdomen and thighs had been laid on a table. The woman's face was gashed 'in all directions'. The nose, cheeks, eyebrows and ears were all partly removed. The lips had been cut by several incisions down to the chin. The neck was cut through together with the other tissues down to the vertebrae.

In short, Mary Jane Kelly had been murdered, and then systematically butchered by the most heinous killer yet known to the British Police, or to the public at large!

Those are the crimes of Jack the Ripper, David, told to you in as succinct a manner as I can condense them to, and of course, to this day no-one has ever named the killer, though the list of apparent suspects has grown over the years as numerous 'experts' have added their own theories to the case. I'm sorry if some of what I've told you has been graphic in its descriptive content, but I assure you I have only told you these things because you must know and understand as much about the Ripper as possible if you are to later understand what I have yet to reveal to you."

"Don't apologise, William," I responded. "I've heard many terrible stories in my time I can assure you of that. Yes, what the Ripper did to those unfortunate women was truly horrendous, but many modern serial killers have far outdone him in terms of the outright savagery of their crimes, I fear."

"Maybe," Forbes went on, "But none of them came back to haunt the living in the present, did they?"

I avoided giving the man a direct answer to that one, and instead glanced at the clock, which read six-thirty. He'd talked for longer than I'd thought, and the first pangs of hunger were now beginning to gnaw at my stomach. Time, I felt, for a break. We had to eat, after all.

"I think that you've reached a good point for us to rest a while, William. Perhaps we should eat, and if you don't feel too tired afterwards, we can return to your narrative?"

Forbes appeared to welcome the thought of a good meal.

"Why, that would be wonderful. I haven't eaten properly for days," he said, "and yes, I suppose this is a good a place as any to stop and refresh ourselves. I hope you'll allow me to carry on afterwards though?"

"Of course. We've nowhere else to run away to, have we? I want to know where this tale of yours is leading, after all."

William Forbes now relaxed once more, his shoulders sagging as he released the tension that must have existed within every muscle in his body. He appeared to shrink before my eyes as he lolled back in the armchair, crossed his legs, and closed his eyes for a full five seconds as though by doing so he could shut out...what?

"Do you want to wait here while I rustle us up something to eat? Cheese omelette and salad alright with you?"

"Sounds excellent, but if it's all the same to you, I'll keep you company in the kitchen. I don't want to fall asleep again, David. You've no idea what those things do to me while my eyes are shut, and my guard is down."

With that, the two of us rose from our seats and made our way to the kitchen where I soon had our evening meal prepared. We sat in a comfortable and companionable silence at the old oak table that served as work surface and dining table in my home, and Forbes looked to me like man who hadn't eaten in days, so quickly did he devour the simple but stomach filling meal I'd prepared for us. It was clear to me that it wasn't only his mind that had been affected by whatever trauma had ensued from his connection with Jack Reid. He had so obviously not taken care of himself in a dietary capacity as well, and as such had laid himself open to illness in more ways than one.

As the pall of night settled over Skerries Rock, and the last of the crockery was washed, dried and put away in my kitchen cupboard, Forbes and I made our way back to the living room, where I poured us both a large brandy before motioning to Forbes to retake his place in my fireside chair. Heavy rain was once more lashing down outside, and the drumming of the raindrops on the windows and the sound of the wind as it skirled around the building appeared to raise the levels of nervousness in my guest once more. He sipped at his brandy, his eyes again furtively glancing around the room, checking for some unseen and unknown apparition to appear perhaps, and then, drawing himself up in the chair, he took a deep breath before continuing his extraordinary tale.

Things were about get remarkably interesting as Forbes now set out to reveal some of what may or not be the true and as yet unknown facts surrounding the Jack the Ripper murders. I couldn't yet envisage just *how* interesting and terrifying his tale would be!

EIGHT

THE CONFESSION OF BURTON CLEVELAND CAVENDISH

"You must understand," Forbes reminded me, "that what I'm telling you is the story as related to me by Jack Reid. I checked the facts surrounding the Jack the Ripper case of course, just to be sure they were accurate, and I can assure you they are. The next section of my story is the part we have to take on trust for the most part, as it relates to Reid's recollection of the journal he says was bequeathed to him by his uncle, Robert Cavendish, and which he himself received in a similar fashion on the death of his father. The journal would appear to have become something of a Cavendish family rolling legacy of evil according to Reid, who, as Robert Cavendish's nephew, became the first non-bearer of the Cavendish name to receive it."

Forbes paused just long enough to look at me as I nodded and urged him to go on with his narrative.

"So, the police were baffled. Jack the Ripper had committed the most heinous and revolting of his crimes, the murder and butchering of Mary Kelly. Despite the offer of a reward, members of various vigilance committees patrolling the streets, and the largest manhunt England had ever witnessed, the murderer was never identified, much less apprehended and brought to justice. Even in the time of Queen Victoria you might think that someone, somewhere would have had an inkling as to his identity, have picked up a clue that a relative or friend perhaps might be behind the killings. Well, David, it appears that someone did!

According to the journal which Reid asserted as having been written by the Ripper himself, the Ripper had visited his father, Burton Cavendish on a number of occasions in the months leading up to, and in the course of the weeks during which he committed the murders. He professed to be suffering from terrible headaches and to the hearing of voices in his head. Cavendish, perhaps blind to the reality of the situation due to his feelings towards the man's mother, chose not to read the signs of his symptoms correctly. As a psychiatrist he should perhaps have recognised the paranoia that appeared to have infected his illegitimate offspring, who was indeed hospitalised on at least two occasions in the summer and autumn of 1888. On both occasions, Cavendish helped secure his release without him being referred to an asylum for treatment of his apparent mental aberrations. This was despite the fact that on one occasion, heavily under the influence of the drug laudanum, the man confessed to being the Ripper to his father, who chose to disbelieve his son. Instead, he put such confessions down as part of the ramblings of a disturbed mind, rather than a true revelation of the facts. The journal even listed a further murder, committed in Leith, near Edinburgh, during the long lull between the killings of Catherine Eddowes and Mary Kelly in London. Jack Reid told me that the journal described in great detail not only the Ripper's journey by rail to the Scottish capital, but also gave a graphic account of the murder of a young Scottish prostitute whose body he disposed of by dumping the remains into the Firth of Forth.

By the time Burton Cavendish eventually accepted the truth about his illegitimate son, it was too late for him to do anything without confessing to his own shortcomings, not to mention his long-ago indiscretion with the man's mother. In a letter to his legitimate son, Cavendish confessed to having visited the Ripper every day after his last gruesome atrocity until he eventually arrived at the final decision that would put an end to Jack the Ripper once and for all. The poor man's mind must have been in a terrible turmoil as he decided to extinguish the reign of terror of Jack the Ripper in the only way that would keep the secret of his birth, and his identity from being made public and bringing shame and ignominy on his family: his illegitimate offspring must die!

Surely, David, we can only guess at the inner turmoil that Cavendish must have endured. There he was, recently united with a son born to the woman he'd loved so many years previously, only to discover that his offspring had grown up to become the most reviled killer in England's history. Then it must have taken a Herculean effort to decide to end the life of the man, who was after all, seriously mentally ill and would today have been incarcerated in a top security mental hospital at the very most. It would seem that Cavendish kept the Ripper under sedation for a number of days while he made his plans for the final 'disposal' of the man, before eventually taking him to the banks of the River Thames, where Cavendish loaded his pockets with rocks to ensure he would sink and then pushed the man under the dark waters of the river, watching him as he sank forever into oblivion. Cavendish then took the journal from the Ripper's lodgings and made sure it remained hidden for the rest of his life. I can't guess as to why he never destroyed the infernal document, but instead, he bequeathed it to his own son, Robert Cavendish's grandfather, with a series of notes and letters written by himself, in which he detailed his own involvement in the case. That journal thus became the twisted and evil legacy that would be handed down through the generations of the Cavendish family, always through the male line.

What Cavendish was obviously unaware of, and his descendants only found out far too late, was that the journal bore more than just the words that told of the deeds of the Ripper. Although it would appear to have missed out a couple of generations, it would appear that the pages of Jack the Ripper's secret journal were imbued in some way with the soul and the living embodiment of the evil that the Ripper had brought to bear during his life. Perhaps one had to be born with a certain mental gene present in order for the journal to carry out its infernal task, but it certainly had a dramatic and eventually lethal effect on Robert Cavendish, Jack Reid's uncle, as it did on Mark Cavendish, Robert's brother, thought to be the man who actually carried out the Brighton murders that Reid was convicted of, only to be exonerated in due course. Of course, on Mark's death, the journal then took a firm hold on the mind of Jack Reid, and the latter-day Whitechapel murders were the result.

It was believed that the journal, if it existed (there always remained official scepticism on that line of thought), had been totally destroyed when Mark Cavendish was killed in a car accident in Warsaw, which saw his body and the contents of his case, including the journal, incinerated in the ensuing fire after the crash. Only fragments remained and were produced in evidence at Reid's appeal hearing and they indeed helped in many ways to secure his release. Those fragments were of course sealed away with the case files, where I imagine they must remain to this day. No-one imagined however, that a section, a whole page of the journal remained untouched, and unharmed by the flames.

On his release from Ravenswood, Jack Reid returned to his parents' home, where he found the last remaining complete page of the journal hidden away in his room, waiting for him to come home and reclaim his legacy. Now David, I think I should bring you up to speed with the facts of Jack Reid's case, in case you're not fully conversant with them."

"I only know what I've read in the newspapers over the years, William," I replied. "I'm sure you'll be able to tell me so much more than the press was ever allowed to report."

"Oh yes, David, I can indeed. I can tell you much, much more. I know you think I'm mad, and perhaps you're right to do so, but maybe you'll change your mind as my story goes on."

"I'm listening, William," was all I could say. I admit to becoming engrossed in his tale. It sounded outlandish and impossible, but then there existed a certain degree of sincerity about Forbes that meant I could do no more than grant him the decency of a fair hearing of his story. I had many questions forming in my mind based on what he'd told me (and indeed, hadn't told me) so far, but I'd agreed to let him continue unhindered as far as possible, and thus, for the moment, I held my silence and allowed him to go on with his tale of events.

Accordingly, as the shadows of evening gave way to full-blown night and the wind whipped in swirling gusts around the solid walls of my croft, William Forbes left the Victorian years behind, and his story arrived firmly in the twentieth century. The shocks, however, were only just beginning.

NINE
THE CAVENDISH LEGACY

"I've no idea what happened to the journal between the time that Burton Cavendish read it and it's re-surfacing years later when eventually passed on to his grandson, Doctor Robert Cavendish, his great grandson and Jack Reid's uncle," Forbes continued.

"From what I can deduce, the effects of the journal don't seem to strike at every generation. Like I said, perhaps there is a gene within the recipient that makes them susceptible to the Ripper's words. Who knows? I do know that Robert Cavendish was the last person before Jack Reid to have close contact with the journal, and although he appeared to be immune to the murderous aspects we've come to associate with Jack Reid, it's certain that reading the journal had a profound and disturbing effect on him. He was involved in a car crash that killed his own father and left Robert in a coma for quite some time. When he eventually awoke from the coma, he insisted that he'd been in the presence of Jack the Ripper and that the Ripper had shown him all sorts of terrible scenes that depicted the awful mutilations he'd carried out on his victims. Cavendish also claimed to have witnessed the tortured souls of the victims, trapped in some kind of limbo from which they couldn't escape. He reported to his wife that he'd been reading the secret journal of the Ripper and yet, it wasn't until some weeks later that he received a call from his solicitor informing his that his father had bequeathed him a package in his will, and that package, Jack Reid swore to me, contained the journal. Did Robert Cavendish therefore dream of the contents of the journal, or was he simply in a coma-induced hallucinatory state as suggested by the doctors? Or, and this is the scary bit, David, did he, during his coma, actually 'connect' in some way with his long dead illegitimate ancestor? Did Jack the Ripper somehow 'break through' time and space and reach out to fill Robert's head with the scenes and sights and sounds that haunted Cavendish for the rest of his life? He died soon afterwards, you see, of a brain tumour. It all happened so suddenly, and no-one was ever able to find out what really happened to Robert, but it's reasonably certain that his mind became seriously unhinged by whatever he'd read, real or imagined. And now, David, we come to Jack Reid himself. From the official records, and from what Reid himself told me, the young Jack Reid had a fairly troubled childhood. The youngster was beset by a sort of 'blood-fixation' and his parents were sufficiently worried by his obsession with all things to do with blood that they sought the help of a child psychologist. Over the years, Reid was also subjected to examinations by psychiatrists, and therapists of all types and eventually, he was thought to have been cured of his obsession. That is, until he bit off the ear of a schoolmate during a playground fracas after the boy had taunted him about being a 'weirdo'. Reid ended up completing his education in a 'special school' for troubled children, but again, by the time he reached his late teens, he was considered free of his previous obsessions and problem behaviour.

Indeed, so well had he progressed that he was able to secure employment as a trainee nurse and became in fact one of the star pupils of his course at his local teaching hospital until the fateful day, when attaining the age of eighteen, he received notification from the family solicitors of his having been bequeathed a legacy from his uncle, the late Robert Cavendish.

That legacy of course turned out to be the journal. According to Jack Reid, he began to read it late one night in the privacy of his bedroom. The first thing he noticed was that the pages felt warm to the touch, as though the aged yellow paper had been infused with a kind of life of their own. The words contained on the page also appeared fluid, and Reid found himself falling under a strange, almost hypnotic spell as he read the words of the long-dead Ripper. The journal, so he told me, exerted such influence over him that he found himself compelled to read on, even when tiredness began to overwhelm him. The Ripper described the most appalling aspects of his crimes, and Jack Reid could feel himself being 'sucked in' as he described it, to the world of Jack the Ripper. He began to actually 'see' the events described on the sickly warm pages, even becoming able to 'hear' the cries of the victims as they gasped out their final breaths. Reid told me that the sights and sounds he witnessed during his reading of the journal were such that he found himself physically appalled and his body began to be wracked with tremors as the full horror of the world of Jack the Ripper became all too apparent to him. Alongside the journal itself were the letters and notes of Burton Cleveland Cavendish, and other notes added through the years by Robert Cavendish and his own father and grandfather.

All of them warned of the fearful consequences that any reader of the journal would be potentially exposed to, and, as I did when Reid first told me this, you're probably wondering why none of the Cavendish men had ever had the sense, or perhaps the nerve, to simply destroy the journal, to end its evil influence, if they so firmly believed in it. Well, from the notes each of his ancestors had placed within the journal, Reid was able to ascertain that none of them had been able to destroy it, as, first of all, they felt compelled by 'something' to ensure that it remained intact, and secondly, each felt that the 'Cavendish Secret' should be carried forward through the generations in order that the truth would always be known to at least one member of the family. It contained too great a secret to be expunged from history altogether, or so the collective thoughts of the Cavendish's believed.

So, Jack Reid completed his reading of the journal, and it appears to have affected his mind so much that he felt the urgent need to seek help in deciphering exactly just what it all meant, not just to him, but to his family as a whole. His mind fought and tussled with all manner of thoughts over the next few days as he tried to decide how to handle the awesome information he'd become privy to. Eventually, he decided that the only person who might have some knowledge of what had happened to Robert Cavendish, and therefore have some insight into what may lie before him, was Robert's brother, Mark. He knew he'd learn nothing from Robert's widow, his Aunt Sarah. This was a male-only secret and perhaps Robert had confided in his brother before his death. For that reason alone, Jack Reid took the decision that would irrevocably change his life. One day, without telling anyone, including his parents, he simply disappeared from home. He knew that Mark had at one time had business interests in the seaside town of Brighton, and it was to there that he set off in search of answers. He acknowledged to me that it was an illogical step, for after all, he had no way of knowing if Robert had ever spoken to his brother of the journal, but, he felt compelled to follow the path he'd set himself upon.

He had little money and found himself living rough on the streets of Brighton at first as he began his search, but of Mark Cavendish, there was no sign. Reid even sent a female acquaintance from back home to the family solicitors in Guildford in the hope that she might find an address for his uncle, all to no avail. In short, he was clutching at straws. Perhaps he'd already become so influenced by the journal into behaving in a somewhat erratic and outlandish fashion. I shan't bore you with the full details, David, but if you've read of the case, as I know you have, you'll be aware that Reid was 'picked up' off the streets by a man named Michael, who feigned friendship with the young man in order to recruit him as a partner in his drug peddling enterprise. What Reid wasn't aware of was that his uncle, Mark Cavendish was in fact the paymaster who directed 'Michael's' movements and when Michael searched through Reid's belongings as he slept and found the journal, he of course stole it and took it to 'the man' as Cavendish became referred to during Reid's trial. For Mark Cavendish, all his dreams had come true. It would seem that Mark was indeed the embodiment of the Ripper in a modern-day incarnation. He quickly used Michael to ensure that Jack was kept well supplied with enough drugs to keep him in a semi- comatose but compliant and easily influenced frame of mind. They turned Jack Reid into a junkie in no time at all by lacing his food and drinks with the drugs.

When the Ripper copycat murders took place in Brighton, Mark Cavendish, through Michael, ensured that Reid was always on the scene so that they could drench him in the victim's blood, photograph him with the murder weapon in his hand, and between them they did enough to ensure that Reid would believe himself to be the killer. The young Jack Reid, already partly disturbed by his encounter with the journal would become the perfect 'patsy' for Cavendish in his evil plans.

I think you know what happened next. Three women were brutally murdered in the exact manner that the victims of Jack the Ripper had been killed. Only the dogged work of Inspector Mike Holland and Sergeant George Wright, helped by ripperologist Alice Nickels, who discovered that the killer had overlaid a map of Whitechapel with one of modern-day Brighton, enabled them to predict where the killer would strike next. So they were on the scene when the third killing took place, though they were too late to save the unfortunate victim who had been killed a day earlier and Reid left in a drugged state on the scene, ready to be picked up and charged with the crimes, as indeed transpired.

Despite his protestations of innocence and his claims that 'The Man' had done it, Reid's insistence that he was a descendant of Jack the Ripper only served to help convict him, by reason of insanity, of the terrible crimes. The trial judge thus sent Reid into the custody of Ravenswood 'Special Hospital' where he remained under the care of Doctor Ruth Truman until the case took a surprising turn.

Alice Nickels and Sergeant Wright were concerned that Reid may have actually been telling the truth at his trial and set out to dig further into his story. Working on the theory that the real killer may have fled the country after the third Brighton killing, with the police getting a little too close for comfort, Nickels checked for similar murders in other European countries and professed herself astounded to find that a series of similar crimes had taken place in Poland. After garnering enough evidence to suggest that another Ripper copycat had been at work, (surely more than a coincidence so soon after Brighton), they managed to convince Inspector Holland to re-open the case. Holland himself visited Warsaw, where he found that the crimes on Polish soil were exact replicas of those in the UK.

When the body of a man who could have been the mysterious 'Michael' turned up, Holland felt he might actually be on to something. Later, the body of another man was discovered, after a horrendous accident that saw the car he was travelling catch fire and crash over the parapet of a bridge in to a river. This time, traces of what proved to be the much disputed journal of Jack the Ripper were found in the car and floating in the river, and the police were convinced that this could be none other than the body of Mark Cavendish, the real 'Brighton Ripper'.

At a subsequent appeal hearing, Jack Reid found himself exonerated of the crimes and controversially set free. I say controversially, because Ruth Truman held out for his continued incarceration, on the grounds that he displayed sociopathic tendencies and could prove a danger to himself and the public at large. No matter, the judges released him anyway.

Her belief proved of course to be tragically vindicated when Reid went on to commit the subsequent series of murders in Whitechapel itself. Perhaps those lives could have been saved if the Appeal Court judges had taken notice of her fears, but that is a matter for their consciences I'm afraid. So, Jack Reid was soon identified as the killer, tracked down to his lair in Whitechapel as I previously told you, apprehended, his mind to all intents and purposes totally immersed in his belief that he was the re-incarnation of Jack the Ripper, and the judge at his new trial had no hesitation in sentencing Reid to his second, and this time, permanent spell in Ravenswood.

And that, David, is, in a small nutshell, the story of the Cavendish family and their strange and at times incomprehensible connection to the so-called Secret Journal of Jack the Ripper."

William Forbes leaned back in his chair and took a deep breath as he allowed himself to relax a little after appearing to have been on a knife edge of tension throughout his narration of the odd tale of Jack Reid and his forbears. He looked me in the eye, as though waiting for me to say something. When I did speak, I confess to feeling a little mystified. So far, he'd told me nothing that would explain his own fears, his belief that he was in some way a target for this so-called evil malevolence of Jack the Ripper that he believed had sought him out across the great divide of time.

I considered my next words carefully before speaking.

"William, what you've just related to me is indeed fascinating, and, if wholly true, of great historical importance, but, you have not as yet told me anything to explain your own condition or belief that you are in some personal danger, or that such danger emanates from Jack the Ripper, who, I firmly believe died over a hundred years ago and who can have no possible bearing on events of today."

"Of course," he replied, "but I'm coming to that, for obviously my own involvement in the case only began after I started to see and record Jack Reid's story. If you'll indulge me a little longer, I'll tell you everything. I'm coming to it, David, truly. I just needed you to understand the full background to what's been happening, and to do that I had to tell you the full story of the Cavendish family and their involvement with the journal."

"Okay, William. Let's say I take what you've told me as factual for the time being, without any queries from me, though I may have some questions for you later. Now, please tell me just how all of this impacts on you and your life."

Forbes took a deep breath, and his body tensed as though steeling himself for some great ordeal. I knew that he was about to reach the crescendo of his story, the part that he believed would convince of the veracity of his tale, and he would obviously want to make it as convincing as possible. He cleared his throat, looked at my lap for a long moment, perhaps checking that the plastic sleeve still sat there, and then, just as he prepared to launch into the next part of his narrative, the lights in the room began to flicker. I assumed the generator was up to its old tricks again, though it shouldn't have misbehaved after my earlier repair job. William Forbes however, saw it as something else entirely and in the flickering light from the overhead bulb I saw his face pale, his whole demeanour changing to one of a man in mortal fear, and he began to shake once more, as his eyes darted around the room and took on that odd hunted look he'd previously exhibited.

As the sound of the wind outside rose once again to a crescendo and the door rattled as though being rapped upon by some unseen hand, the lights at last guttered and failed plunging the two of us into almost total darkness, broken only by the iridescent orange-blue flames of the log fire, and William Forbes, unable to control his terror any longer, his face contorted in horror, let out a blood curdling scream. His demons had returned!

TEN

A PHONE CALL IN THE NIGHT

"God help me! He's here," screamed Forbes into the darkness, his voice a falsetto of fear and panic combined.

"There's no-one here, William," I retorted, trying to remain calm, though Forbes's reaction to the extinguishing of the lights certainly succeeded in giving me a moment or two of illogical panic. Almost as quickly as the lights had flicked off however, they returned, bathing the room in the safe, warm glow that should have brought Forbes back to the world of reality. They didn't. His face had become a mask of sheer terror. Whatever lurked within his mind, real or imagined had taken such a hold on William Forbes that it was soon apparent to me that this time, his panic bore deep seated roots. He certainly believed that someone or something was with us, in that room. His eyes flashed their terror and his brow dripped with the sweat of fear. The intensity of the wind outside my croft had gathered and the howling of the burgeoning gale added to the feeling of isolation and loneliness of my island home and that, perhaps, also had an effect on him. I couldn't be sure. All I knew was that I had to find a way to end his torment, even if only temporarily.

As Forbes thrashed around in the chair, his mind a mass of confusion and dread, I continued to speak calmly to him:

"William, it was just a slight fault in the fuel line on my generator, the one that provides me with all my power. There's no mains electricity here on the island. These things happen now and then. It's really nothing to panic about. There's no-one else here, just you and me. William, please listen to me. You're safe here. Do you remember where you are? You're on Skerries Rock. I'm David, remember? Doctor David Hemswell. You came to me about the strange things that have been happening to you. I'm trying to help you, William, and I will help you if you'll let me. But first, you must calm down, please."

Slowly, very slowly, Forbes began to lose that terrified hunted look. His bodily spasms grew less intense and his rapid breathing returned to normal. Eventually, he relaxed and sat, slumped in the chair, looking for the entire world a broken man. Only now did I realise just how much his inner fears and beliefs, however illogical, had affected the man. No matter that I remained keen to hear the rest of his story. My own experiences as a doctor first, and a psychologist second, made me aware that what the man sitting in front of me needed at that time was rest, preferably the kind of rest that comes from a decent night's sleep. Forbes had of course told me that it had been a long time since he'd enjoyed a full night's sleep.

"William," I began when I considered him ready to resume normal conversation once more. "Are you okay now? That was quite a scare you gave me."

"I'm so deeply sorry, David. Really, I am. You see, I know you still don't believe me, but he really is with me, in me, somehow, and when the lights failed I just knew it was him, or at least I thought it was him, coming to infest my mind with those terrible images and sounds once again. I don't want to experience those things any more. They're just too terrible to contemplate."

"I presume by 'he' you're referring to Jack the Ripper again?"

"Of course I am. You'll understand more when I tell you the rest of the story. I wish to God I'd never heard of Jack Reid, certainly that I'd never accepted the task of becoming his legal confidant. If I'd never gone to Ravenswood, never spoken to him, heard his awful tale and come into contact with that awful document," he nodded in the direction of the plastic sleeve on my lap, "then perhaps none of this would have happened, at least, not to me. I daresay some other poor soul would have ended up like me, but I'd rather that had happened than this."

"Look, William, I know you want to tell me the rest of your story, but really, it's getting late. It's almost eleven thirty, and you're in no fit state to continue. I can give you a sedative, something to help you sleep and we can start afresh in the morning. I think a good night's sleep and a decent breakfast on waking will do you the world of good. What d'you say to that?"

Forbes sighed, whether through tiredness or resignation I couldn't say, but his body suddenly sagged against the back of the chair. It was perhaps a relief to him that he wasn't being forced to relive the full story in one sitting. At least, that's how I read it.

"Perhaps you're right, David. I really do want to tell you everything, but maybe your suggestion of a rest is the right one. I'd welcome the sedative you mentioned. It might be the only thing that will enable me to sleep without being carried away by the terrible events that usually haunt me in my sleep."

I quickly went into my bedroom, returning a minute later with a syringe loaded with a reasonably powerful sedative, designed to put Forbes to sleep for at least eight hours. Before he allowed me to administer it however, Forbes made me hand over the plastic sleeve containing the page from the Ripper's journal, which he quickly locked in his briefcase. I'd steadfastly stuck to my agreement not to read it until he told me to, but at that moment I wished that I'd been able to cast a quick glance at it during the course of our first evening together. Forbes had remained adamant however, that to read it, even to touch it without the protective sleeve could have serious repercussions for me, and even during his previous bout of terror I'd managed to resist a natural curiosity, and maintained a resistance to the temptation to take a close look at the contents of the sleeve. In a way, with its removal from my possession I admit to feeling a slight gratitude to Forbes for removing any chance of me giving in to further temptation through the night.

Forbes obediently rolled up his right sleeve and sat quietly as I administered the injection. That done, I led him to the spare bedroom, where he quickly undressed, and changed into a pair of blue striped pyjamas as I rolled back the duvet for him. He slid beneath the warm covers of the bed just as the sedative began to take effect, and I stayed with him until, a minute or two later, he fell into a deep sleep. Despite the fact that the sedative would keep Forbes soundly asleep through the night, I left the bedside lamp on as I took a last look at my guest/patient, as I now thought of him, before withdrawing from the room, leaving the door ajar, just in case...well, just in case.

With Forbes safely tucked up for the night there was little more I could do other than lock up the house and turn in myself. Perhaps Forbes's paranoia had rubbed off on me a little, because, despite my scepticism surrounding his Jack the Ripper tale, I decided to take a quick turn around the outer environs of my home before turning in. I donned my thick Parka and a pair of sturdy leather boots, and, halogen torch in hand, made a quick tour of the area immediately surrounding my home. I soon carried out my external examination of the croft and its outbuildings, satisfying myself that there was nothing and no-one present, apart that is, from Forbes and myself. There were no other buildings on Skerries rock and in such a gale, the breaking wave crests that struck the rocky shore were instantly transformed by the driving wind into a bitingly cold salty rain-like squall that swept right across the tiny spit of Skerries Rock before carrying on its course towards the sheltered side of the island, disappearing once more into the darkness, falling into the narrow span of ocean that divided my home from the mainland. As such, there existed no hiding place for any self-respecting human being on the Rock. As for the ghostly spirits of long-dead serial killers, however, I really couldn't say.

Returning to the welcome warmth of the croft, I locked and bolted the very solid front door. The oak tree of which it had once been a part probably withstood such Atlantic gales for many a century. Now, it formed a beautifully crafted barrier between me and the storm that swept across the Rock. I swiftly divested myself of my wet outer clothing, and sat for a few minutes in my fireside chair, recently occupied by the now-sleeping William Forbes. I yawned, but, before turning in for the night, I decided there was one more thing I had to do. I picked up the telephone and dialled a number from memory. It might be midnight, but I knew from past experience that the owner of the number I was calling would certainly be up and about at the witching hour. It was one of her favourite times of the day.

After only three rings, the phone at the other end of the line was picked up and a firm though polite voice answered with a simple, "Hello?"

"Kate, it's me, David Hemswell."

"Why, David, how wonderful to hear from you."

There was no, '*What time of the night do you call this?*' or '*Why are you calling me at such a late hour?*' I knew the lady too well to expect anything less than that simple everyday greeting, no matter the hour, day or night.

"Listen Kate, I think I need your help."

"You still on that God-forsaken rock in the middle of the Atlantic Ocean?"

"Yes, but it's not quite in the middle, Kate, just a mile from the mainland."

"Oh, fiddle-de-dee. Such minor details. You say you need my help?"

"That's what I said, Kate."

"Then say nothing more, dear boy. I'll set off tonight and be with you some time tomorrow. Any ferries running your way?"

"I'm afraid not, but ring me when you arrive in Balnakiel and I'll skip across in my motor launch and pick you up."

"Motor launch eh? My, aren't you the grand one?"

"Oh stop it, Kate. It's not nice to mock."

"Mock? Who's mocking? You sound like a grand landowner from another era, David. Can't wait to see that place you've shut yourself away from the world on."

"Kate, I haven't…. Oh, never mind. I can never win an argument with you, can I?"

"Ah, the boy is learning at last," my friend laughed down the phone. "Expect me when you see me, then," she said, and I could imagine the broad grin spreading across her face as she spoke.

"Wait. Don't you want to know what it's all about?"

"Oh no, dear boy, and spoil the surprise? If you say you need my help, then my help you shall have. Now, good night to you. I have to pack a few things and get the old banger out of the garage."

"That 'old banger' is a ninety-six, Bentley Convertible, Kate. Hardly a battered old wreck, now, is it?"

"I suppose it'll do until something better comes along. Now, David, please, will you allow an old woman to get on? It's a long way to the middle of the Atlantic."

She chuckled devilishly.

"Okay, Kate, and...thanks."

She spoke no more, and I heard a click as she replaced the receiver at the other end. At last, I heaved myself up from the chair and made my weary way to bed. As I finally laid my head upon my pillow that night, I felt that at last I'd done something positive in the case of William Forbes. He needed far more than I alone could give him. That much was for sure, and as I closed my eyes, I smiled softly to myself, and wondered what Forbes would think of the redoubtable Kate Goddard!

ELEVEN
KATE'S ARRIVAL

THANKS in the most part to the sedative I'd administered to Forbes, the night passed peacefully, with me achieving my full quota of six hours sleep. Nothing went 'bump' in the night, and I witnessed no ghostly manifestations. Clearly, whatever William Forbes felt had followed him to Skerries Rock had no evil intent toward me.

I rose early, as was my habit, and looked in on my guest. He appeared to be in exactly the same position I'd left him in the previous night, sleeping sonorously, also due to the effects of the sedative. I chose to leave him to wake naturally and set about preparing breakfast.

The bacon, eggs and beans were ready to be served, and, before I could make a move towards checking on my guest's state of wakefulness, he appeared, fully dressed in the kitchen doorway.

"Smells good," he said, greeting me with a smile that belied his appearance of the previous night, when all manner of terror had gripped him and sent him into paroxysms of fear and dread.

"You seem to be feeling better," I replied. "Hungry?"

"Yes please. You won't mind if I leave shaving until later?"

"Feel free, William. There's no one here to insist you shave at all, come to that. You probably feel a little weary after the sedative I gave you. It'll wear off soon though."

"I am a little lethargic," he said as he sat opposite me at the kitchen table. Breakfast was soon behind us and I deliberately left it until after he'd eaten to tell him my news.

"But why?" Forbes asked after I'd told him of my late-night phone call to Kate Goddard, and of her impending arrival at Skerries Rock. "Why do you need someone else here? I thought it would just be the two of us. You said I could count on your discretion. Why invite this Goddard woman?"

"Because, William, from what I've observed so far, your case presents certain characteristics that fall well into Kate's field of expertise. Much of what you've told me so far relates to the history of the 19th century crimes of Jack the Ripper and the more recent ones of Jack Reid. The rest, however, your 'visions' and the sounds you insist you've heard, and the feelings of being victimised by the soul or the spirit, call it what you will, of Jack the Ripper, appear to me to possess more than a passing link with the supernatural, or the paranormal. That, my dear William, is where Kate Goddard fits in.

Kate lives in Scarborough, in the upmarket Atlantis apartment complex, from where she carries out her own, very well documented investigations into things that perhaps might be dismissed by the established scientists and psychological medics of this world. I met her during the time I lived in the town, and, rather than dismiss her as many might have done, I became very friendly with her and though I may remain a little sceptical about some of what she does, I've learned to trust her enough to understand that there are indeed things in this world that we can't always explain away by the application of science or psycho-analysis. Trust me, William, if anyone can help me and therefore help you to explain what's happening to you, it's Kate Goddard, and it will have been well worth me asking her to come and assist us."

Forbes remained sceptical and appeared disappointed that I'd brought in outside help. I, however, had made the decision, and firmly believed that Kate would have much to offer as Forbes's story gained momentum.

"Well, there's not a lot I can do about it is there?" he spoke quietly.

"Like I said, William, trust me. I know what I'm doing. You came to me for help, and Kate is the person best-placed to assist me in giving you the assistance you require."

Forbes capitulated.

"Very well, let's see what she can do. When will she arrive?"

"I'm expecting her to phone me on her arrival in Balnakiel after lunch, maybe later in the afternoon. When she does, I'll go pick her up from the village in the launch. You can come with me or stay here to await her arrival. The choice is yours."

"No way am I staying here on my own, David. You can't ask me to do that."

A momentary flash of fear showed in his eyes once again, and then disappeared as quickly as it arrived.

"I didn't ask you to, William. I said it's up to you."

"Then it's settled. I'll accompany you in the launch. Anyway, now that you've explained about her, I'm anxious to meet your mysterious friend. Maybe she'll understand the things that have been happening to me without being quite as doubtful as you."

"That's right, William. But please remember, it's not that I totally disbelieve you. I just don't know exactly *what* to believe. Kate will help me sort it out."

Having spent the remainder of the morning showing Forbes around my tiny island, taking in the sea bird colonies and the dramatic view from the cliffs out to the rolling Atlantic, lunch was a casual concoction of cold meats and salad, composed of my very own freshly grown produce. Soon afterwards, the telephone rang, with Kate Goddard announcing her arrival in Balnakiel. Forbes and I were soon on our way to collect my latest house guest, as I piloted the launch, as fast as its motor would allow, hugging the coast all the way in the now calmer and less threatening inshore rollers.

"Good God, man, she's eighty if she's a day!" Forbes exclaimed, as I pointed out the diminutive figure of Kate Goddard waving to us from the harbour wall as we neared port.

"Seventy-five actually," I corrected. I'd deliberately not mentioned Kate's age earlier, as for me, it was irrelevant. To someone like Forbes, perhaps it might have a negative effect. We'd soon find out. "Don't let her age put you off. Kate's as sharp as a knife, believe me."

"I hope so," Forbes replied, adding, "Hope the old dear doesn't have a coronary while she's with us. It's a long way to the hospital."

I could have mentioned my own fears for Forbes, should he need immediate psychiatric care, but I declined the opportunity to do so. It would have served no useful purpose.

I guided the launch in to a smooth docking beside the jetty and hailed the lady standing some ten feet above us.

"Ahoy there, Kate."

"And the same to you, Captain Bluebeard" she retorted.

"Shouldn't that be Blackbeard?" I laughed up at her.

"Blue, black, who cares? Now, how the dickens do I get on board that old skiff of yours?"

"Wait there, Kate, I'll help you."

Leaving Forbes on board, I ran up the steps to the top of the jetty, and in seconds, Kate and I were involved in a deep embrace, one that signified the meeting of two exceptionally good friends. Kate was dressed in a bright yellow sou'wester, heavy sea boots and a pair of rather inelegant but highly practical waterproof trousers that would have looked more at home on a trawlerman.

"Before you ask," Kate spoke before I could get a word in, "I borrowed the clothes from Martin Humbold back home. He's the skipper of the fishing boat, Sally B, and he advised me they were the best thing to wear in this neck of the woods."

"You mean you woke a trawler skipper in the middle of the night to borrow his clothes?"

"Oh, he didn't mind at all. He and I are old friends, a bit like you and me, David."

"Well, good for Martin. Is that all your luggage?" I asked, pointing to an old-fashioned brown leather suitcase that stood at her feet.

"Indeed it is, dear boy. You'd be surprised how much a lady can pack into one of those wonderful old cases. I didn't know how long I'd be here, so I brought enough clothes to last me a week. If I have to stay any longer I'll be hoping you have a darn good washing machine in that hovel of yours."

"Croft, Kate. It's called a croft, and it's certainly not a hovel, I'll have you know."

The two of us hugged again and then burst out laughing. Kate had an irascible sense of humour that could rub some folk up the wrong way. Luckily, I wasn't one of them. I found her witty and amusing and loved her as I would a favourite Aunt.

"Better come and meet my other guest," I nodded in the direction of the launch where Forbes stood waiting for us to join him.

"Oh yes, please introduce me, David. Then, not another word about the case until we reach your island. I want to enjoy the adventure of this short sea cruise if that's okay with you."

"Your wish is my command, dear lady," I replied, taking her hand as I led Kate down the sea-slippery steps from the jetty and in a few seconds, on to the deck of the launch.

William Forbes greeted Kate cordially as I introduced the pair, though his face registered surprise when I told him that Kate wished to know nothing of his case for the time being. I cast off the mooring rope a minute later, and we headed out past the breakwater into the open sea. Kate positioned herself on the small bench seat that ran from the wheelhouse to the stern of the launch, while Forbes stood looking through the windscreen at the open sea ahead of us. I set course for home and as the sea was by now almost a flat calm I was able to do some people watching as I held the helm on a steady course. William Forbes appeared to me to be staring at some unknown point on the horizon, looking at, or for, something only his mind could comprehend. He was edgy and uneasy, and he held himself stiff, legs planted well apart to steady himself and one hand holding on to the side of the tiny cabin. Now and then he cast a glance at me, and then at Kate, but his eyes soon returned to that distant point, searching perhaps, but for what, or who?

As for Kate Goddard, I soon realised why she'd asked to enjoy the ride to Skerries Rock in silence. I remembered how her mind worked as I noticed that throughout our short and uneventful voyage, her eyes never once left the rock steady form of William Forbes. She was studying him, his demeanour, his body language, everything about the man, and he hadn't the faintest idea that he was being scanned by one of the sharpest brains it had been my good fortune to meet in many a year.

I finally broke the silence on board with a hearty "Land ho!" as Skerries Rock came into view, and then, and only then, did Kate assume the guise of an excited elderly lady, eager to cast her first glance at my island home.

"Oh, I say," she exclaimed. "Isn't it all rather delightful? Small, but delightful, David. A bit on the wild side too, I should say, but then, you are a bit of an adventurer aren't you, darling boy?"

"Glad you like it Kate," I responded and then winked at her and nodded in the direction of my other passenger. Kate knew that I'd caught on to her strategy and she winked back, conspiratorially.

"Oh, I do, darling, I really do. Can't wait to see this little croft of yours. I do hope you have a goodly supply of gin on hand, David. I shall be most disappointed if you haven't."

"Don't you worry Kate. I even have a supply of tonic and fresh lemons, too. You shan't have to forego your favourite tipple while you're here."

"Excellent," she grinned broadly. "And you, Mr Forbes, are you a G & T man may I ask?"

"Eh, what? Sorry," Forbes spluttered, his mind quickly returning from one of those far off points I was getting used to. "G & T did you say? No, actually, I'm more a brandy man myself, or perhaps a fine malt now and then."

"Ah," said Kate, adding that snippet of information to her mental database on William Forbes.

"Come on, you two," I shouted above the sound of the breaking waves. "We're here. Help me manoeuvre her into the boathouse then we can all get to know each better up at the house over a nice cup of tea."

"But David, dear boy, it's not a house, it's a *croft!*"

William Forbes simply couldn't understand why Kate and I burst into paroxysms of laughter after her last remark.

"Oh, come on. Let's go," I grinned as I led the two up the short pathway that led to my home.

I led the way, carrying Kate's suitcase, with Forbes close behind me and Kate bringing up the rear. I knew without looking that her eyes would never once have left the walking figure of William Forbes. Kate really is the best at what she does.

TWELVE
FIRST IMPRESSIONS

Thirty minutes later, Kate, William Forbes and I sat comfortably in front of my glowing log fire as we sipped tea, and Kate devoured an unhealthy supply of chocolate chip cookies from my supply of biscuits. Forbes had graciously given up the spare bedroom and Kate's case was swiftly unpacked, and her clothes hung in the wardrobe. I'd set up a camp bed in my office which Forbes assured me would suit him admirably.

Divested of her outerwear, Kate now sat in a warm but hugely oversized fisherman's style sweater, (another loan from her friendly trawler skipper), and a pair of well-cut blue jeans that made her look somewhat less than her age. Slight of build and with black hair that showed only traces of grey, Kate resembled an archetypal granny, though one with a wit and a mind as sharp as a university don, which she'd been, at one time in her past.

"So, Kate, please tell me exactly what it is you do. David was a little reticent in his description of your talents and specific field of expertise, though he's told me you're the best person in the country to help with my problem."

Forbes was doing his best to appraise the new arrival, though I knew that by now, Kate was well ahead of him in that department, having studied him from the moment she first set eyes upon him.

"Well, Mr Forbes, or may I call you William?" He nodded his assent. "William it shall be then. I'm what some people call a paranormal investigator, though I prefer to think of myself as a simple reader of people and situations, an observer of the unusual traits that some of my fellow human beings exhibit from time to time. Over the years my talents have, I admit, brought me into contact with a great many people who have had what they term as 'supernatural' experiences, and I've been able, in some cases to either verify or debunk such occurrences. You see, William, too many people are prepared to dismiss the supernatural, as though it has no part to play in the modern world, and yet I firmly believe that much of what is termed 'supernatural' is in fact a manifestation of our own minds, as though some of us are able to make things happen without knowing quite how or why it takes place."

"So you're saying that if something is supernatural it's really being caused by the mind of the person who experiences it, whatever *it* is?"

"It's a little more complicated than that, William. I've had contact with many people of different beliefs, spiritualists and church people, and out and out atheists, who hold no religious beliefs at all, and yet, over the years, I've found evidence of such happenings being experienced by them all. So, no, I don't dismiss the supernatural out of hand. What I'm saying is that sometimes however, we can be to blame for our own experiences, when our minds allow themselves to be taken over by an idea, or a specific fear for example."

"When someone is seriously disturbed, mentally, you mean? You and David think I'm crazy, is that it?"

"Not at all, William. David has asked me to come and listen to your story with him because he feels I'm better qualified than he is to make a decision or pass judgement on the 'paranormal' elements of your tale, which he tells me is quite astounding so far. As you were about to enter the phase of informing him of how this phenomenon has affected you, he felt a second opinion from someone with more experience in such matters would be helpful. He is a very clever man and has wide ranging experience in all aspects of criminal behaviour and psychological traumas, but he knows just how important this is to you and he simply felt I could help. I hope you don't mind."

When she was being totally serious and left the joking side of her nature behind, Kate Goddard could be a very formidable and persuasive lady. Her charms had obviously done the trick when Forbes replied:

"In that case, I'm delighted that you agreed to travel all this way to add your undoubted skills to trying to help me end this once and for all."

I now decided it was time to get things moving. It was growing late in the afternoon and I wanted Forbes to move on with his story, but there was something that had to be done first.

"Kate, I think you and William need to go over what he's already told me before we can make any further progress. Would you mind telling Kate your story so far, William?"

"Of course," said Forbes, and Kate added,

"Perhaps you could leave the two of us for an hour or so, David. I'd like to hear William's story so far in private so I can assess it independently of any theories you may already have formulated."

"No problem," I replied. I knew that Kate would be able to add to her already growing mental data on William Forbes far more effectively from a one on one discussion with him and I soon left the two of them closeted in my sitting room as I made my excuses and made my way to the boat shed, where I spent a useful hour tidying up the equipment stored there and performing some basic routine maintenance on the launch's engine.

By the time I returned to the croft, Forbes was just arriving at the break off point he and I had reached the previous night, so I quickly left them to conclude the first part of the story and disappeared into the kitchen to put the kettle on. I guessed they'd be thirsty by the time they finished, and I was correct in my assumption when I re-appeared with a tray some ten minutes later.

"Ah, excellent, refreshments!" said Kate. "I wondered when the catering staff would show up again."

"Cheeky bugger," I grinned at her. "Next time it'll be your turn to make the tea."

"Oh now, David dear, what a way to treat a guest. Now be a good boy, shut up and pour!"

"You're incorrigible, Kate Goddard." I replied, laughing as I spoke.

"But of course I am, darling. Why do you think no man would ever lead me down the aisle to live forever imprisoned in Holy matrimony?"

"Because, dear lady, the man hasn't yet been born who could cope with your wicked sense of humour or your acid tongue. You forget, I've seen you at your worst, as well as at your best, Miss Goddard."

Appearing to ignore me completely, Kate turned to face Forbes.

"He's quite right you know, William. I'd have made a most unfortunate catch for any poor unsuspecting man who'd had the misfortune to snare me in marriage. I suspect divorce would have featured very strongly in any such liaison in my life."

"Oh, I'm sure you're both quite wrong," said Forbes, politely. "I've found you to be a most agreeable lady in the past hour or so. You've listened patiently and without interruption to my story so far, with the ultimate politeness."

"Indeed I have, William, but then again, you haven't asked for my hand in marriage, have you?"

Kate burst out laughing, a very loud and raucous laugh that I knew all too well. I couldn't help but join in and then, much to my surprise, and I suspect Kate's as well, Forbes joined in. It was the first evidence of any levity he'd exhibited since I'd met the man and I felt relieved that, at least for a few seconds, a spot of humour had pierced his waking terrors and enabled him to smile at last.

The brief interlude for tea and yet more biscuits over, Kate asked if she could speak to me in private for a few minutes before Forbes took up his story once more. Forbes made no objections and Kate helped me clear the tea things away and we retired to the kitchen for a quick conference.

"Well?" I asked as soon as the kitchen door closed, leaving the two of us shielded from Forbes's sight and hearing. "I know you've been watching him from the moment you saw him from the dock in Balnakiel. Any thoughts?"

There was no jocularity about Kate Goddard as she replied.

"There's something odd about our Mister Forbes," she said. "I can sense something, though I can't quite put my finger on it, not yet at least. Don't get me wrong David. I'm not saying he's a fake, certainly not. There's a great disturbance happening in and around William Forbes, I don't doubt that for a moment, but there's also an aura I can't quite grasp."

"An aura?"

"Yes, well, two to be precise, and that's what's confusing me. There's an overwhelming aura of fear, that much is certain. When I say fear, I mean mortal dread. He's surrounded by it, though it doesn't all emanate from Forbes himself. It's as if there's more than one of him, if you know what I mean, or at least, more than one element of fear present within him. And then there's the second aura, and that's the one that disturbs me the most, David. There's a malevolence about it, and it's slowly wrapping itself tighter and tighter around him. He doesn't know it, but his mind is slowly opening itself up to the great power that this aura brings with it. I don't quite understand what's happening here, but I do know that William Forbes is a man in great turmoil, and that you were very correct in calling me in the middle of the night. This man needs help, David, and he needs it now!"

You must remember that I'd told Kate nothing of the facts surrounding Forbes and his visit to consult with me. She knew nothing of the tale he'd told me about Jack the Ripper, or his spirit at least, being 'after him' as he put it. So far, all she knew was the first part of the story as Forbes had related it to me the previous night. And yet, here she was, telling me things which, at the very least, made me think that there just might be something in what Forbes had told me, unbelievable as it may sound. I far from believed in him entirely, but Kate's words certainly made me feel a little more well-disposed towards my guest's story. The look on my face at that point must have spoken volumes, because Kate looked me in the eye and said:

"What? You know more than I about all this, David. Have I said something pertinent already?"

"Very pertinent, Kate. Until you spoke just now I was perhaps prepared to write Mr Forbes off as an over-imaginative crank who'd been scared to death by his meetings with a serial killer. Now, I'm not so sure. Perhaps you'll realise why when

Forbes goes on with his story and tells you exactly why he's so terrified. I haven't heard it yet, of course, but I am privy to a little more information than you, and that's why your words just now have given me pause for thought. I'm presuming Forbes didn't tell you any more than...?"

Kate raised a hand, halting my question in its stride.

"Not a word more than I asked him to. And that was simply to relate to me his story up to the point you and he left it last night. He told me of the Burton Cavendish affair and the birth of the child, right up to Jack Reid's second and final period of incarceration at Ravenswood. He delivered the whole thing as he would a lecture to a group of students. I particularly asked him to be as brief and as succinct as possible, without elaboration. He did very well, David."

"And he showed no signs of being gripped by fear, or panic, or anything like that?"

Nothing at all. It was odd though. While he was telling me his story his eyes kept darting around the room as if he was looking for someone or something. Strange also that he can retell such a lengthy tale without notes or some form of written aids."

"I thought that too, and yes, his eyes were constantly monitoring the room while he spoke to me too."

"If I didn't know better, David, I'd swear he was searching for a connection to a presence neither you nor I are aware of, almost as though he were seeking approval for the way he was relating the tale."

"Good God, Kate. That's a massive leap in intuitive deduction, if you don't mind me saying so."

"As I said, it was just a fleeting feeling. I could be very wrong of course, and in fact I hope I am. I'd hate to think there was some ethereal entity sharing your lovely home with the three of us."

"Oh, come on Kate. That's enough of that kind of talk if you don't mind. Carry on like that and you'll end up scaring me, and I don't scare easily."

"David, my dear, if I carry on like that, and if there is anything like that lurking in the ether here on Skerries rock, I'll damn well end up scaring myself!"

Kate smiled, and wasn't entirely convincing if that smile was meant to reassure me.

"I think we should be getting back to our friend in the other room," I said, trying to drive the conversation back to a less supernatural level.

"Agreed. It's time we both heard the rest of Mr Forbes's story."

With that, the two of us once again joined William Forbes, who sat waiting patiently for our return, his hands clasped together on his lap; his eyes still carrying that faraway look, though the smile with which he greeted our return appeared warm and genuine enough.

"Hello, have you agreed on the degree of my madness yet?" he asked, half laughingly.

"All I can say, William, is that I don't think you're mad at all." Kate replied.

"Neither do I," I added slightly less convincingly.

"Then, would you like me to tell you the final, awful part of my story? I warn you now, it's almost driven me to despair and if the two of you can't help me then I fear it won't be long before I find myself in an early grave."

"Oh, come now, it can't be as bad as that, surely?" I asked.

"Can't it? I'll let you judge that for yourselves. Now, to get back to Jack Reid and my involvement with that damned lunatic homicidal maniac."

Forbes took a deep breath, Kate and I involuntarily held ours, and he launched into the explanation for his ultimate terror and the reasons for his being here on Skerries Rock with me, trying to cling on to the *final vestiges* of his sanity, as he put it. I admit to being totally unprepared for what was yet to come, though I suspect, with hindsight, that Kate already had an inkling. She'd read Forbes like a book so far, and maybe she was a page or two ahead of me as he began.

THIRTEEN
A QUESTION

"Do you think we could have the lights on? Forbes asked as he began.

I rose and complied with his request, figuring it would make him feel more comfortable as the shadows of early evening began to cast their pall over the island, and the windows of my croft darkened in response.

"Thank you, David," he said as I returned to my chair, and once again, the voice of William Forbes led me, this time accompanied by Kate Goddard, into the strange world of the so-called Cavendish Legacy.

"So, my meetings with Jack Reid continued, with him relating his story to me, much as I am now relating it to the two of you. Reid went into far more detail than I've imparted to you, by the way, but I felt a fairly detailed overview would suit you better, rather than an actual blow by blow account of every sentence of conversation we exchanged."

Kate and I nodded our agreement, though she did take the opportunity to ask a question.

"William, you mentioned that Jack Reid died recently. Like

David, I've heard all about Reid and his crimes. Who hasn't, unless they've been stranded on a desert island for years? No pun intended David. I don't recall reading anything in the press about his death. What happened to him?"

"His death was reported, but at the request of the Home Office, the press co-operated in releasing only a low-profile account of his demise. The authorities believed that enough publicity had accompanied Reid in life, without some sort of media circus greeting his death. I don't know how they got the various newspaper editors to agree, but they did."

"Ah, the Home Office has far reaching powers, William. They could have issued a notice to the press that would force them to comply with their request on the grounds of national security or of it being a public interest issue. They can't quite gag the press, but they can make sure the press is co-operative, under threat of prosecution and shut downs. Those powers were brought in as part of a little-known raft of anti-terrorism legislation soon after we entered the twenty first century. They weren't popular with the press, but they've been obliged to comply."

"I see, of course, I should have realised, but my mind hasn't been working very well, as I've already told you. Still, as a member of the legal profession I should have known."

"Not necessarily," I replied. "You are, or were, primarily concerned with Civil law as opposed to criminal cases, so the legislation wouldn't have been something you encountered much in your career."

"Perhaps," said Forbes. "Anyway, back to Jack Reid, and the matter, and the manner of his death. I'd visited him on three occasions by the time I discovered he was terminally ill. It was the day of my fourth visit, and Ruth Truman called me into her office for a private conversation before I met with Reid. She didn't mince words.

"Jack Reid has been complaining of severe headaches for some weeks, as you probably know, Mr Forbes?"

"Yes," I replied. "He's mentioned those headaches on a number of occasions."

"Medical tests have revealed that Reid has developed a brain tumour. The prognosis is not good. In fact, such has been the rapidity of the growth, added to the fact that the doctors say his condition is inoperable, and it is estimated that Reid has less than two weeks to live. I suggest that any business he has with you be concluded as soon as possible, Mr Forbes, for obvious reasons."

"So it was that I learned of the death sentence that nature appeared to have passed on Jack Reid, serial killer. It struck me as more than coincidental that he'd been struck by the very same malady that had led to the death of his uncle Robert Cavendish. I wondered if perhaps such tumours might run in the family, be hereditary, maybe. No-one seemed prepared to give me a satisfactory answer to that question, despite me asking a number of doctors, all of whom appeared to hold differing views on the subject. Reid died sixteen days after my final visit to Ravenswood. There wasn't much of a funeral for him. His body was eventually released to his parents, who had it cremated, and his ashes scattered. No memorial stands anywhere to commemorate the life of Jack Reid."

Forbes fell silent for a moment and Kate took the opportunity to speak once again.

"So, the Ripper, or the Cavendish legacy whichever you call it, died with him?"

"I wish that could be true, oh, yes I do," said Forbes, becoming agitated. "But, that's sadly not the case. You'd think, wouldn't you that if the curse was going to live on, it would do so through the surviving members of his family, his father maybe? But it appears that the curse seems to miss out certain members of the family, though always it has struck at least one member of each generation."

"But how could such a terrible burden fall upon your shoulders, William. You are not a Cavendish."

"No, I'm not, am I?"

Those last words were spoken almost cryptically by Forbes, a nuance of voice that wasn't lost on Kate, who picked upon it right away.

"You're keeping something back from us, William" she spoke bluntly.

"I don't mean to keep anything from you, either of you, but please, I should return to my story. Only when I've told you everything in the correct order will you perhaps begin to understand."

"Then perhaps you should return to your intriguing tale," Kate replied. "I'm sorry for the interruption."

"That's okay. You needed to know something, and you asked. Now, where was I? Oh, yes, I've already told you about the circumstances surrounding Reid's first period in Ravenswood, the trial, the conviction and his subsequent exoneration of the Brighton crimes. There was no doubt about his guilt in the case of the Whitechapel murders, and no legal argument in the world that could keep him from being locked away from society for a second time, this time, for good as it turned out.

One of the most surprising things about the time I spent with Jack Reid was that I became extremely impressed with his level of intelligence. Aside from being polite, well-mannered and appearing to be in control of himself at all times, the man had an extremely high I.Q. and I've since come to understand that many psychopaths and sociopaths are in fact highly intelligent people. He'd spent many hours during his time at Ravenswood in the hospital library. Now, unlike a prison,

Ravenswood is designated as a 'special hospital' so the library there enjoys a far greater selection of books than a normal prison facility would hold. Reid also had access to a computer and apparently spent a lot of time researching history on the internet. Before you ask, Doctor Truman told me that certain sites are 'blocked' by the authorities, so that inmates are unable to access, for example, internet porn sites and so on.

Reid went on to tell me that after his uncle, Mark Cavendish had carried out his devilish plan and the murders in Brighton and Warsaw, he, Reid, worked out that his Uncle, Robert Cavendish, must have been the one in his particular generation who was spared the full effects of the Cavendish legacy. True, reading the journal had a devastating and perhaps fatal impact on the psychiatrist, but Jack became convinced that Robert must have confided in his own brother, Mark and that somehow, Mark became the recipient and therefore the carrier and implementer of the curse as far as his generation was concerned. The two brothers had apparently always been close, and yet after Robert's death, Mark disappeared from the radar so to speak, selling his business interests and leaving the country, without telling anyone where he was going. Mark Cavendish must have spent years preparing for the eventual bloodbath in Brighton, and Jack Reid's search for his uncle, and the subsequent discovery of him by Mark's young henchman must have been like manna from heaven for the older man. Jack Reid became the perfect fall guy for Cavendish, and it's quite obvious to all concerned that Mark Cavendish must have been one seriously deranged individual to go to the lengths he did to perpetrate his own heinous crimes, and attempt to implicate his own nephew, or to be more precise his second cousin, though he'd always been referred to as 'uncle', in those terrible murders.

I digress, however. Jack Reid told me that after his release from Ravenswood he returned home, and that was where he found the remaining segment of the journal, the one you're now holding now, David. Remember not to remove it from that plastic sleeve, won't you?"

I nodded. Forbes continued.

"Within a few short days, Jack Reid began to feel as though a 'presence' as he described it, was watching his every move. We must remember that when Reid first received the journal as a young man of eighteen he read it quickly, was horrified at its content and then stuffed it in his bag when he left home. It remained there until stolen from him by Mark Cavendish's young accomplice and the pages then fell into the hands of his uncle, quite literally. If, as Reid put it, there was something evil and malevolent in those pages, Mark Cavendish held it so often that it must surely have worked its evil effects on him. With Cavendish dead and the journal apparently destroyed, that should have been the end of the matter for all time, but that one page survived, and Jack Reid thus became, somewhat belatedly, the unwitting recipient of the curse of the Cavendish family. Having read the words on that page, David, and having felt the warmth and the stickiness that seems to emanate from the page itself, Reid began to experience strange dreams, almost hallucinogenic, so he told me, in which the victims of Jack the Ripper, and those of his uncle, Mark Cavendish reached out to him in the form of terrible apparitions. Their screams were the most terrible sounds he had ever heard in his life, and when they weren't screaming, they moaned and groaned as though they were being crushed or tortured, their breath, if you could call it that, being slowly forced from their bodies with no way of it ever returning. The mouths of those apparitions, so he said, were like the open jaws of an enormous shark, or a whale, with a gaping maw and what appeared to be the entrance to a black, cavernous interior from which, Reid instinctively knew, there would be no returning from were he to be sucked inside. So he found himself continually running, trying to escape from the apparitions, the shapeless and yet all too real forms that were searching for him, reaching out to him. He was a descendant of the Ripper, and he just knew that those creatures were hellbound on his destruction, as he was after all the living embodiment of the man, or should I say men, who had so hideously snuffed out the lives of those poor women.

Into those dreams there came another figure, one who he once again recognised immediately, not by his face, because Reid insists he had no face, but by his actions, by his appearance and by his voice. It was at this point in his story, David, Kate, that Jack Reid told me of his first and most terrifying 'meeting' with the manifestation of Jack the Ripper himself!"

FOURTEEN
JACK

The flames from the log fire in the grate cast dancing shadows round the room, and the occasional soft crackling sound of a log settling into a new position as it burned down added a certain atmospheric quality to the room as Forbes went on with his story.

"Jack Reid found it harder and harder to concentrate on his everyday life and on his job valetting cars as the dreams and the feeling of being 'possessed' began to take its toll on him. He'd managed two nights with no dreams, or should I say nightmares of the Ripper's victims when, as he put it to me, he faced for the first time, the ultimate horror of a direct contact with what he described as the spirit of Jack the Ripper. He'd fallen into a fitful sleep, as had become the norm ever since he'd found and re-read the journal page, and now, after the brief respite of the previous couple of nights, his mind descended into the darkest pit that hell could provide, or at least that's how he described it to me. With his reference to hell, I couldn't help but think of the way the 'Dear Boss' letter from the Ripper to the press at the time of the original murders began, *From Hell*.

Like all of his dreams/nightmares, this one apparently began with him apparently walking along a dark, cobbled street, devoid of any street lighting. The end of the street was always in view, though, walk as he might, he never seemed to draw any closer to that end, where a distinct junction could be seen, one exit right, one left. He knew instinctively that he had to reach the end of the street and take one direction or the other, but, first, he had to get there. As he walked along that filthy, slime ridden street, he could just make out the outlines of windows in the buildings he walked between. Those windows appeared to be blackened out or covered with ragged pieces of cloth to keep the weather out. The air was still, and the fetid stench of human excrement added to that of horse dung and other animal by-products assaulted his nostrils. He knew he was in the middle of the biggest and most foul slum area in old London town. He was in the cess pit of human degradation that was Victorian Whitechapel!

His feet made no sound upon the cobbles. Reid described the feeling as that of walking, but at the same time hovering just above the surface of the street as though he were there, but not really a solid fixture in the scene in which he now found himself. He continued walking, moving past the dilapidated buildings, and the blanked-out windows, yet still the end of the street appeared no nearer.

Suddenly a piece of black sackcloth covering one of the broken windows flapped back, inwards towards the room beyond, despite there being no wind, and Reid stopped dead in his tracks. From within the dark and derelict innards of the hovel, a mournful sound emanated and drifted out into the dark street. Reid covered his ears as the sound grew to a piercing shriek and then, unable to take his eyes from the window casement, he saw a skeletal hand groping through the opening, trying to pull itself out into the street. Something appeared to be holding it back, and, unable to help himself, Reid drew nearer to the opening until he saw the most terrifying sight. Attached to the skeletal arm was the emaciated body of a woman, yet not a woman any longer, a pitiful and worm infested parody of a human being, a living corpse, it's mouth nothing more than an empty hole, no teeth, no tongue, just a gaping black cavity from which that awful keening screeching continued to pour forth.

As Reid drew to within touching distance the creature seemed to sense his presence and its blank, blood-red eyes suddenly appeared to lock onto him, holding him in their dead gaze. He described feeling frozen in time, unable to move or speak as he watched the terrible writhing of the apparition as it struggled against some unknown and unseen bonds, still trying to claw its way into the world outside.

As the screams grew to a horrifying crescendo, Reid suddenly caught sight of another figure, in the shadows behind the awful creature. Before his eyes could attempt to focus on the other being, he sensed more than saw the second creature raise an arm in the darkness and then, to his ultimate horror the arm flashed down towards the back of the woman thing and the terrible corpse-like creature simply exploded before his eyes. There was no sound, just a colossal and terrible torrent of blood that gushed from the creature and splashed in a river of crimson all over the figure of Jack Reid. His mouth opened but no sound came. He tried with all his might to utter a scream of horror, but though his mouth opened, and his lungs felt as though they might burst, only silence issued forth. His clothes were covered in the stale, rancid sticky blood of the dead thing that had disappeared before his eyes and as movement returned to his limbs he began to run. He ran and ran, still trying to reach the end of that awful street, though again, the end with its inviting junctions seemed as far away as ever.

And yet, the strange part of the dream was that although he drew no nearer to the end of the street, he knew he was moving past the decrepit buildings as they appeared to flash by him as his legs carried him as fast as he could go. As he dashed for what he hoped would be safety more of those awful skeletal hands began to appear from behind the darkened windows of the buildings. Pieces of cloth, rolls of old newspaper, all the ragged pieces of materials that had been used to block out the windows from the effects of the weather were suddenly strewn aside as those awful creatures of darkness reached out, trying, so he thought, to drag him into their terrible and blood soaked world. As he passed each one, the screams began, and as he rushed past the groping hands, each one disappeared in an explosion of blood, in the same way the first apparition had apparently been destroyed from within by some other fearful creature of the night.

His face, hair, his clothing, all reeked of the copper-sweet smell of blood as he ran headlong towards the seemingly unapproachable exit from that street of nightmares. His hands flailed as he tried to clear the blood from his face, to prevent it clogging his eyes, his nose and his mouth. He retched, feeling the bile rise as he tasted that terrifying red cocktail and tried to breathe without inhaling the sticky red blood of those awful creatures of the dark.

And then, as quickly as the screaming had begun, the street fell silent, silent as the grave. Reid looked down, astonished to see that all traces of the vile smelling, cloying blood had disappeared from his clothing. He reached up and felt his hair. It was dry. He swept a hand across his face: it too was dry.

To his further astonishment, as he looked ahead he saw that he stood a mere ten feet from the end of the street. The two-way junctions lay so close he could reach it in seconds. He could make out the lights and the sounds of the streets that lay beyond as his mind came to realise he was within yards of safety. One second, he'd been running and making no forward movement, now he stood so close to the way ahead he could almost feel the warmth of the well-lit streets that lay beyond the dark street of horrors he'd struggled to escape from.

He needed no forcing onwards towards the light and then, just as his feet reached to within a yard of the junction, a long, dark shadow fell across his path, surrounded by an unearthly glow, backlit from the gas lamps on the street behind it. Jack Reid stood stock still, his instincts telling him straight away exactly who now stood blocking his path. His eyes fell to the ground, to the point where the shadow began at the feet of the newcomer. Black polished boots rose from the foul-smelling street surface, though they bore none of the filth that was such a feature of the cobbled surface. Above the boots, clean, dark grey trousers led up until they met with the hem of a long, black frock coat. Reid continued to raise his eyes until the head, or what should have been the head of the newcomer appeared in his view. Where that head should have been Reid saw a black, swirling mass of something he couldn't even begin to describe to me. At best, he described it as a sort of cloud, shaped into the semblance of a human head, but with no eyes, mouth, ears or visible sign of hair. The whole thing carried a stench, more foul than the all-pervading odour of decrepitude and effluent that rose from the filth of the street itself. Despite the lack of visible organs, he felt that the thing could see him quite clearly; a notion confirmed when the mass appeared to flash from the effects of some kind of internal light, and the most unearthly voice Reid had ever heard emanated from deep within the creature.

"*At last, we meet, young Jack, and what a handsome young gent you are,*" it said, in a voice that Reid swore to me could have come from the deepest, darkest, recesses of Hell. "*You know me, Jack, so you mustn't fear me, for I am you and you are me. You know this, do you not?"*

Reid couldn't speak, and then, he realised that the voce he was hearing had no earthly voice at all. The words were reverberating in his brain, as though planted there by the foul creature that stood before him.

"*That's correct,*" said the beast in confirmation of his realisation. "*You don't need to speak, just think of me and I'm with you, Jack, and I hear you, and can speak to you from within your very own soul, for the soul is something we share. You saw those creatures in the street? Do you know who they were? They are what's left of our victims, Jack. Six from Whitechapel, 1888, three from Brighton, and two from Warsaw. They are condemned to stay trapped here for ever, and each night I return and they are forced to relive the sublime torment as I consign their souls to Hell once more. Are their screams not the most exquisite sound you've ever heard? You see the empty windows Jack? They are for the others, those yet to come, those you will send to join me!*"

Reid could hardly believe it. This was the most evil incarnation of Hell that he could have possibly imagined. Here was, without doubt, none other than Jack the Ripper, confirming not only that Jack was his descendant, but that the two of them somehow shared the same, evil, black-hearted soul.

Not only that, but the thing was telling him that he would join him in the terrible litany of murder that had so obviously spread its tentacles through the previous century and more.

"*We'll meet again soon, Jack, very soon,*" said the creature, as it suddenly began to swirl into nothingness before his eyes. The last thing Reid remembered of the dream was the sound of music as the thing that had once been the living, breathing Jack the Ripper floated away into the night. The song was one he'd never heard before, but he knew by its sound that it was old, incredibly old, perhaps a Victorian music hall tune.

The Ripper was gone as suddenly as he'd appeared and Jack Reid woke up screaming into his pillow. He clicked on the bedside light in his room and looked around, but all was quiet and still. There was no-one and nothing in the room but him. His hands trembled as he pulled back the bed covers and made his way to the bathroom where he splashed his sweat-covered brow with cold water. As he did so, he looked at his reflection in the mirror. The sight of his own face seemed to mock him as he realised that not only did the Cavendish legacy carry a fearful curse, but that he was somehow inextricably linked, heart and soul, to the infamous Whitechapel murderer. No matter how hard he'd tried to fight it, Jack Reid now knew what destiny held in store for him, and though he swore to me that he did everything he could in the coming weeks to avoid the inevitable, there was nothing he could do to prevent the bloodletting that would eventually cause the streets of twenty-first century Whitechapel to run red once more!"

FIFTEEN
KATE'S REVELATION

"William, please! I need you to stop, right there. There's something I have to speak to you about," Kate suddenly interjected animatedly.

Something about the description of Reid's dream had obviously struck a chord in her mind and it was quite clear that she needed instant clarification of whatever it may be before allowing Forbes to continue. Forbes appeared quite relieved to have an opportunity to stop and draw breath. He visibly relaxed and it was only at that moment that I realised just how rigidly he'd been holding himself throughout his narration. He allowed his shoulders to sag a little and he leaned back in his chair, rubbing his neck which was clearly stiff and sore from his having held it in one position for so long.

"What is it Kate? What's wrong?" I asked, unsure what she would say next.

"Yes, Kate?" said Forbes.

"Your description of Mr Reid's dream was extremely lucid, William, almost *too* lucid, I venture to say."

Forbes's eyes suddenly assumed that odd, hunted look as

she spoke, and I could see him becoming tense once again after only a few seconds of being at rest. Kate continued before he could respond to her assumption.

"I can quite understand him giving you a graphically vivid picture of what he saw, heard and felt during his nightmare, but for you to relate it in the manner you've just done to David and I without a single note of guidance to aid your recall of his words leads me to believe that there is much more to this dream than you're letting on to us."

"You...you know, don't you?" Forbes exclaimed; his face visibly paling as he spoke. He'd turned a deathly white, all evidence of the previous ruddy redness in his cheeks disappearing in an instant. I might have been mistaken, but I could have sworn that his hair, thin as it was, actually stood on end as a new fear appeared to take a hold of the man and sweat began to break out on his brow. Unfortunately, as yet I'd no idea what Kate alluded to and I waited with bated breath for the explanation for Forbes's sudden terror.

"What do I know, William? Please, tell David what you think it is I already know, that you haven't told us yet."

"Yes, please, one of you tell me what's going on," I pleaded.

Forbes seemed to have turned to jelly, his whole body language indicating he was in no state to speak of the matter. He sank into his chair, his eyes once more darting around the room looking for whatever it was that appeared to terrify him earlier. As his mouth moved, the only sounds that emerged were incoherent mumblings. It was therefore left for Kate to say what perhaps he would have done if he'd been able.

"The reason William is able to relate the dream in such detail and with unerring accuracy is because, David my dear boy, the nightmare he's describing was not exclusive to Jack Reid. If I'm not mistaken I think we'll find that William here has experienced the images and the terror of that dream at first-hand. In short, he's relating to us his very own nightmare, am I correct, William?"

Kate's words cut through Forbes's terror and he responded almost instantly, as though, by revealing her deduction, she'd relieved him of a great burden.

"Yes," he sobbed as tears began to stream from his eyes. "How did you know? How on earth did you work it out?"

"It was quite easy really, old chap. No-one could possibly have related the imagery you just conveyed to us with such intensity unless they'd gone through the experience personally. There was no way you could have simply heard it from Reid and then told it to us in the way you did. You may not have realised it, William, but as you spoke, your body grew more tense by the second. With each step along that awful street you described you sunk further into yourself, your eyes shrank, and your breathing grew more rapid. You were reliving the experience in your mind, and though you fought hard to keep your voice on an even keel I could read every nuance in your tone, and it didn't take a genius to put two and two together."

"Er, excuse me," I butted in. "I'm not exactly a numbskull, Kate, and I certainly didn't work it out."

"That's because you weren't looking for it, David, my dear boy. You see, not only did I read it in what William was saying, and how he said it, almost from the beginning of his telling us the story of the dream, I was actually *expecting* it."

"You were?" I asked.

"Really?" asked an incredulous Forbes. "But, why? How? I don't understand how you could have been expecting that the dream was as much mine as Jack Reid's."

Now, the reason for me asking Kate Goddard to join me on Skerries Rock would begin to reveal itself. This was why she was here, and why I was very glad she'd agreed to help me in the strange case presented by William Forbes. Kate looked deeply into the eyes of the man sitting opposite her, and she spoke quietly and gently as she revealed the first results of her own 'examination' of Forbes.

"From the first moment I met you, William, I knew that something was troubling you very greatly. I don't mean that I could see were a worried man, that kind of thing. Anyone can see such things in their fellow human beings. No, I could sense something malevolent hanging over you, the presence of an aura of evil that wasn't directly a part of you. In fact, I feel there are two auras surrounding you, William, both of which are fighting a battle of wills, perhaps to take control of you, or at least your mind. I do know that you've sensed these things yourself, and that's why you are constantly searching with your eyes for the things that you feel are attempting to assault your psyche. It's an illogical act of course, because although you can feel them you most definitely can't see them. Now, am I on the right lines with my initial hypothesis?"

Forbes appeared stunned.

"But, yes, that's exactly what's happening. You're amazing, really. How on earth, I mean, how could you...?

"It's what I do William, and I suspect that David here had an idea of these things, but couldn't really work it out for himself, but his subconscious mind knew enough to make him call me in to assist him, and you. The human mind is capable of so much more than people imagine, William. You, David, almost everyone has certain abilities that under normal circumstances never reveal themselves. They are simply lying dormant but when great danger or trauma takes place, quite often this latent sense, let's call it the 'sixth sense' for want of a name, can click into place and gives us the so-called 'premonitions' or ' hyper-sensitivity' that are often evident in such cases. David felt something in you that he instinctively knew he couldn't handle, but that inner sense told him that I could help and, hey presto, here I am."

"Yes, I see, well, at least I think I do. But, Kate, don't you see? If I've been having the dream it can only mean one thing!"

Kate nodded, I merely felt confused. 'Auras' are not something that fall into the everyday remit of a clinical psychologist. Although I'd sensed that William Forbes had problems that might call for Kate's special brand of expertise, her current train of thought had left me a little outside the loop.

"What William is saying," she explained, "is that if he is experiencing the same dream, or nightmare, whatever you wish to call it, then somehow, he believes that he must have some connection with Jack the Ripper. So far, it would appear that only members of the Cavendish family have been affected by contact with the journal, and if Reid was to be believed, that particular family, from Burton Cavendish's offspring to the present day, are all loosely descended from the same bloodline as the Ripper. Therefore, and I assume this is the question you've been asking yourself, William; why should you, a solicitor with no previous connection to the Cavendishes or the Reids, find yourself under this kind of psychological assault?"

William Forbes now appeared totally in awe of Kate as he gasped,

"Why, yes, that's it exactly. You're an amazing lady, Kate. You've worked it all out in next to no time. As you say, if I'm dreaming the same things as Jack Reid did, then does it mean I'm also somehow a relative of Jack the Ripper? I don't see how I could be, but there doesn't seem to be any other logical explanation, does there?"

"There are always the possibilities of other explanations William," Kate replied. "Whether they are valid or not, or whether they will stand up to scrutiny is another matter of course."

"And these auras you mentioned?" I asked, not wanting to lose the thread of the conversation and how it all connected the case together.

"Ah, yes, the auras," said Kate. "First of all, I believe that William is currently surrounded by two different but very real auras. Number one, and this is the one that I feel is the most dangerous is the one that is trying to take control of his mind and is without doubt a strong and malevolent force of evil. The other, not as strong as the first, is by no means an evil force, but one that if given the opportunity to overpower the first, may just prove to be the route to William's eventual salvation from the curse of the Cavendish family if that is indeed what we are facing."

"Then you can actually *see* these things?"

"No, David, I can't see them, but I do feel them, sense them if you like, with that other sense I was speaking of earlier. I don't consider myself to be special in any way, but perhaps I've managed to develop that particular sense more than others, and that gives me this innate ability that you and others have found useful in the past."

"So, do you think you can actually help me?" pleaded Forbes.

"I hope we can, William," Kate answered positively. "The first thing we will need to do is to investigate the history of your family, if that's okay with you. We must try and discover if there is any possible connection between you, your ancestors and the Cavendish family."

A thought hit me.

"There is another possibility, Kate. One of those 'other' possibilities you were speaking of earlier, perhaps."

"Go on David."

"Well, so far we're assuming that all the latent evil, the Jack the Ripper stuff and all that was passed on in the genes of

Burton Cavendish. Certainly, some of his genes must have borne the Ripper's make-up or it would be inconceivable that it would have affected his family through the generations, but we should remember that the Ripper had a mother too. According to Reid's story, the journal mentioned that she ended her life incarcerated in a mental asylum. Isn't it therefore safe to assume that she bore as much responsibility for creating the insanity of the Ripper as Burton Cavendish? Isn't it possible that William is descended not from the Cavendish line, but from the family of the Ripper's mother?"

Kate Goddard smiled a knowing smile as she spoke once again.

"You know David. I really do think you are developing a talent for this kind of thing. I had nursed that thought in my mind for the last few minutes and I wondered if perhaps you might pick up on it too."

"Oh my God!" Forbes exclaimed, a look of shock permeating every aspect of his face. "You really do think I'm a descendant of that vile murderous beast don't you?"

"As I said, William," said Kate, solemnly, "there are always other possibilities, so yes, we must consider this one very carefully and diligently if we are to assist in saving you from the fate that has befallen so many of the Cavendish family through the years."

"Saving me? You mean you really think the Ripper is trying to get me?"

"Get you? Well yes, perhaps, but not in the way you currently believe. I would hazard a guess, William, that if the journal holds the power that the Cavendish family have believed it to possess over the last hundred years or so, then there is a very real danger that you may be the next one to be pulled into its nightmare world. If you're not incredibly careful, and if we fail in the task ahead of us, you may conceivably be the next Jack Reid, or the next Mark Cavendish."

Forbes's mouth fell open, though he uttered no sound at all. His face registered total shock, as I think mine must have done too. At no time up to that awful moment had I considered the terrible potential scenario Kate had just outlined. Now, however, I was forced to confront the possibility that the middle-aged man in the fireside chair in my cosy little home on Skerries Rock might just be destined to be the next incarnation of Jack the Ripper!

As for the man himself, William Forbes sat hunched, a beaten man to all appearances, as tears began to run down his face and his body began to shake uncontrollably.

The terrible silence in the room, broken only by the steady ticking of the grandfather clock, ended as Kate brought us back to the present:

"I think," she said quietly, "we had better start looking into William's background sooner, rather than later, eh, David?"

I nodded, saying nothing, my mouth dry as old bones, feeling as dumbstruck as the man in the chair, who continued sobbing quietly.

SIXTEEN
A SHADOW IN THE NIGHT

THE SOUND of waves crashing over the rocks that littered the bay on the Atlantic side of Skerries Rock mingled with the eerie rushing of the breeze hurrying in from the open ocean to form a dissonance of nature's reverberation in our ears as the three of us stood looking out into the darkness, from the cliff top. It had been Kate's idea to drag William Forbes from the sanctuary of the fireside into the open air in order that he, and we, come to that, might attempt to clear our heads before proceeding further with our strange inquiry. I'd expected Forbes to put up some sort of opposition to the idea of an evening stroll after the shock of Kate's earlier revelation, but, perhaps because she'd earned his trust and admiration so quickly, he'd made no protest at the suggestion and instead agreed to Kate's idea with apparent enthusiasm.

Dressed in warm coats, fishermen's sweaters, thick winter trousers, scarves and wearing sturdy boots, topped off with a selection of Peruvian Alpaca wool hats I kept in the croft, we would have appeared an odd trio to anyone who might have seen us on that cold, windswept evening. As it was, there was no-one to see us. We three were the entire population of my island. Even the sea birds had called it a night and not even a passing gull or kittiwake swirled in the air above us as we stood, each lost in our own thoughts for over ten windswept minutes. There wasn't much to see to be truthful. At that time of evening, with the vast backdrop of the Atlantic stretching out for a thousand miles from the coast of my tiny island home, the horizon soon blurred until sea and sky became one and the same to the naked eye. Only the pale visage of a faraway half-moon and the occasional twinkling of a distant star in the vast panoply of space broke the gloom that met our view as we continued to stand, buffeted by the wind and lost to each other and to the world as we communed with the powers of nature for a short eternity.

What the others were thinking about I couldn't say, but I was caught up by the thought that William Forbes could be in some way related to the infamous Jack the Ripper, and thus, perhaps, to Jack Reid through some distant family connection. If so, could he really be destined to follow in the footsteps of the original killer? Would he, like Mark Cavendish and Jack Reid find himself wielding the bloody knife that would end the lives of some poor innocent woman or women at some hitherto unknown point in the future? I looked at the back of Forbes's head. He was, without doubt, the least Ripper-like creature I could imagine, but then, as no-one knows what Jack the Ripper looked like in the first place, I supposed that to be a nonsense. Why would the Ripper appear different to any other so-called 'normal' human being? As a professional I knew that killers come in all shapes and sizes and that the most mild and inoffensive looking person can in fact be transformed into the most terrible killing machine, capable of intolerable cruelty and savagery when faced with the right motive and circumstances.

The others appeared equally lost in their own private

world of thoughts, and for those few minutes a kind of peace and tranquillity reigned over Skerries Rock,

until Kate's voice broke us from our reverie at last.

"I think we should be getting back."

"You do?"

"Yes, David. There is much to do, and pleasant though it is standing here communing with the power of nature, we really should return and begin our efforts to help poor William."

"Why did we come out here in the first place if there is so much to do, Kate?"

"Because, dear boy, even my mind needs a break from time to time. Such were the images portrayed by William's story that I was becoming overwhelmed with a sense of great evil and malevolence that had somehow managed to permeate the solid walls of your charming home. In short, I needed fresh air, and the chance to think logically about our next step."

"And what is our next step, Kate?" The question came from Forbes who had moved a few paces closer so he could hear our conversation. I could tell that he felt tense and afraid. The tremble in his voice betrayed any sense of normality he might be struggling to maintain.

"Why, dinner of course!" Kate still had the power to shock me, and her reference to something as mundane as dinner when Forbes appeared almost on the verge of a nervous breakdown certainly took my breath away with no lesser force than the strong Westerly that buffeted us as it gathered pace with the coming night.

"Dinner? Now?" Forbes spluttered. "But what about…?"

"We can do little more tonight, William," Kate retorted. "If we are to effectively research you family background there are certain steps we must follow, certain pathways to tread that are not open to us at this time of the night."

"David has the internet," he pleaded.

"Yes, of course, and there is much that may be gleaned from the world-wide web," she replied. "But we may require far more than can be gathered from a mere internet search engine. The information we seek is, I think, well hidden in the mists of time, William. If not, you would, I'm sure be aware of any, what shall we call it…er, anomaly in the recent history of your family?"

"I'm not aware of any such anomaly. My parents, grandparents and great grandparents are all well documented."

"Yes, I'm sure they are, but what about their brothers, sisters, nieces and nephews, cousins, illegitimate offspring, and so on?"

"Good Lord, how on earth do you expect to trace all of those?" I asked.

"Tomorrow morning gentlemen, I shall place a telephone call to a friend of mine. He is a historian and an expert in the art of genealogy. If anyone can conduct an extremely fast search and come up with a fairly accurate and concise family tree depicting your ancestry, William, I guarantee it will be Miles Prendergast."

I'd never heard of Prendergast, and asked Kate about him as we walked back to the croft, a slightly crestfallen Forbes walking a few paces ahead of us. He'd obviously expected more from the night than the prospect of a meal and an early night. I doubted he'd sleep much anyway, after Kate's earlier revelations.

"Miles Prendergast, David, is a professor of history. He is based at one of the older colleges at Oxford, though he hails originally from Scalby."

"Ah, another Scarborough boy."

"Precisely. He and I sort of grew up together in the village and have been lifelong friends. He has one of the finest minds I've ever encountered. About twenty years ago he took up genealogy as a mere hobby yet became so intensely involved in researching various projects that he quickly became an expert in the field. When we've eaten I'll ask William to write out as much information he can about his ancestry, and in the morning I'll contact Miles and ask him to do a fast genealogical search and create a family tree for Forbes."

"But, is it possible to do such a thing as a fast search for something like this?"

"Believe me David, if anyone can do it, Miles Prendergast can. When I impress the urgency of the matter upon him, I'm certain he'll get back to me very soon, in a day or two perhaps. Then again, the Forbes family background may be extremely easy to trace in which case he may be able to do the job much sooner than that."

"I just hope you're right, Kate. Apart from the fact that there is a chance that Forbes might actually go completely off his head if this thing drags on much longer, what the hell do we do if what you suspect turns out to be true and he does become some sort of 'Clone of the Ripper' while he's here on the island?"

"Ha, I'm glad to hear you haven't lost your sense of humour dear boy," she laughed.

"I'm not laughing, Kate. I'm bloody serious" I chided her.

"Of course you are you lovely man. But listen, if Forbes does indeed go totally bonkers while he's here, I'm sure you can do something to restrain and sedate him until we can get him to a hospital, am I right?"

I nodded.

"Good, then all we have to worry about is the possibility that he might suddenly become filled with the blood lust of the Ripper, and as there are no prostitutes here on Skerries rock for him to disembowel and mutilate, I think we're relatively safe from that eventuality."

I was about to reply but she cut me off.

"Listen, David. Nothing like that will happen. Trust me. Forbes is still in control of himself, no matter what he may think. If there is a malevolent presence that's followed him here to your home, it has a lot to do yet in order to gain control of his mind, and, this time it has me to contend with, not just William Forbes and his weakened state of mind."

"I hope you're right, Kate. That's all I can say."

There was no time for more, as we'd arrived at the door of the croft. Forbes had reached home a few seconds before the two of us, and he now stood, framed in the light from the interior of my home as held the door open for us. It was then that I saw something that sent a chill down my spine and caused the hairs on the back of my neck to stand on end. There was no-one standing in the doorway apart from William Forbes, whose shadow was cast forwards by the light behind him so that it reached out to greet us as we neared the door. Yet, I could swear that there was another figure standing just behind the man; taller, leaner, and indistinct in detail, yet undisputedly human in form. And yet, no, not human, for the thing, if it was real, seemed almost gaseous, amorphous and unreal, seeming to hover and linger around the form of William Forbes rather than being stood in any fixed point. It was then I realised that the thing, whatever it was, actually appeared to emanate from *within* Forbes, to be a part of him, an extension that grew from his body, slowly and surely growing in size until I felt sure it would totally engulf the man, who seemed completely unaware of its presence.

Just in case I thought I was imagining the vision I was being subjected to, Kate suddenly grabbed me by the arm, forcing me to stand stock still beside her.

"You see it too?" I asked, breathlessly.

"Shh" she urged, and as we watched the strange sight, the

thing, whatever it was, began to recede back in to the body of William Forbes, until in less than five seconds, it had withdrawn completely and there was nothing but the standing figure of the man who waited to greet us as we entered my home once again.

"Say nothing, David, not a word," she whispered as we followed Forbes in to the living room, back to the light and the welcoming warmth of the fire that continued to burn and crackle softly in the hearth.

As we divested ourselves of our outer clothing, I was filled with the desire to ask Kate what she thought we'd just witnessed, but I respected her urgings to silence, and held my questions back. Perhaps, later, when Forbes fell asleep, I might find the opportunity to ask her, but for now, she seemed determined to keep the incident from Forbes. Whatever had just happened to William Forbes, whatever that thing was, it was plain to both Kate and I that he had no inkling of it, and that was the obvious reason for Kate not wanting to scare him any more than he was already.

That seemed all well and noble of course, but it did little to calm my own shattered nerves and the first thing I did after ridding myself of my outer garments was to grab the whisky bottle and pour myself a large one.

"I say, are you alright, David? You look a little shaky" said Forbes as he watched my trembling hand pouring a large measure of the amber liquid into the glass.

"I'm fine, thank you William," I lied. "Just a little chilled from the walk, that's all. Would you both like a drink?"

"Ah yes, just the thing to warm us all up," Kate replied cheerfully. "Gin for me and a brandy for you, eh, William?"

"Yes, lovely."

"Excellent! And then I think, we should see about that dinner, David."

She was good at this, I had to admit to myself. How she could carry on as though nothing had happened after what we'd just witnessed, I found difficult to comprehend, but then, Kate Goddard had always been an exceptional woman, and I was heartily glad that I'd made the decision to call her.

As we sat sipping our pre-dinner drinks, and the warmth of the room banished the chill from our bodies, William Forbes, appearing much more cheerful than he had an hour previously, probably thanks to Kate's therapeutic walk, turned to me with a smile on his face.

"This is an excellent brandy, David. Mmm. That's better. Very warming. You know, you quite surprised me when you rushed in just now and grabbed that whisky bottle. If you weren't such a professional and doctor and all, and if I didn't know you better, I might have imagined you'd just seen a ghost."

I laughed: a very silly schoolboy giggle more than a laugh. As Kate looked at me, fixing me with a stare that called for my continued silence, I couldn't think of a word to say.

SEVENTEEN
THE MUSIC OF THE NIGHT?

Dinner that night tuned out to be a muted affair, with little conversation passing between the three of us. I'd done my best to prepare a reasonable meal in a short space of time and the cheese omelettes with salad and baked potatoes went down well with both Kate and Forbes. I felt that every one of us really wanted to say something, but that something held each of us back from voicing our thoughts. In my case, it was of course the strange incident surrounding our return to the croft. What on earth had that thing been that seemed to appear from within the body of William Forbes? I thought that perhaps it might have been the manifestation of one of those auras that Kate had mentioned earlier. If not, what else could have caused such an event? The fact that Forbes appeared not to have possessed any knowledge of the manifestation, or what was happening in him or around him at the time made the whole affair seem even stranger. Of course, there was nothing I could do to find out more on the subject until Kate and I could be alone. She'd made it quite obvious that I wasn't to speak of the matter in front of Forbes, so I forced myself to be patient. I had little choice in the matter.

I had the idea that Kate was also thinking about the same thing. The fact that both of us had witnessed the strange occurrence surely meant that whatever it had been, it was indeed real and not imaginary. There was no way I could conceive of Kate and I having shared a hallucination. I felt sure, as I finished the last of my meal that she was as anxious as I to speak of the matter, and somehow, I felt it an issue of importance that we pack Forbes off to bed as soon as we could, without making it too obvious that we were trying to get rid of him.

Forbes himself ate in almost total silence, only asking Kate a couple of basic questions about her proposed call to Miles Prendergast the following day. He wanted to know just how much information Kate expected him to provide in order for Prendergast to conduct his search, and Kate asked him to sit down after dinner and write down the names, places and dates of birth, if he knew them, of as many members of his family as he could, going back, if possible to the late nineteenth century. Approximations would have to do, she told him, if he was unsure of any of the information. She felt certain that Prendergast would find what he needed as long as he had something to go on. That was when, with dinner coming to a close, Kate played her master stroke.

"I think, William that you would concentrate far better on producing what we need for Miles if you retire to the spare room and sit quietly where you can think in peace. David and I will certainly not disturb you and you can take your time in trying to think of all the information we need."

"Yes, of course. Peace and quiet, the best thing by far," he agreed and soon after, he took himself into my spare room armed with a notepad and a ballpoint pen, ready to wrack his brain and provide Kate with the names and details of as many members of his family as he could think of. At last, Kate and I had the opportunity to discuss the earlier phenomenon.

Before we did however, there was something else on Kate's mind which she brought up the moment the door to the spare room closed behind William Forbes.

"David, have you noticed something odd about William's behaviour?"

"You mean apart from strange apparitions appearing from his body and half-scaring the living daylights out of me?"

"Actually, no, that's not what I mean."

"Then, what exactly are you talking about, Kate?"

"I mean the fact that he's hardly mentioned the Ripper, or his fears and the meetings with Reid at all since our discussion before we went for a walk."

Kate was quite correct of course. Since admitting to experiencing the dream, and after Kate announcing her 'possibilities theory' and her intention to contact Miles Prendergast, Forbes had fallen eerily silent on the whole subject. Bearing in mind his behaviour and demeanour over the previous twenty-four hours, it did seem odd that he'd said little on the subject from the time we'd left the croft until he'd left us to write up his family history in the spare room.

After a moment pondering on Kate's observation I replied with the only theory I could drum up.

"Psychologically speaking, it may be a case of 'a problem shared' and all that. Having finally found the courage to admit that he is experiencing the dream, and revealing his innermost fears to us, it could be that some of his fear and terror has subsided, at least temporarily. By sharing his problem perhaps he feels he's now on the way to finding a solution and escaping what he believes to be some kind of supernatural 'possession' if that's the right term. That might be the explanation."

"And then again, David, it might not," Kate looked glum. "There's no doubt in my mind that William remains terribly afraid. Everything in his body language points to it, and of course, there was the manifestation you and I saw on our return to the croft."

"Ah, at last! I wondered when you'd get round to that. At least it's good to know I wasn't imagining it, but why didn't you want to talk about it in front of Forbes? Surely he needs to know about it?"

"Perhaps he does, but not yet, David. Tell me, I need to know exactly what you saw, to understand whether your vision matched mine, or whether we saw 'it' in different manifestations."

I soon confirmed to Kate that what I'd seen tallied exactly with her recollection of it.

"What was it, Kate, a ghost?"

"No David, not a ghost. I've been doing what I do for a lot of years, and believe me, I've so far failed to definitely confirm the existence of one single ghost. There are a great many things in and around us in this world that can't always be explained, but the existence of 'ghosts' as commonly perceived is yet to be confirmed or denied. There is no proof, either way, I'm afraid."

"Then what is all this paranormal stuff you investigate?"

"David, let me explain something to you. when I say there are no ghosts, what I mean is that there is no proof that the individual spirit of, say, your grandfather, can return to earth and haunt you in some physical sense, you know, ghostly white floating figures on the stairs at night and all that. That's not to say that there aren't recorded instances of supernatural occurrences that can't be easily explained. When I spoke of the 'auras' surrounding Forbes for example, they may very well be the auras of earth-bound spirits, unable to find rest due to some terrible happenings during their lives, or deaths. Maybe, and this is mere conjecture, the evil that was contained within the soul of Jack the Ripper was so great that it is impossible for it to depart for wherever such souls go after death, and that somehow, that evil has succeeded in trapping the souls of its tragic victims in some kind of limbo, a hellish world where they must forever live out a repeated scenario that always ends up in the same way, with the victims falling prey once again to their earthly murderer."

"Jack Reid's dream!" I exclaimed.

"And poor William Forbes's dream too, it would now appear," Kate added.

"Yes, of course, but what has that to do with his silence and the thing we saw."

"Let's suppose for a minute that my original hypothesis was correct, David, that there are in fact two separate auras surrounding William Forbes."

"Like, good and evil perhaps?" I ventured.

"Almost, but not quite. Certainly, there is intense evil, but as for the other, I see it as being calmer, less violent, but whether it is acting for good or for some other, hidden element of malevolent intent, I can't yet say. I do believe though, that what the two of us saw was a manifestation of one of those auras. Normally such things wouldn't be visible to the naked eye, but perhaps, just this once, the conditions, the light of the room beyond and the intense darkness outside where we stood contributed to make the sighting possible."

"So you're saying we shouldn't really have seen it?"

"Under normal circumstances, no. but we did, and the fact is inescapable. Somehow, David, you and I have seen something that very few people have ever seen. I doubt there are more than a dozen people on the planet who can have witnessed such as we did tonight."

"But what the hell do we do about it? Was that Jack the Ripper do you think?"

"I don't think so, David, no. If it had been, I think there would have been a greater 'charge' in the air, and I suspect Forbes would have been beside himself in one of his panic attacks. No, I believe that what we saw was the manifestation of the 'other' aura, the unknown one, the calmer one, and for some reason, it has managed to make Forbes's mind withdraw slightly within itself. It's as if the thing has helped him to shut out the awful reality of the dream, the terrible consequences that may yet be visited upon him. Like I said, this other aura may or may not be acting in Forbes's best interests, but for now, I believe it's making our task easier by keeping him placated, almost like one of your sedatives."

"Huh, I think I'd rather place my faith in one of my sedatives than in some jiggery-pokery mumbo-jumbo aura character."

"David, my dear boy, I'm surprised at you! If I didn't know you better I'd swear you're taking the mickey out of me and my noble profession."

"I'm sorry if it sounded like that Kate." I guess my words had wounded her professional pride and I was contrite as I went on. "You know how much I respect and value your opinions. It's just that this whole affair is beginning to get me a little rattled. I've always known what you do, and have shown a keen interest in your work, but never quite as close-up and personal as this, that's all. A lot of what you're saying is mystifying to me, Kate, and I'm not used to being mystified, I can tell you that."

"Of course you're not, David. You're a professional, a psychologist who is used to dealing with the workings of the human mind on a *human* level. You're not used to seeing what can happen to the human mind when something inhuman makes an appearance and that, believe me, is what we're faced with here."

Kate appeared mollified by my apology and I felt confident to continue.

"Alright then, Kate. You're the expert and I'm the novice in this supernatural, paranormal stuff. If I wasn't involved and you were in charge of the investigation, if Forbes had simply contacted you for example, what would you do now?"

"What I suggest *we* do now my friend, is wait until Mr Forbes completes his task in the other room, and then we try and spend a pleasant few hours before retiring to bed. I don't think we're going to find out much more from the strangely reticent Mr Forbes tonight, at least, not unless the current force that is keeping him quiet releases its hold on him. That's why I don't want to mention the aura to him, David. If this rather passive entity leaves him, it's highly likely that the other, very violent one will replace it, and that is just what we want to avoid. I fear that each time that vile creature, whatever it may be, takes a hold on William it lessens his resolve and his will to resist it, and if it is in some way a manifestation of what was once the soul or the spirit of Jack the Ripper, then we had all best watch our backs."

As Kate's words died out, the door to the spare room opened and William Forbes stepped back in to the room, the firelight casting a ruddy glow to his cheeks that I suspected would be absent in normal daylight. He appeared to have remained in his calmer state, and he greeted us warmly, holding out a piece of A4 paper in his hand as he drew closer to Kate.

"Well, that's about the best I can do," he said as Kate took the offered sheet of paper from his hand.

"That's fine William, really," she said after casting a cursory glance at the handwritten document. It will give Miles something to go on, and that's all I asked of you, thank you."

"So, what now?" he asked.

"Now, we relax. At least, we try to," she replied, taking Forbes by the arm and leading him back to my favourite fireside chair, where she soon had him comfortably seated, feet up on the footstool that she'd brought over from the side of the hearth.

No sooner had Forbes laid his head back against the upright of the chair back, than his eyes appeared to grow heavy. He yawned, and said very quietly,

"I say, I'm so sorry, but I feel so very tired. Must be all that thinking and writing. I hope you won't mind if I close my eyes for a moment or two."

Forbes was asleep in seconds.

"Good," said Kate. "He needs to rest."

"Great," I said. "And how do I get him to bed if I can't wake him later? He's no small lump to drag through the house, you know."

"Oh, fiddlesticks, you're a darn sight stronger than you pretend, David Hemswell. You'll manage if you have to."

Before she could say another word, I held up my hand, stopping her in her tracks.

"What is it?" she asked, sensing instantly that I'd stopped her for a good reason.

"Did you hear that, Kate?"

"Hear what?"

"Coming from outside, I'm sure of it."

"Sure of what, David? What did you hear? There's no-one else on the island."

"Oh forget it. It must have been my imagination. It was nothing, I'm sure."

"David, you're infuriating me. Please, will you tell me what you heard, or at least what you *thought* you heard?"

"Oh, very well," I replied, rather sheepishly. "Just for a few seconds, even as we were talking, I could have sworn I'd heard the faint tinkling of music coming from somewhere outside the house."

"Music? Outside, on a night like this? What kind of music was it, David?"

"Well, that's just it, Kate. You remember what Forbes said about the dream, about the music he'd heard when the figure appeared at the end of that terrible street?"

Kate's face was solemn as I said, "It was a piano, playing Victorian music, Kate, just a few bars, but very definitely the kind of stuff that was played in Victorian Public Houses and Music Halls!"

EIGHTEEN
DISCORDANT MELODY

THERE WAS NOTHING OUTSIDE, naturally. Kate had made no effort to ridicule or dismiss my sudden outburst, but instead had taken me by the hand and led me to the door. Forbes continued to sleep peacefully in the chair, and the two of us made a careful exit from the front door and stood surveying the immediate environs of my home.

"I told you I'd probably imagined it," I said, as we stood in the darkness listening to the wind as it drummed up a small symphony of its own as it whipped around the outbuildings and across the yard outside the croft.

"Probably is never good enough for me, David," Kate replied, leading me further from the door, away from the comparative safety of the warmth and the light, further into the darkness. A shiver ran through my body as I recalled the all too fleeting sounds I'd heard.

"You really heard something didn't you?"

"I thought I did, but perhaps it was just the wind."

"And would the wind be capable of producing a sound that would bring to mind a Victorian piano melody?"

"No, of course not, but with all that's going on around us at the moment, perhaps my imagination decided to play a trick on me."

"Listen, David, I dismiss nothing, and at the moment I'm neither believing nor disbelieving what you may have heard. Tell me, is there any way you might be able to recall the melody of the sounds you think you heard?"

"No way, Kate. I'm sorry. Even if it really was the sound of music, it was too short and indistinct for me to even attempt to recall it, or hum it, or try to identify it. Why, do you think it's important, somehow pertinent to the case?"

"Look, if you heard something, and it was a Victorian melody, I'd say for sure it has something to do with the case. However, if it was a fleeting trick of your imagination, then we have nothing to worry about, do we?"

"But just supposing it *was* music I heard. Then what?"

"Well, my old chap, then we have to ask where on earth such music could have originated from, as the entire population of this island of yours consists of you, me and the sleeping man back there in your sitting room. Not only that, but how the hell could anyone re-create the sound of a piano out here?"

Just then, the sounds of melodic tinkling brought the two of us up with a start. Kate took hold of my arm as I almost jumped out of my skin, until, a sudden realisation hit me and I began to laugh, hesitatingly at first, then with gusto as I led Kate along the narrow path that led to the back of my home.

"What the...? Where are we going?" she demanded as I almost dragged the poor woman along in my wake.

"There, look!" I shouted against the wind as I pointed towards a small shed that stood a few yards from the rear of the croft, where I kept my tools.

Kate's eyes followed the direction of my outstretched arm until they came to rest upon the reason for my agitated run around the croft. There, hanging from the overhanging eaves of the shed, was a rather large, steadily swaying and tinkling wind chime, its bars blowing and colliding in the wind, creating its own musical rendition of a random and unknown melody.

"See, I told you it must have been my imagination, but maybe my ears also picked up the sound of the wind-chime, which would have sounded as though in the distance from the front of the house in the living room, and my mind simply magnified it into the Victorian melody I thought I heard, probably suggested subconsciously by Forbes's story and the mention of the music when he encountered the dream apparition."

"Maybe," Kate shouted above the developing gale, and she began to drag me back around the house towards the warmth of the living room. "We'll talk about it indoors, shall we?"

It all sounded pretty conceivable to me, and I nodded and allowed her to lead the way back to the house. For some reason, despite the plausibility of my theory, and the concrete evidence of the swinging wind-chime, I had the distinct feeling that Kate wasn't totally convinced, and, as we entered my living room once more, and I set eyes on the sleeping figure of William Forbes, the source of everything taking place around us, I admit that neither was I.

"You don't think it was the wind-chime, do you, Kate?" I asked as soon as we'd made sure Forbes was still deeply asleep, and unable to overhear us.

"I don't know quite what to think yet."

"But if it wasn't, then where the hell could the music be coming from?"

"Where the Hell, exactly," said Kate with a very solemn look on her face.

"What? You mean you think it might actually have come

from beyond the grave? Oh, come on Kate. You can't really mean that, surely?"

"I've told you, David. I'm dismissing nothing and accepting nothing for the moment. Best to keep an open mind on the whole situation until things begin to clarify themselves. I really could do with having another word with our sleeping friend over there."

"So, let's wake him."

"Yes, I think we should. I need to ask him something and in light of what you may or may not have just heard, his answer could prove very important indeed."

It took me a good minute to wake Forbes. He was in such a deep sleep that rousing him from his slumbers required calling his name, shaking him, and even pulling the footstool away from under his feet until his eyes opened and he looked up at Kate and me with a bleary-eyed stare that told me he wasn't sure where he was for a moment or two.

"Ah, back in the land of the living, am I?" he asked as he at last focussed his vision and smiled at me as he stretched and ran a hand through his wispy hair.

"I take it you slept well? No bad dreams or nightmares this time, eh?"

"Quite so, David. I haven't slept so well in ages. How long have I been out?"

"A little more than an hour, that's all,"

"Yes, sorry we had to wake you," said Kate, "but there's something we need to ask, and it is important, or we wouldn't have disturbed your much-needed sleep."

"Please, it's perfectly okay. What can I tell you?"

"Well, William, you mentioned to us that in your dream, you recalled hearing music in the background when you first saw the figure that you assumed to be the Ripper. Have you any idea what that tune might have been?"

Forbes's face paled as he allowed his mind to focus once again on his memories of that awful nightmare scenario he'd described to us in such terrifying detail.

"Well, obviously, at first, I had no idea what the music was. Jack Reid had described hearing the same thing of course but in his psychologically disturbed state there'd been no way he'd made any effort to identify the tune. When the dream returned to me for a second, and then a third time I found that the tune remained within my memory during my waking hours, you know, like one of those irritating TV commercial jingles you can't shake from your mind. I'd never heard the tune before, but I decided to try and find out what it was. I'm not the most tuneful of people so the best I could do was hum the damn thing. My colleagues at the firm must have thought I was crazy as I walked into various people's offices asking them if they'd ever heard of this particular tune. Of course, none of them had. The few outside acquaintances I had also looked askance at me when I began humming the tune to them and they were equally at a loss to name the tune. I tried visiting my local music shops, but again drew a blank. I've tried and tried but despite my best efforts I've never been able to identify it. It's always the same whenever the nightmare hits me, but I'm beginning to think I'll never know what it is and what significance, if any it has to.... wait a minute! Why are you asking me about the music all of a sudden? It must be important if you've woken me just to ask me about it."

"Well, just before we woke you, David could have sworn he heard the sound of music coming from outside the house. We both went out, but of course there was nothing and no-one in sight. The wind is getting stronger out there, and then we stumbled across the wind chime hanging from David's tool shed and we thought that maybe the wind and the chime might be playing tricks with David's mind, particularly as you'd already mentioned the music. We thought maybe his mind had simply heard the chime and associated the sound with your tune from the dream."

"Hum it for me, William," I said, wanting to hear the tune in full and see if I could recall the few bars I thought I'd heard earlier.

Forbes took a deep breath, and appeared to disappear in to the deepest recesses of his own mind for a few seconds, and then he began to hum, softly at first, and then with greater intensity as the tune progressed. It was a strange, haunting melody, quite obviously Victorian or even earlier in origin. They don't write music like that anymore. Although I'd earlier only heard a few distant bars of what I'd identified as music, it took only a short time for me to raise my hand in a signal to Forbes to stop his rendition. He fell silent and looked at me, waiting for my response. Beside me, Kate stood rigidly, waiting for my response. I think she knew in advance what I was going to say.

"That last bit, there's no doubt in my mind. It wasn't my imagination Kate. Don't ask me how, or why, but that's exactly what I heard coming from outside. Now, for god's sake tell me how the wind could play a trick like that. In fact, I'm begging you to tell me that the wind *could* play a trick like that!"

William Forbes stared up at me from his position in the armchair. Kate took hold of my arm gently and looked up into my eyes with a look I'd never seen on her face before. I began to feel for the first time, that perhaps even Kate Goddard had been touched by a frisson of fear as she answered my plea.

"David, you know as well as I do that the wind couldn't have done that. Gentlemen, it is my firm belief that it has become imperative for us to identify that song. It is, I believe of great importance somehow, As yet I don't know how or why, but the fact that it repeats itself every time you experience the dream William, and that you too have heard it, though why I didn't also hear it I don't know, must mean it is of great significance with regard to William's situation."

It was at that moment that the lights went out, the room was plunged into subdued fire-lit darkness and William Forbes let loose a piercing, penetrating scream that made me imagine that every banshee in Hell had descended upon him!

NINETEEN
THE JOURNAL

"Dammit!" I shouted, as Kate did her best to calm the screaming figure of William Forbes. "Must be the bloody generator again. It happened yesterday. I thought I'd fixed it."

"Obviously not," Kate called to me over the sound of Forbes's wailings. "William! For God's sake man, calm down," she cried as she gripped him by the shoulders and shook him, attempting to break through the fear and panic that had gripped him with the failing of the lights. He continued to scream, oblivious to her pleadings.

It wasn't even pitch dark in the room. The glow from the log fire provided sufficient light for us to be able see relatively well, but the sudden plunge from electric light to firelight had done the trick and plunged Forbes back into his twilight world. He quite obviously connected the power loss with the things that were happening to him.

"He's coming, I know he is!" he suddenly shouted, his face a mask of terror.

"Who is? Who's coming?" Kate asked the question as calmly as she could, trying to alleviate the panic that clearly flowed through Forbes's entire being. At least he'd stopped that awful screaming.

"The Ripper. He's going to kill me. I know he is."

"Why would he want to kill you?"

"I don't know. But, if he doesn't why is he doing these things to me?"

"What things, William? What exactly is he doing to you that you haven't told us about?"

"What? I don't know. It's just that it all went dark and the shadows moved and…and I can feel him."

"What do you mean, feel him? Feel him where, William? Is he here, already, in this room?"

I marvelled at Kate's tactics. Gradually, she was teasing small snippets of information from the terror-stricken man. A few seconds earlier, Forbes had said the Ripper 'was coming'. Now, that had become 'He's here'. A subtle change, but one that Kate had picked up on immediately. With each answer, Forbes provided her with more of the data she needed to work with in order to solve the mystery into which we'd been plunged. For a few seconds however, he fell silent until Kate began to urge him onwards.

"Come on, William, please, tell me, is he here in the room? Is that why you're so afraid?"

"No, of course he's not in the room, you fool" Forbes was becoming hysterical.

Kate remained calm and passive as she slowly coaxed the conversation along.

"So, where is he? You say he's here, so tell me, exactly *where* he is?"

"He's here," shouted Forbes again, this time manically hitting himself on the chest with the palms of his hands. *"Don't you understand? He's right here, inside me!"*

At last! Kate had managed to force it from him. William

Forbes, in his hysterical state, obviously believed that Jack the Ripper had somehow taken over his body, or at least had become a part of him. How, I don't know, but it was plain that Forbes believed it. Kate turned to me.

"David, go and do what you have to do, but please leave us and go and get that damnable generator of yours working. We need the lights on, and fast."

"But what about…?"

"I'll be fine, really. Now go!"

Pulling on my weatherproof parka from the coat stand by the door I hurriedly exited the house and made my way to the generator room outside. Loathe as I was to leave Kate alone with the trembling figure of William Forbes, she remained adamant that I go and get the lights working. She'd assured me she was safe with Forbes, though I wasn't too sure about that. Even so, something about Kate Goddard made people do as she asked, me being no exception.

Repairing the generator took me all of five minutes. The problem, which I identified almost immediately, turned out to be nothing more than a blown fuse. I kept spares in the tool shed, and soon returned with a replacement, popped it in its place in the fuse box and peered through the darkness to the croft, where I could see the lights come on as power was restored. I wasted no more time in the generator room and hastened back to the house as quickly as my legs would carry me.

I swept through the door fully expecting Forbes to still be shaking and exhibiting the signs of his earlier terror, yet, in the few minutes that it'd taken me to change the fuse in the generator room, Kate appeared to have succeeded in calming the man down completely. He now sat calmly, as did Kate, who'd seated herself in the armchair directly opposite Forbes's position.

"Is everything...?"

"Everything's fine, David," she assured me, cutting me off in mid-sentence. "What was the problem?"

"Just a blown fuse, nothing more serious than that. It happens sometimes with these old fuse boxes. Maybe one day I'll get a modern board fuse board fitted with circuit breakers, but for now, the system is still pretty much in the dark ages. How are things in here?"

"The second the lights came back on, William calmed down immensely."

"Yes, I'm so sorry for my outburst," said Forbes to me, looking very contrite. "I must have sounded like a crazy man."

"That's okay, William." I smiled at him, feeling a large degree of sympathy for the obviously disturbed individual who'd sought my help and now seemed to be going through a rapid mental deterioration. "So you don't think Jack the Ripper is inside you after all?"

"Actually, David, I do," he said in all seriousness. "It's just that Kate here has managed to convince me that I may be in error. We're just talking it through now."

"Oh, in that case I'm sorry to have interrupted the flow of your conversation."

"It's not a problem, David," said Kate. "William, as you know, kept screaming at us that Jack the Ripper was going to 'get' him, then of course he thought that the Ripper was inside him. Now, as I've just explained to him, if Jack the Ripper was really trying to get him or harm him he would hardly be doing it from inside the body of the person he wanted to hurt, now would he?"

There was a kind of logic to Kate's words, but I'm not sure if even she felt convinced by what she'd just said. I could see that Kate was trying hard to mollify Forbes, but her argument fell apart if one considered that the spirit of the Ripper, if it really existed, might be trying to gain control of Forbes and the only way to do that, at least to my way of thinking, would be for that spirit to enter, or possess Forbes's body and mind. I think she knew what I was thinking because she then said:

"Of course David, there are other possibilities as I've said from the start, but we mustn't let William here fall prey to fear of the dark and things that go bump in the night must we?"

"Yes, Kate was just about to explain those other things before you came in." Forbes added, with a degree of composure he'd lacked a few minutes previously.

"Ah, then you must continue, Kate," I said, wondering how she could get through the next few minutes without telling Forbes that he might in reality be possessed by the Ripper, if one believed in such things of course.

Kate gave me one of those, *'Leave it to me'* looks before continuing.

"As I was saying," she went on, "I don't believe you are in any physical danger, William. Whether this is or is not a manifestation of Jack the Ripper that is affecting you, and remember, you haven't told us the whole story of your visits to Jack Reid yet, I can see no reason why it should wish to harm you. You have done no harm to it, or him, or whatever, and most spirits, if they are indeed spirits, have no power to harm human beings. I believe whatever is happening to you is taking place on a psychological level and as such you are safe from physical harm. On the other hand, I can logically understand that, if you are indeed a descendant of Jack the Ripper, then a connection of sorts may exist between you."

Forbes drew in a breath, stunned at the thought.

"Don't worry; we are here to help you. Now listen, I also don't believe that the paper you entrusted to David is harmful to anyone but a descendant of the Ripper himself. I'd like to take a look at it in a moment if you please, David. You see,

William, I believe that the journal did exist but you must remember that if we are to believe Burton Cavendish, it was he who 'disposed' of Jack the Ripper, his illegitimate son, and so the journal was never passed on to a soul by the Ripper himself, but by Cavendish, so we cannot assume that any malevolence was passed on directly by the Ripper through his journal."

"Wait a minute," I interrupted. "Are you saying that any evil that comes from contact with the journal comes not from Jack the Ripper but from Burton Cavendish?"

"I don't know," Kate replied, barely pausing for breath as she went on:

"But, I do believe we need to look closely at every aspect of the journal to the best of our abilities. That's why I wish to read that paper, William. You see, it appears odd to me that the effects of the journal are intended to strike at members of the Cavendish line, but have not affected every generation since Burton's death. From what our friend William has gleaned from Jack Reid, and I know there's more to come before you say anything, William, it would appear that neither Cavendish's own son, or his offspring, Robert Cavendish's grandfather, or his father were affected. Even Robert, though disturbed by his reading of the journal, didn't become a crazed copycat killer like Jack Reid did. Robert's younger brother Mark apparently did, though we are led to believe that the journal was always passed to the eldest son, therefore Mark was never intended to come into possession of it. He must obviously have been made aware of the journal's existence by his brother and perhaps the mere knowledge of it triggered a psychological effect on the man. So, what are the criteria for the journal to work its so-called magic? Why would the Ripper place some sort of curse on his journal, when we assume, he wasn't intending to die at the hands of his own father, and therefore had no precognition of his demise?

Something just doesn't add up in my mind, though I admit I could be very wrong. What I do suspect however, is that in order for the journal to affect a person they have to carry a certain genetic coding, a particular gene that makes them highly susceptible to the effects of the journal, which we have to assume are genuine, even though we don't understand them."

"And that gene, of course, we have no way of identifying or predicting," I replied.

"Exactly," said Kate, who then turned to face Forbes. "As for you, William, the possibility exists that you are a descendant of the Ripper, through his mother's side, and are therefore in danger of being affected in some way by the journal, even though you possess only one page of it."

"But," Forbes protested, "I know who my grandparents and great grandparents were. My great-grandfather was killed in the trenches during the First World War and my great-grandmother dies soon afterwards. I was told all about them as I was growing up. My grandparents all lived to ripe old ages and my father was a respected solicitor, as I was until recently. None of them were serial killers, and I'm damn sure I'd have known if we had a Jack the Ripper copycat in the family."

"But that's just it, William, don't you see? You and your family wouldn't have known. No-one knew who the Ripper was, let alone who his family were. Burton Cavendish didn't actually name him in his letters, and you have no idea what your great-grandfather did or didn't do in his private life. If he'd been committing a series of murders after dark I doubt he'd have publicised the fact, now would he?"

"I don't know what to think any more," said Forbes. I'm really rather confused.

"So am I," I added.

"Look, the way I see it we need to do three things," Kate

said gaining the attention of both me and Forbes. "First of all, we need to get Miles Prendergast to research William's family background, post-haste in the morning. Where did the majority of your ancestors live by the way, William?"

"Mostly in the country, I believe down in Devon."

"Thank you. Where was I? Oh yes, secondly, we need to try and identify that melody that seems to play a part in the dream. I don't know why, but I feel it has some significance in whatever is going on. If you can hum it and David can record it we can take steps to identify it. I have a friend who has extensive knowledge of the Victorian era, theatre, music hall and so on. She may be able to help us identify it. You do have a recorder, I presume, David?"

"Yes, of course, we can record it straight onto my computer and send it to your friend if she has the internet."

"Oh, she does, most definitely, and Kate, do you have a friend who can help in almost any eventuality?"

She laughed.

"Oh, come now, David. You should know by now that I have a most extensive network of friends, both personal and professional. There's not a lot I can't find out if I really need to."

"So it would seem," I replied, at which point Forbes chimed in once again.

"Er, excuse me, Kate, but you mentioned *three* things we have to do? That's only two so far."

"Oh, yes, number three. If I may, I'd like to take a look at that page from the journal now."

"You okay with that, William?" I asked as I reached down to pick up the plastic sleeve containing the page, which had fallen to the floor beside my chair when I'd left the room earlier. Slowly, I stretched my arm out to offer the sleeve to Kate. As her fingers came within a couple of inches of mine, we both sensed the sharp intake of breath that emanated from Forbes.

Kate turned to face him directly.

"William, it's all going to be okay. Don't worry. The page can't hurt me, or David come to that. We're still not entirely sure if it can cause any effect on you, are we?"

Forbes said nothing but nodded imperceptibly. Kate at last took the plastic sleeve from my grasp and with no hesitation, withdrew the musty old yellowed page from within. Without waiting for Forbes or me to say a word, she simply began reading from it.

> *Blood, beautiful, thick, rich, red, venous blood.*
> *Its colour fills my eyes, its' scent assaults my nostrils,*
> *Its taste hangs sweetly on my lips.*
> *Last night once more the voices called to me,*
> *And I did venture forth, their bidding, their unholy*
> *   quest to undertake.*
> *Through mean, gas lit, fog shrouded streets, I wandered*
> *   in the night, selected, struck, with flashing blade,*
> *And oh, how the blood did run, pouring out upon the*
> *   street, soaking through the cobbled cracks, spurting,*
> *   like a fountain of pure red.*
> *Viscera leaking from ripped red gut, my clothes assumed*
> *   the smell of freshly butchered meat. The squalid,*
> *   dark, street shadows beckoned, and under leaning*
> *   darkened eaves, like a wraith I disappeared once*
> *   more into the cheerless night,*
> *The bloodlust of the voices again fulfilled, for a while...*
> *They will call again, and I once more will prowl the*
> *   streets upon the night,*
> *The blood will flow like a river once again.*
> *Beware all those who would stand against the call,*

I shall not be stopped or taken, no, not I.
Sleep fair city, while you can, while the voices within are still,
I am resting, but my time shall come again. I shall rise in a glorious bloodfest,
I shall taste again the fear as the blade slices sharply through yielding flesh,
when the voices raise the clarion call, and my time shall come again.
So I say again, good citizens, sleep, for there will be a next time...

Her voice trailed off as she read the last, chilling line, penned by no less than the Whitechapel Murderer himself, we all believed. Rather than launch into a discourse on her view of the document, she stood quite still, saying nothing until I felt I had to prompt her. For God's sake, we needed to know what she thought!

"Well?" I asked, as Forbes stood open-mouthed, waiting for her to speak.

"Oh dear," she said quietly, shaking her head as she spoke. "Oh dear, oh dear, oh dear. I do apologise, gentlemen. I fear that I may have been terribly wrong about everything, and this document confirms my error completely."

As she slumped into the armchair beside the fire, and I stepped forward to make sure she was okay, I could have sworn my mind suddenly filled with the sound of music, a silly, Victorian melody, just for a second or two, and then, silence...

TWENTY

AN ETERNAL ENTITY?

"How could I have been so stupid? I see it all now."

I'd never seen Kate quite so crestfallen. She was usually so sure of herself but something she'd read on that decrepit page had quite clearly shaken her belief in herself.

"Come on Kate. Don't be so hard on yourself. We're all shooting in the dark, so to speak, aren't we? After all none of us have ever encountered anything quite like this phenomenon of William's before."

"Yes, I know dear boy, but you see, I'd become so convinced in my mind that Jack the Ripper couldn't have been behind all of this, that it must somehow be connected to the Cavendish family, through something that Burton did, that I was prepared to dismiss the obvious."

"Will you please tell us what you found in your reading of the journal page?" asked Forbes. "I've read it and re-read it so many times, and apart from it being the apparent rantings of a madman or a psychopath, I don't see what else it can mean."

Kate passed the page to me.

"Read it again, to yourself, David. Tell me if you see what I see."

I did as she asked but, like Forbes, found myself unable to discern what Kate was getting at and what had disturbed her so much that she actually doubted her own abilities.

"I'm sorry Kate. I can't see what you're so obviously seeing. You're going to have to tell us, I'm afraid."

"It's right there, at the end," said Kate. "All the way through his rantings, he's making it quite clear that he's referring to the murders, the ones he's already committed. He speaks of 'voices' of a blood lust that must be fulfilled. Do you realise he never once refers to himself as being the one responsible for any of the killing? It's always them, the voices."

"Surely a symptom of his paranoia," I ventured.

"Perhaps, and perhaps not, David. You see, as he gets to the end of the page I believe he reveals far more than you may think. Listen. This is what it says.

Beware all those who would stand against the call,
I shall not be stopped or taken, no, not I.
Sleep fair city, while you can, while the voices within are
   still,
I am resting, but my time shall come again. I shall rise
   in a glorious bloodfest,
I shall taste again the fear as the blade slices sharply
   through yielding flesh,
when the voices raise the clarion call, and my time shall
   come again.
So I say again, good citizens, sleep, for there will be a
   next time...

Let's take it one step at a time. 'Beware all those who would stand against the call.' To whom do you think he's referring?

"The police, or perhaps the authorities, anyone who would get in his way and try to stop him?"

"That's what I thought at first, but no. I believe his meaning is more literal. Beware all those who would stand against the call, *of the voices*. In other words, anyone who does not respond to the call when they receive it."

"But," I replied as realisation of what she was saying hit me; "you're intimating that perhaps he, 'Jack the Ripper' wasn't the first one to receive this mysterious 'call'. That perhaps there may have been others before him?

"And after him, David, yes."

"I'm sorry, I'm not following you," said a confused Forbes.

"What Kate's trying to say is that she thinks Jack the Ripper may have been just one of a number of killers who were in some way influenced by these so-called 'voices'. There could well have been others before him."

"That's right." Kate confirmed.

"But, surely, we would have heard of other Ripper type killers in the past if there'd been any?"

"There've been plenty of serial killers in the past, William. It was mere coincidence that Jack the Ripper's murder spree coincided with the rise of the popular tabloid press in London, so his crimes received massive publicity. Others before him may have been just as bloodthirsty but history has failed to record the full details of their crimes."

"I see, I think."

"Kate is also hinting at the possibility that these 'voices' could be the reason why certain members of the Cavendish family committed their crimes. They were the only ones attuned to whatever the voices really are."

"Precisely! I do believe you're becoming a believer, David,

my dear boy," Kate said, grinning at me. "You see, these 'voices' may not be voices at all, at least not as we recognise the word 'voice'. Perhaps the song you heard, or the dream itself is the way this thing, whatever it is, speaks to you, or to whoever it infects. The dream or the means of communication could even be different for each individual subject. Now, look at the end words on the page.

> *I am resting, but my time shall come again. I shall rise in a glorious bloodfest,*
> *I shall taste again the fear as the blade slices sharply through yielding flesh,*
> *when the voices raise the clarion call, and my time shall come again.*
> *So I say again, good citizens, sleep, for there will be a next time...*

I think 'my time shall come again' means that the thing that is possessing the Ripper will in fact return, but not necessarily in the next days or weeks, but at some time in the future. It's a logical assumption that people would think he's referring to the immediate future, but I have my doubts, especially when the last line states

'*sleep, for there will be a next time.*'

He's warning us, telling us that there will be another like him returning at some point in time, to do it all over again, and again."

"You're asking us to believe an awful lot of supposition there, Kate," said Forbes, who I could see wasn't overly impressed with Kate's interpretation of the page.

"Yes, I am, William, and I could be wrong. I've said that all along, but David asked me here to give my opinions, and that is precisely what I'm doing. If you can better them, then please, go ahead."

"I can't, of course and I'm not trying to belittle your idea. It's just a lot to accept, that there is some malevolent force travelling through time, 'infecting' people and turning them into serial killers."

"Oh, I don't know," I said. "We've been trying to find the elusive 'rogue gene' that turns people into serial killers for years. Maybe there isn't one. Maybe it's this thing, whatever it is, that's ultimately responsible for some of the worst excesses at least."

"So, what do we do? How can we stop it?" Is it going to infect me next?"

Forbes looked worried, really worried.

"We stick to my plan," said Kate. "First thing in the morning, we contact Miles Prendergast and get him to do his stuff, and in the meantime, David, can you get your computer ready to record William's rendition of that song?"

"Sure," I nodded and left the two of them as I went into my office and fired up the computer.

Less than ten minutes later, after I'd been joined by the others, William Forbes had recorded his own rendition of the Victorian melody that plagued him and that I instantly recognised, though I remained puzzled as to why I should have heard those few bars of the song, apparently coming from outside, earlier that evening. Though he'd only been able to hum it, there was no doubting the similarity between his version and what I'd heard, so, satisfied that it was as accurate as we could make it, Kate quickly took over the computer and sent a copy of the recording, with a request to try and identify it, to her musically minded expert, without of course giving away the true details of why she wanted it identified.

"There!" she said with a hint of satisfaction in her voice. "It's sent. If anyone can tell us what that song is, it's Christine Westerman. If she's at home, she should acknowledge receipt of my message and the music file and with any luck we'll have an answer by the morning, unless of course she recognises it right away in which case we may only have to wait a short time."

The name Christine Westerman was new to me and I wondered how, and from where, Kate knew her.

"I've never heard you mention Christine before. Is she a contemporary of yours, Kate?"

"No, not really, David. She's half my age for a start, around fortyish I think. She lives in Whitby, and I met her when someone told me she could help with anything to with audio and musical matters, and I got in touch with her and we became friends. She's helped me a few times with helping to ascertain the validity or otherwise of a number of so-called 'supernatural noises' and of course, they've all been fakes so far. She has a real reputation as an authority on music through the ages, and she's a particular fan of the Victorian and Edwardian eras, and there aren't too many pieces that she'd be unable to track down and name, believe me."

"Let's hope so," said Forbes. "Especially as you believe this tune to be so important in helping to find out what this is all about."

"As I said before, William, I may be wrong, but yes, I do feel it's vital we find out what that music is. After all, if it weren't, then why on earth should David have heard it too, earlier tonight? I have a feeling that once we identify that music, and if Miles Prendergast can give us an accurate record of your family tree in double-quick time, we might just find ourselves making progress in solving this mystery, and how it affects you."

"And don't forget, Kate, we may learn more from the rest of

William's story. There may be more clues to come in what we haven't heard so far."

"But of course," Kate agreed. "Perhaps we should continue, if you don't feel too fatigued, William?"

"No, of course I don't mind, and I'm not too tired at present. That short sleep earlier this evening has refreshed me a little and I do so want to tell you and David everything in an attempt to get to the bottom of all this."

"Then I'll go make us some hot coffee and we can go sit round the fire and let William carry on with his tale, eh?"

"Excellent idea, David," Kate agreed and then pointed to the 'mail received' icon of the screen of my computer. "Look, David. Maybe that's a reply from Christine."

It was indeed a reply from Kate's musical friend, though she'd not identified the song immediately, either because Forbes's hummed version was too indistinct, or perhaps it was a really obscure piece that would require extensive research on her part. Either way, her e-mail promised Kate that she'd be in touch again in the morning. She diplomatically made no inquiry as to why Kate needed to know the title of the song. To her, I supposed it was just another challenge, like you or I might enjoy a crossword puzzle. There being nothing to keep us tied to the computer I switched off and left the two of them to settle down by the fire while I went to the kitchen. I returned a few minutes later with a pot of hot coffee, and a tray of assorted biscuits and the three of us were soon settled once again in front of my log fire, the shadows of its flames continuing to dance around the room, reflecting on the walls in a one-dimensional ballet reminiscent of the figures in a whirling Victorian zoetrope moving picture machine.

With the coffee pot drained, and the biscuits left mostly untouched, and with the ticking of the grandfather clock the only accompaniment to his voice, William Forbes at last prepared to return to the story of his meetings with serial killer Jack Reid. As he did so the clock began to strike the midnight hour, and the sound of the wind that whistled its way around the croft carried deceptive hints of things that may or may not be waiting just around the corner for us as we readied ourselves for what was yet to come. As the final chime died away, William Forbes cleared his throat and began to speak.

TWENTY-ONE
JACK REID'S CONFESSION

Forbes took up his tale once more as Kate and I sat listening attentively.

"So, the visits to see Jack Reid continued. I became quite friendly with his psychiatrist, Ruth Truman, and though she would never discuss details of his illness and his treatment with me, for professional reasons, she grew to be quite forthcoming about his general demeanour and attitude, always at pains to let me know whether he was in a receptive mood or not each time I arrived to speak with him. If he was in one of his occasional sullen and uncooperative moods, I found it hard to justify my time with him as he'd say extraordinarily little and would really do no more than go over what he'd told me on previous visits. Thankfully, that only occurred a couple of times and the rest of the time he was quite lucid and animated during our time together.

I continued to find it difficult to really get to grips with his reasons for wanting me, or at least, someone, to record all the things he wished to tell me, and why he felt the need to record his thoughts for posterity. At last, on my penultimate visit to

Reid, he gave me a hint of those reasons. He'd just received the diagnosis of his terminal illness, and though it had hit him hard, he quite clearly wished to make sure I knew everything he wished to communicate to me.

During my previous visits, he'd given me an illuminating description of all that had happened to him from the day he'd inherited the journal through to his first and then his second trials. He told me of his relief after being released following the appeal after the Brighton killings, but that, even then, he knew that destiny, or fate, whichever one I cared to choose, held something more for him. The dreams were what haunted him most of all, particularly the one I've described, the one that I've experienced for myself. With each reoccurrence of that one dream, he felt as though he was being drawn further into the dark web of fear that surrounded the life of the Ripper. Reid was, in his own words, *'being drawn inexorably towards a conclusion over which he held no control.'* By the time he began committing the murders in Whitechapel, he believed he no longer maintained any control over his own actions.

As he described these things to me, I began to realise that his words were an indication that, contrary to the belief of the courts and the psychiatrists, Jack Reid was in fact more lucid and intelligent than anyone had given him credit for. You see, he wasn't making excuses, or rolling out the old, *'it wasn't me guv'* ploy. He knew he'd done it, committed those terrible murders, and he knew that he was being held in Ravenswood as part of society's retribution for his crimes, but, he also knew that something inside him had been compelling him to commit those acts at the time of the murders, something he couldn't describe and that no-one would probably have believed. The fact that he knew he wasn't in control of himself, that was it, you see. *He knew.*"

I thought I was beginning to see what Forbes was getting at. So did Kate, who rapidly interjected.

"A madman, or a psychopathically damaged person would not have known, at the time, that he was not in control, is that what you're getting at?"

"Precisely. Reid kept repeating to me that he was under the control of Jack the Ripper, and that nothing in Heaven or on Earth could have prevented those murders. I finally realised that I'd been called upon by Reid to receive his final 'confession' if that's what you'd like to call it. The world saw him as nothing more than either a monster or a crazy man. I saw a quite different Jack Reid to the monster the tabloid press had created. By the time I left Ravenswood that day, I realised that Jack Reid wasn't a madman, he was a frightened one!"

"This is all very well," I said, "but surely every psychopath or sociopath in the recorded history of crime has come up with similar reasons for their cries."

"Not quite," said Forbes. "Here you had a man who'd been tried, committed and then acquitted and then tried again for a different set of murders that he *did* commit, and who had nothing to lose or to gain by telling me these things. He knew he'd never be released, even before he received the death sentence that the doctors had delivered by way of his illness. When he told me that he believed the page of the journal in his possession had somehow received an infusion of the evil, or the essence of the soul of Jack the Ripper, he wasn't speaking to me as a deranged man might. He spoke in a cold, matter-of-fact, take it or leave it way that left the decision to believe or disbelieve him entirely at my discretion."

"And this confession you mentioned?" I asked.

"That was just it, David. His confession was simply the things I've told you. He couldn't help himself because at the time of the killings he simply *wasn't* himself. Not in a psychiatrically diagnosable illness way, as most people would assume, but in actual fact! He was so afraid and so desperate for his words to be recorded on paper so that future generations might realise just what had happened to him."

"Did you discuss any of this with his psychiatrist?"

"No David, I couldn't. You know as well as I do that our conversations were subject to attorney/client privilege. I had to keep everything confidential, unless and until given permission by my client to reveal what he'd told me. You think of course that she would have repudiated his beliefs and put it all down to his illness."

"Yes, William, I do. Jack Reid was seriously mentally ill and yet you appear to have believed his inane ramblings just because he happened to put them across to you in a calm and civilised manner."

"Well," said Forbes, with a note of hesitation in his voice. "There was one more thing that kind of swayed me to believe him rather more than I might have disbelieved him."

"And that was...?"

Forbes reached into his cavernous briefcase once more and withdrew a large brown envelope, from which he extracted a single sheet of A4 paper and passed it across in my direction.

"Please, read this." He said as I grasped the sheet of paper he proffered. "Reid gave this to me the very last time I saw him before his death."

Anxious to read the document, written by the murderer himself, so close to his death, I immediately began to read aloud, for the benefit of Kate.

Dear Mr Forbes,

I write these words as I wish to record my final thoughts

on the matters we have discussed, so that you might have a permanent record of certain aspects of our time together. That I have been responsible for the deaths of others is a matter of record. Whether I was the actual 'cause' of those deaths is another matter entirely. As I've taken great care to explain to you, my problems began solely with the receipt of the journal of my ancestor, known to history as Jack the Ripper, on the death of my uncle, Robert Cavendish. From that awful day until today my life has been one long torment. I won't go into the details of the case of the 'Brighton Ripper' for which I was incarcerated in this awful place only to be later exonerated and released. The events that took place are well documented and I'm sure by now you are well aware that I told the truth at all times during and after the original investigation. As for the murders in Whitechapel, again the facts are well known and yes, I was the killer, which I have never denied, though you are also now aware of how the crimes came to pass.

You are also privy to the knowledge that my days are numbered. The tumour in my head is growing larger by the day and will kill me sooner, rather than later I fear. I say this in the hope that you and those who may read this in the future will be aware that I have no reason to lie or mislead you. I am protecting no-one and stand to gain no monetary advantage from this statement. I'm sure the press would have paid good money for my words, but what good would it have done me?

So, for the final time, I say to you that my family is possessed of the soul of that infamous murderer, Jack the Ripper. What is all the more galling is that at no time did any of my antecedents mention the real name of the man who killed the women of Whitechapel over a hundred years ago so I cannot even go to my death with the knowledge of the identity of the man who has plagued and bedevilled my life.

It is my firm belief that somehow, the Ripper, whoever he was, managed to infuse every ounce of the evil that dwelt within his soul into the pages of that terrible journal as he wrote it and that the mere possession of the journal has been sufficient to bring great misfortune upon my family through the last hundred years.

I wish for you to attempt to confirm my belief, though of course the results of any such investigation will not be known to me before my death. That, in itself, should assure you of the sincerity of my belief. I confess to you now that I indulged in a great deal of research prior to selecting your employer to act for me in this matter and within the list of names of the solicitors they made available to me something drew me to your name. I cannot say why, but I felt as though it were pre-ordained that you would be the man to record this final statement from me.

So, I hope you will agree to fulfil what has now become my dying wish. I beg and implore you to investigate the possibility that the journal does indeed carry within it the means to inflict such horrors on the living souls of the present. You'll need help to do so. I have used my time here in Ravenswood well and have made great use of the access I have been granted to the computers. I'm convinced that only a man of letters, one with a psychological background and a proven record of dealing with cases of a criminal nature will be suited to the case. Such a man does exist. Although you may think a paranormal or supernatural connection is required in order to carry out this investigation, you must first ally yourself with an established and credible psychological profiler and investigator. The name of the man you must enlist if he is willing, is Doctor David Hemswell, formerly resident of Scarborough, and now the owner and sole resident of a small island off the coast of Cape Wrath, Scotland. I'm sure, if you approach him directly as a result of a request from me, he will refuse his help. You should therefore look into his background and discover a means of approaching him without using my name, initially.

I implore you, Mr Forbes, go to Hemswell. He's the only man for the job, I assure you. There will be plenty of ways to approach him without using my name. The police are always calling on him. There will be various senior officers who will be able to put you in touch with him, I'm sure. After all, you are a respected man, a solicitor, and it won't seem unusual for you to be seeking his help in a case.

If, between you, you can determine the truth of what I've been telling you all these weeks, I will be vindicated. The world will know that I was never the monster they believe me to be, but the mere dupe, a pawn of a power so great that it has lasted a century and more.

I will die soon, Mr Forbes, and therefore whatever you discover cannot affect me one way or the other in this world, but, and I know it's a lot to ask, you may just be responsible for saving not only my name, but my soul!

Please believe me when I say again, I am not the crazy and deranged beast in human form they all believe me to be. I am as much a victim as those who died at my hands, but only you, and perhaps Doctor Hemswell, can prove it.

With my deepest respect.

Jack Reid

Forbes at last fell silent. Kate stared, not at him, but at me. I sat stunned, though only for a few seconds, and then my voice broke through the silence in the room. Rather, not so much my voice as a tirade as I realised that Jack Reid had planned this meeting with Forbes all along.

"Jack Reid mentioned me by name? He told you to seek me out? Why? How did he know about me? I thought you said you'd got my name and contact details from Chief Inspector Gould.!"

"I said I'd got your telephone number from Mr Gould, David, that's all. I didn't actually say that he'd given me your name, if you remember? I couldn't tell you the truth, not right away. As Reid said to me, there was a good chance you'd have rejected me out of hand if I'd done so."

"But, why me?" I asked again, with slightly less anger in my voice.

"As he said, he'd done his research. He felt you were the best qualified man for the job."

"But I had to bring in help, didn't I? Kate's here and she knows far more about this than I do."

" Perhaps he expected you to do just such a thing. He was intelligent you know, not a moron. I've long suspected he had it all worked out even before I visited him for the first time."

Kate broke into the conversation.

"Don't be too hard on William, please David. He was, and is, following his client's instructions. His responsibility lies with the client first, as you know."

Kate was correct, of course, though I couldn't shake the feeling that I'd been used, played like a chess piece both by Reid and William Forbes. I knew it was too late to back out, we'd come too far, and I tried to suppress my anger and focus on what Forbes had just read to us.

"Okay, William, I forgive you," I lied. "At least we now know why he wanted you on his case. He's seeking some kind of peace after death. He honestly believed in his story; that much is for sure. I suppose the least we can do is carry on and try to discover if there can possibly be any truth in those beliefs."

"I think you're right," Kate concurred.

"Thank you, both of you," Forbes spoke with a hint of apology in his voice. "I would have told you sooner, honestly, but now is the appropriate time to do so. I had to make sure you were committed to the case before revealing the letter to you. I'm sorry for the deception, really I am."

The more Forbes apologised, the more I felt used, but there remained little to be gained by allowing my anger to take control of the situation. Kate had been correct of course. The solicitor was acting on the instructions of his client, and dead or alive, his responsibility remained to that client and to do his best to see those instructions through. I wondered however, if Forbes had any other nasty little surprises up his sleeve, but for now, refrained from asking.

"Is there anything else to add to the story, William?" asked

Kate as I subsided into my chair, my anger for the moment placed on hold.

"Only that two weeks after he gave me the letter, Ruth Truman phoned my office. Reid was dying and had little more than a day or two left, at most. He'd requested a last visit from me, and the doctor assured me that if I wished to comply with his request, it had better be soon.

I arrived at Ravenswood the following morning and, sure enough, Reid looked near to death as I looked at him lying hooked up to various monitors and drips, a doctor and nurse hovering not far from the bed."

'"He doesn't have very long" Ruth Truman whispered to me as I drew near to his bed.

"Reid certainly appeared weak and forlorn as I finally stood right up close to his prone figure."

"You came," he said in a very quiet voice, almost a whisper.

"Yes, Jack, I'm here" I replied.

"I have one last thing to give you," he gasped, the mere act of speaking appearing to cause him discomfort. "Doctor Ruth, if you please."

"Ruth Truman walked to the small bedside cabinet and opened the single drawer in the fixture, withdrawing an envelope, large enough to hold an A4 sized document. She handed it to me. I looked at her inquiringly."

"It's okay, it's allowed. It's just a sheet of paper that he wants you to have. He says it's part of the Ripper's journal. I've seen it many times in our sessions, and it can't do any harm for him to want you to have it. You are his solicitor after all, and all his effects would probably go to your firm anyway for future disposal."

"I took the paper and looked at Reid. He smiled and sighed as though a great weight had suddenly lifted from him."

"Take it, Mr Forbes. You'll know what to do with it when

you read it later. Don't forget, see Hemswell. You must see Hemswell."

"Jack Reid suddenly slumped back against his pillows. The doctor and nurse who'd been standing to one side now moved forward. Ruth Truman placed her hand on my arm and drew me back a couple of paces as the medics stepped in to do their work. There appeared little they could do, and within a few seconds, the machine that had obviously been monitoring Reid's heartbeat began to beep, a long continuous and shrill sound that boded no good at all for the man in the bed. The doctor placed a stethoscope to the patient's chest as the nurse held up his wrist and checked for a pulse. Within seconds the nurse replaced Reid's hand on the bed cover and the doctor withdrew from the bedside, turning and speaking to Ruth Truman as he did so."

"He's gone."

"There had been no attempt made to resuscitate Reid. I'd expected them to shock him back to life, but Ruth Truman later explained to me that Reid had firmly requested no such action be taken when the time came. He'd wanted to die naturally and as peacefully as possible, and in that, he did at least receive his final request. The rest was now up to me, and I left Ravenswood with a heavy sense of responsibility on my mind. That night I sat and read the document, the infernal page from the journal. The very next night the dream came to me and has haunted me ever since. I lost no time in doing everything I could to find a way to contact you and as I so obviously succeeded, here I am!"

"Well," I replied, "that's some tale, don't you think, Kate?"

"Some tale indeed, David. Tell me William, when you read the page from the journal, was it in the plastic sleeve as it is now?"

"No, it was loose, just a piece of old yellowed paper, or so I thought."

"And now of course, you believe, as Reid did, that it somehow contains the residue of the soul of Jack the Ripper?"

"Yes, I do. I most definitely do. Surely the pair of you must think there's something in it by now?"

"I'm certainly concerned about all of this," I replied. "And I'd like to know why I heard that music, especially as Kate didn't hear a thing."

"I'd like to discover the answer to that one too, David," said Kate.

"So, where do we go from here?" asked Forbes, looking worried and yet relieved at the same time. He clearly felt better for unburdening himself with the revelation of the letter from Reid but obviously still harboured worries about what the future held in store for him, and perhaps for all of us.

"It's very late," Kate replied, pointing to the grandfather clock which registered almost one a.m. "I think we all need some sleep."

"But, what if the dream comes back?" Forbes looked very worried again.

"David, would you be prepared to give William a large sedative, one that will put him into a deep sleep until morning, with your permission of course, William?" she asked.

Forbes nodded his agreement.

"Yes, of course. A heavy sedative should preclude any chance of you dreaming," I said, rising from my chair to fetch my medical bag.

"Then I suggest we do no more until morning. There's been no reply from Christine as yet, and we have Miles Prendergast to enlist to our cause when daylight returns."

"Very well, Kate. It looks like it's bedtime for the three of us. William, you were kind to offer to sleep in the camp bed, but with the sedative in you, I'd rather you slept in my bed. I'll rough it for tonight."

Forbes made no argument, and I quickly injected him with the sleep-inducing sedative. Within a few minutes Kate had retired to the spare bedroom and Forbes was safely tucked up in my bed, the effects of the sedative already having sent him into what I hoped would be a long, deep and dreamless sleep.

As I stretched out as best as I could, fully clothed on the camp bed soon afterwards, I found it difficult to close my mind to all we'd experienced that evening, particularly the contents of the letter from Jack Reid. What Forbes had said made sense of course. Reid had researched his case carefully and found my name through reputable sources on the internet, and yet, I felt uneasy. There were other, equally qualified psychologists out there. Why me? I continued to ask myself, why me? I lay there for a long time, listening to the wind as it whistled around my lonely and isolated home. Just before intense tiredness at last caused the weight of darkness to force my eyes closed for the night, I could have sworn that the wind changed its tone very imperceptibly until the notes of a delicate and eerie melody began to play upon the breeze. Sleep came at last, as everything turned black...

TWENTY-TWO

A NEW DAY DAWNS

Incredibly, I slept through the night with not a single disturbance. I guess I'd been so tired that an earthquake might have found it difficult to rouse me once my eyes had closed and sleep took its blissful hold. I'd half expected to suddenly find myself sharing that terrible dream that Jack Reid had somehow passed on to William Forbes. Thankfully, no such terrors beset my sleeping mind.

Rising from the camp bed, I stretched, loosening the muscles in my neck, which ached slightly from the less than comfortable sleeping position imposed upon me by the bed. My clothes felt stale and dirty, but I decided not to risk waking Forbes by entering my room for clean ones. Better to let him sleep and wake naturally after the large dose of sedatives he'd received the previous night. Instead, I busied myself in the kitchen. As I sat at the table enjoying a cup of hot coffee and freshly buttered toast, Kate walked sleepily through the door.

"Morning, David."

"Hello, Kate. Sleep well?"

"Like a baby, surprisingly. You?"

"Same here," I replied, making no mention of the lingering thoughts of the melody that plagued my last waking moments.

"I think perhaps we were all far more tired than we'd imagined. William is still snoring his head off in your room. I popped my head round the door just now."

"He's been through the mill a bit hasn't he? He's definitely going through an intense psychological trauma. I'm not even sure we can help him, Kate. If all of this is really just a manifestation of a delusional mind…"

"Do you really believe that, David, after all we've heard and seen so far?"

"You know, for a minute I'd forgotten that damned aura, or apparition, or whatever it was we saw, Kate. So much happened last night it's a little difficult to separate reality from fantasy."

"It was real enough, David. You have to believe me when I say again that there is much we still don't understand about the afterlife, or the power of the human spirit."

"For now, Kate, I'll go along with whatever you suggest, and I'll keep my mind open, but to tell you the truth, I'm not sure about any of this anymore. The sun is shining out there, the wind has dropped, and the sea birds are serenading us with their usual dawn chorus, and it's hard to think of some evil entity walking the earth in perpetuity on such a day."

Kate walked to the window and looked out upon the crisp, clear dawn that nature had provided. Skerries Rock stood bathed in sunlight, though the constant Atlantic breeze would ensure that temperatures didn't rise much above mildly warm. In the near distance she could see the rising slope that led to the cliff top, lush swathes of billowing grass forming a writhing sea of green leading all the way to the cliff edge.

"It's beautiful," she said quietly, and then, "but evil knows no boundaries, David. It takes no account of beauty, of sunshine or darkness. We see the blue sky and the birds, hear the sound of the waves breaking on your island shores, and watch the soft white clouds as they float past, carried by the breeze that comes from nowhere and disappears into oblivion far from here, and yet, no matter how idyllic such a vista may appear, the malevolence that is hanging over us lies waiting, perhaps floating on that very breeze, or disguised in the white tops of the surf, and we must be vigilant."

"Very eloquent, Kate, and so true," said a voice from the doorway.

"William, good morning. How are you today?" Kate responded as Forbes walked in to the kitchen. Like me, it appeared he'd slept in his day clothes, everything looked crumpled and worn, as did the face of my strange and troubled guest.

"Better for the long sleep," he replied, "but worried, very worried. I'm so afraid of what might happen to me, and perhaps to you as well. I fear I may have brought trouble to your home, David, and if I have, I apologise."

"You haven't had another dream, have you?" I asked.

"No, it's not that. I think, however, that Jack Reid must have had some reason for suggesting you as the man to help me solve the riddle of the journal, and if he did, perhaps it bodes badly for you too. I wish to God I'd never set eyes on the man, never accepted the case from my employers, and most of all, I wish that I'd never roped you in to this madness that seems to be engulfing me."

"I appreciate your sentiments, William, but it's a bit late for such thoughts now. You're here and we can't turn the clock back. If something supernatural is taking place, then believe me, we have the best ally in the world right here in the form of Kate."

"Why thank you, kind sir, I'll try not to disappoint you." Kate smiled as she spoke. "Now, perhaps William, you and I should eat something as David already has done, and then I must get busy. First, I'll ask you to boot up your computer, David, and we'll see if Christine has replied yet. Then a phone call to Miles Prendergast will hopefully set things in motion on the family tree investigation."

Half an hour later, after I'd showered and changed into fresh clothes, I left Forbes to do the same as Kate and I powered up my computer. Sure enough, a further reply from Christine Westerman was waiting for us, sent barely a quarter of an hour earlier. Though she hadn't identified the melody as yet, she stated that it sounded strangely familiar. She'd made the best of Forbes's hummed version and had done her best to re-create it on her piano and had then recorded the tune. She thought that perhaps one or two notes weren't quite right, but it shouldn't stop her identifying the tune, given time. She hoped to have an answer for us later in the day. I felt disappointed at the lack of an instant result but, as Kate pointed out, there must have been thousands of music hall or popular songs and ditties written in the Victorian era. For Christine to have come up with an instant answer had been hoping for a little too much, too soon. Kate replied to Christine's email and thanked her for taking the time and trouble to help us out. She stressed the importance of discovering the tune's name and perhaps its origin, again without telling her friend exactly why we needed to know, and why we were in a hurry. She gave Christine Westerman my telephone number and asked her to call if she found the name of the tune, rather than email us. Christine agreed. There was nothing more to do now but wait.

As Forbes emerged from the bathroom looking slightly less crumpled than before, Kate left the two of us together as she took up residence in the living room in order to phone and explain our needs to her other friend, Miles Prendergast. As the morning seemed such a pleasant one, I invited Forbes to accompany me on a walk around the island, and he readily agreed, anxious I thought, to get some fresh air in his lungs and escape from the slightly claustrophobic atmosphere that had developed in the croft over the last twenty four hours. Donning our outer coats and hats, we popped our heads around the living room door and I quickly but politely interrupted Kate's conversation and told her our intentions. She was already deep in conversation with Miles Prendergast, (I assumed) and we left her to it and made our way into the fresh air.

"Do you really think that you can help me get through this?" asked Forbes as we stood on the cliff top peering out at the almost infinite expanse of the Atlantic Ocean that reached out to the horizon before us.

"With Kate's help, we've every chance" I said, though I still struggled to convince myself even as I replied to Forbes's question. "A lot depends on what she's able to discover today. She obviously thinks the song is of great importance and if she can find a connection between your family and that of the Cavendish's, she may have an idea what to do next."

Forbes rubbed at his eyes. The wind, or his emotions clearly causing tears to run down his cheeks.

"Are you okay?" I asked.

"Yes, it's just that my life has changed so much in these last few weeks. Here we are, staring out at the most incredibly beautiful panorama and I should feel stirred by it, awed, even, but all I can think of is that terrible dream and the awful feeling that something terrible is about to befall me, despite Kate's reassurances."

"Everything will work out, you wait and see," I replied, trying to sound far more confident than I felt.

A cormorant wheeled in a tight arc above us and screeched its call as if to summon reinforcements in its daily hunt for fish beneath the waves. A little way out to sea I saw a pair of dolphins break the surface and leap in happiness from the water, only to splash down into the surf in seconds and disappear from view. Nature was in its element before my eyes and yet we, Forbes, Kate and I, were slowly being pulled from our own natural element into another, darker world, an unknown and perhaps dangerous place where the forces of nature might not prevail.

I glanced at my watch. Incredibly as it seemed to me, we'd been away from the croft for over an hour. It felt like no more than twenty minutes or so. The time had arrived for us to get back and discover if Kate had achieved anything as yet. Forbes willingly followed in my footsteps as we trudged back along the path. He was as anxious as I to hear what Kate had discovered, if anything.

A few minutes later, divested of our hats and coats, we returned to the living room of my croft where Kate sat, reading from a sheet of paper which by its appearance she'd obviously printed off from my computer.

"Any news, Kate?" I asked as Forbes and I flopped down into two of my comfortable armchairs.

"Oh yes, David, my dear boy" she spoke animatedly, excitement in every word. "I do indeed. Yes, I have news. Just wait until I tell you!"

TWENTY-THREE
TRANSFORMATION

"Well, come on, Kate. Don't keep us waiting," I implored as she rose from her chair, placing the sheet of paper on the coffee table in the centre of the room.

"Yes, please tell us what you've found out," Forbes added.

"Right then, here goes," she began. "To begin with, Miles Prendergast has been more than helpful, as I knew he would be. I explained what we were looking for, and then at his request, I e-mailed the information you gave me on your family, William, as he and I chatted on the phone. He received it in seconds and after perusing the document, he sounded very hopeful. It seems the university has a rather special computer programme that can do the work of a dozen researchers in hours as opposed to days, or weeks. As you were able to provide some perfectly accurate information on your antecedents, Miles believes that he should be able to conjure up the information I've asked for by the end of the day."

Kate paused. I knew that her information appeared positive and of a hopeful nature but what she'd just told us certainly didn't warrant the excitement she'd displayed on our return. I knew there was more to come.

"Stop holding out on us, Kate. You've found out something else, haven't you?"

"As it happens David, yes I have. Thanks to Christine Westerman, I can now tell you the title of that strangely enigmatic tune."

"That was fast work," I said.

"I told you she was good," Kate smiled.

"So, what is it?" asked Forbes. "Do you think it has any special significance, as you suspected it might?"

"Oh yes, William. It has significance alright, as I'm sure you and David will agree when I tell you more about it, again thanks to Christine."

"So, *what is it?*" I almost begged, growing impatient with my friend who definitely appeared to be dragging the moment out, perhaps for theatrical effect.

"Sorry David. I shan't keep you in suspense for another moment. But, please humour me for a minute. Come to your office and I have something to show you on your computer.

"Don't keep us in suspense, Kate, just tell us what it is, please."

"I'm going to do better than that, David. I'm going to let you hear it in full."

"Good Lord," Forbes exclaimed. "But how?"

"The magic of the internet, William," Kate replied. "Christine has a wide circle of friends who share her passion for nineteenth century music and she apparently sent copies of her own recording to a number of them. One of them not only contacted her with an almost instantaneous reply but also suggested a certain website where people place videos of all sorts of things. There was a home-made copy of a short video there, with the song in question being used as the background to the subject matter."

"At least tell us the title before you show us the video," I pleaded.

Kate smiled as she replied, "The song is called *A Violet from Mother's Grave*."

"Never heard of it," I said.

"Me neither," Forbes added.

Kate's face assumed a deadly serious look as she continued.

"Ah, but it isn't the song itself, or the title that gives it the significance in this case, but rather the circumstances surrounding one particular rendition of it. Christine told me that the song was a popular little ditty, as she called it, in the days of Queen Victoria. It would probably have passed into total musical oblivion as have most of the songs from that era had it not been for one single event that meant it would forever play a part in the singular saga of the murders of Jack the Ripper."

"Bloody Hell," I gasped.

"This 'event' you mention. What was it?" asked Forbes, his face drained of colour as Kate's words sank home.

"Quite simply, gentlemen, my friend Christine informed me that *A Violet from Mother's Grave* was the song that Jack the Ripper's final victim, Mary Kelly, had been heard singing in her miserable little home, by a passing witness, on the night of her murder. In fact the words of the song were probably the last words that anyone apart from her killer heard from her."

"Oh, my God," Forbes staggered backwards and only a firm grip on the back of an armchair prevented his legs from buckling from under him.

"Dammit, Kate. You suspected it would be something like this, didn't you?" I said, as my mouth dried up and my temples began to throb from a sudden and quite violent headache.

"I wasn't certain, but I did have a suspicion that the music would have something to do with the Jack the Ripper case," she agreed. "I never dreamed it would be something with such great significance to any of the individual murders."

"Then it must be Jack the Ripper who's after me!" Forbes exclaimed, now verging on the hysterical.

"For God's sake, William, calm down," Kate ordered in that unflappable, not-to-be-argued-with voice of hers. "If the music does indicate that the spirit of Jack the Ripper is haunting your dream, and I admit it looks that way, it doesn't necessarily mean he's 'after you' as you put it."

"But why else would he be doing this? And why should David have heard the song on the wind last night? What has he got to do with all of this apart from helping me to find out exactly what's going on?"

"I don't know yet, but maybe just the fact that he is helping you is reason enough. Perhaps the Ripper, if it is the Ripper, is trying to tell David something. Perhaps that's what he's doing to you to, simply trying to tell you something. Maybe there's a significance in the dream that none of us have seen yet. Jack Reid was a relative of the Ripper. You, as far as we know, are not. Therefore logic dictates that you have experienced the dream either as a result of the power of suggestion, having heard it described in detail by Jack Reid, or because, if this is a case of a supernatural entity, it is trying to communicate with you. The same goes for you, David. It may be trying to tell you something, something that you can learn from the song."

"But why? What the hell have I got to do with it, apart from trying to help William to solve the riddle of the journal and its effects on the Cavendish family and on him of course?"

"Maybe this entity, or the Ripper, or whatever it is, is trying to help you solve the riddle by focussing your attention on the song?"

"But the damn song means nothing to me! I don't see how it could be a clue to anything. And why didn't you hear it too?"

"I still don't have any real answers, David, so we'll all have to be patient. I have an idea forming in my mind, but until I can get my thoughts clear on the matter, I'll say nothing, at least for a while."

"So there's nothing we can do for now?" came the question from Forbes.

"We can watch the video and let you hear the tune as it must have sounded when sung in the Victorian era," Kate replied as she finally managed to get Forbes and me to stand behind her as she sat down in front of my computer screen.

She quickly nudged the mouse across the mouse mat and my screensaver cleared to show the site she'd already mentioned, and which was set up to show one particular video. She clicked on 'Play' on the screen and the video began to play. Immediately, the haunting melody of *A Violet from Mother's Grave* began to play, followed by the voice of a singer who appeared to have copied the Victorian style perfectly. The song sounded very much as I imagined it would have done when performed by a Victorian Music Hall singer all those years ago. I almost forgot to take notice of the video images, but when I allowed myself to focus on the pictures on the screen, I saw that the video was in fact someone's short but touching tribute to Mary Kelly, a kind of tribute to her life, and a memorial to her death.

The video maker had assembled a collage of images, mostly copies of press cartoons and photographs from the time of the Ripper murders, and included a couple of highly disturbing images of the mutilated, or rather the butchered remains of Mary Kelly, all of which assumed a great poignancy when played back to the accompaniment of that sadly haunting melody. I closed my eyes for a couple of seconds and could mentally conjure up an image of the frail and perhaps hungry young woman who despite the deprivation of her grim and seedy existence, managed to remain upbeat enough to sing to herself as she breathed out the last few hours of her too-short life.

I cast a quick glance at Forbes. I'd only ever heard those few bars of the song that drifted to my ears on the wind, but William Forbes had heard so much more of the song in his dream-state, and had heard it so much more often than I. Now, his face appeared ghostly white, as the scratchy, haunting sound of the melody screeched at us from my computer speakers.

In an instant, Forbes had transformed back into the trembling, terrified figure that both Kate and I had witnessed over the previous two days. Terror danced in the suffering look evident in his panic-stricken eyes, darting all-round the room, once again searching for some unknown and unseen assailant perhaps. His hands shook, his skin assumed a deathly pallor and his legs would probably have collapsed from beneath him if I hadn't anticipated what was about to happen and guided him into a small office chair a few feet from where we stood.

The final strains of *A Violet from Mother's Grave* signalled the end of the short video, and Kate turned to look at me and the now slumped figure of William Forbes.

"That's it," she said with a sort of finality.

"It's bloody spooky, hearing it played through the computer like that." I said. "William, are you okay?"

The crumpled face that looked at me as Forbes raised his head from his hunched position confirmed to me that he certainly wasn't okay. It was a look I'd seen before, as he'd appeared when he withdrew into that dark and very private world where his own dark thoughts and unearthly fears and terrors held him in their thrall. I had the distinct impression that William Forbes's mind, disturbed enough already by all that had happened to him, and by the fear that had remained lurking just beneath the surface these last few hours, had now descended further along the path towards irrevocable breakdown.

His lips moved, but not a sound came from his mouth. His hands were now clasped tightly together on his lap, as though by gripping them in that way he could stop the tremors and the shaking that now pervaded his entire being. If that had been his hope, it had failed. From the top of his head to his feet, the man had become a quivering mass of terror-stricken humanity. Kate and I looked at each other, then back at the man in the chair.

"Hearing the tune sung like that might just have sent him over the edge," I said, as Kate rose and moved across to try and bring the trembling man out of his terrible anxiety and fear attack.

"I should have anticipated this," Kate replied as she took hold of Forbes by the shoulders, gently but firmly attempting to remonstrate with him. "Come on, William. Don't leave us now. Try and snap out of it. We need you, as much as you need us. We can only help you if you're here to guide us through certain aspects of all of this. Please, William, don't crack up on me now."

Her attempt failed. I also did my best to help Forbes recover from this latest attack, but as the minutes ticked by, his eyes seemed to sink further into their sockets, the tremors in his body increased and he began to drool from the side of his mouth. There was now little doubt in my mind that we were losing him, at least in terms of any form of coherent behaviour.

"We have to get him to lie down, David," Kate insisted. "Can we manhandle him to the bedroom, do you think?"

"I think we can do that," I responded. "But why the

bedroom? Can't we get him to lie on the sofa in the sitting room?"

"The sofa will do, David, but what I want more than anything is for you to get your medical bag and prepare a bloody large dose of that sedative. I think William needs to be out of it for a while, if we're to get anywhere in this matter."

"Kate, what is it you're not telling me?" I asked, suddenly aware that my friend's face had assumed a genuinely concerned look.

"David, look at him. Look very closely. Can't you see what's happening?"

I did as she asked and looked intently at the shaking figure of William Forbes. As I did so, I became aware of exactly what Kate was getting at.

"He looks different," I gasped in surprise, as the face of the man in my office chair appeared to visibly alter before my eyes. His brow had narrowed, and now presented itself with deep furrows and creases evident. His eyes, already sunken into his head through what I'd presumed to be fear, now bore a feral look and blazed with an intensity that sent a shiver down my spine. Even his mouth appeared smaller, his lips pinched and his teeth showing as yellow and uneven, whereas I would swear that the night before, he'd possessed a perfect set of pearly white ones.

"Jesus Christ," I shouted as I realised what was taking place. "He's changing! What the hell is he becoming, Kate?"

"I don't know, David, at least not yet, but we have to sedate him. We must keep whatever it is that's inside him quiet and at bay until we figure out what's happening. He could be very, very dangerous if we don't know what we're dealing with."

"Come on then. Let's not waste time," I urged, as together, Kate and I lifted the still shaking and trembling figure of William

Forbes from the chair and, his feet dragging along the carpeted floor, we managed to struggle through to the sitting room where we deposited the almost dead weight of his now writhing body on to the sofa. Forbes appeared to be struggling and failing to hold his own in a fight against something that attacked his very internal being. His head thrashed from side to side and his arms began to flail around, as though attempting to push some unseen attacker away. His breathing was rapid and panic-stricken, and I place a hand on his chest and could almost feel his heart trying to burst through his ribcage, so fast had his heart rate become.

"David, the sedative! Quickly man."

Leaving Kate with him for no more than a few seconds I dashed to my room and grabbed my medical bag. As I returned to the living room, a terrible maniacal laughter suddenly burst from the lips of the man on the sofa.

"Hurry, man, hurry. Look at him" Kate urged, a hint of desperation creeping into her normally controlled and even voice.

Rushing to the sofa I looked down at Forbes, lying there with that awful sound issuing from his lips. In addition to the terrible unearthly sound of that laughter, I was stunned by what I saw.

"Kate, what the hell's going on? His eyes..."

"I know, hurry, David, the sedative, *now!*"

I quickly pulled his sleeve up and plunged the needle into his arm. Within seconds of doing so, William Forbes fell silent and his eyes began to close. I looked one more time at those eyes before they finally closed. I hadn't been mistaken. William Forbes possessed brown eyes; of that I was certain. Before he'd fallen into the drug induced slumber however, I'd seen them change from their normal appearance as they'd become engorged with blood, until all that peered out from his eye sockets were two, blood red orbs that could only have had their origins in Hell itself.

I stood back from the sofa, looked down, and realised that my own hands were shaking. I looked at Kate. Her face registered the shock we both shared at what we'd just witnessed.

"Kate, what the hell just happened here?" My voice trembled.

"David, my dear, dear boy. I don't know. I really don't bloody well know!"

That was when I first saw the tears running down her face.

"Whatever it is, I do believe we are all in terrible danger," she said before collapsing into the computer chair, deep worry lines furrowing her brow.

"Was it the aura?" I asked, trying to find some reason for the manifestation we'd just seen.

"David, I meant what I just said. I have no idea what the heck we've just seen, but an aura couldn't possibly manifest itself in such a grotesquely physical form, I'm sure. I can only hope that whatever it was somehow dissipates before he wakes up."

"Do you have any other friends who might be able to help us?"

"David, I've never in my life seen anything like this before, and I can assure you that none of my friends or colleagues have either. This is something so unearthly that I have no words to describe it, no words of comfort to offer to you or myself." I paused, my mind racing as it tried to compute the mass of thoughts, both logical and illogical that ran through it in mere milliseconds. When I spoke again I almost feared to utter the words that came from my own mouth.

"Kate, do you really think that the spirit, the essence or

whatever, of Jack the Ripper just materialised within the body of Forbes, right here, before our eyes?"

Kate Goddard's eyes fell to the floor, unable to look directly back in my direction. She sat there silently as Forbes lay, breathing deeply in his sleep and I stood staring at her. Finally, wordlessly, she gave a gentle nod of her head, and I shivered. Whatever warmth had existed in the room a few seconds earlier had deserted me and I felt tendrils of fear and panic rise within me as the stench of the grave filled my nostrils and the terror that had previously belonged exclusively to William Forbes reached deep with me and took a firm hold of my soul.

TWENTY-FOUR
A WALK ON THE WILD SIDE

Despite the early hour, I poured Kate a large gin and tonic and myself an exceptionally large Napoleon brandy. Recent events certainly justified the large measures. The two of us sat, quietly stunned, in front of the unlit log fire in my sitting room. The lack of warmth and absence of the fire's comforting glow added to the all-pervading chill that had crept into my home as we attempted to make sense of what had just taken place. Forbes continued to sleep deeply on the sofa. I'd assured Kate that the large injection of sedative I'd given him would keep him out for hours.

"I have to admit, I'm bloody scared, Kate," I said as I drained my glass and quickly poured myself another.

"You wouldn't be human if you weren't," Kate acknowledged. "I'm pretty shaken up myself, and I've seen a few things in my time, believe me."

"That, that thing in there, is it still William Forbes, or has he become something inhuman, possessed by something we still don't understand?"

"I hope to God he is still William Forbes," Kate replied.

"My own theory, and it's based on no real evidence, David, so don't quote me on it, is that William Forbes *is* still there, lying on the sofa, but that there is something else lying there with him, *in him*, in fact."

"Wait a minute. Didn't he say to us once that Jack the Ripper was inside him? Could that be it, Kate?"

"Look, David, we're staring straight into the unknown here. I'm sure you began this whole thing thinking that Forbes was a bit of a wacko, a man who'd come too close to a serial killer and who couldn't handle some of the stuff he'd learned from Reid, am I correct?"

"Spot on, actually," I replied. "I thought he'd come up here and that I would be able to listen to him and offer some advice on how to clear his mind of the preoccupations he'd developed and send him home feeling refreshed and relieved. Instead, all of his nightmares have somehow become mine and yours too and we seem to be dealing with a real case of some kind of evil manifestation."

"Demonic possession, perhaps," said Kate, thinking aloud rather than in reply to my words.

"I've heard of such things, though I never gave them much credence, at least not until now. You think that's what we just witnessed?"

"David, we won't really know much more until Forbes wakes up. What I do know is that the change in him appeared to begin as soon as the tune stopped. It was as if the music reached into him and triggered a response."

"Yes, and what a response! Those eyes, Kate. They looked hellish. Could that really have been blood that we saw filling his eye sockets?"

"It looked like blood to me."

"But, how could such a thing happen?"

"I don't know, but let's go take a closer look at William. He's fast asleep so it should be safe enough."

I followed Kate as she rose and together, we approached the supine form of Forbes as he slept sonorously on the sofa. Sure enough, trickles of what could only be blood were evident, trickling from the sides of his closed eyelids. Very gently, I lifted one eyelid, my intention being to confirm or deny the presence of those awful blood-filled orbs we'd so recently recoiled from.

"Kate, look!"

Kate joined me as we looked into Forbes's right eye. The redness was there, but was no longer as intense, and the eye gave us the impression of being severely bloodshot.

"Certainly not what we saw earlier," Kate confirmed.

I thought hard for a moment before speaking once again.

"Blood vessels," I said.

"Pardon?"

"Burst blood vessels, Kate. That's what I think happened earlier. Something caused the blood vessels in the eyes to rupture, causing an immediate and very frightening reaction for anyone witnessing it. It had to be a very severe reaction for the eyes to appear filled with blood the way they did. Every single blood vessel must have burst simultaneously and yet now, just a short time later, they appear to be repairing themselves and, if I'm not mistaken, in a few hours Forbes's eyes will have returned to normal. Only an intense shock to his system could possibly have caused such a thing to happen. It's almost as if his optical senses suffered from a great shock that his ocular nerves couldn't contend with."

"You mean he saw something that his eyes refused to believe or that caused such mental anguish in him that his brain simply told his eyes to shut down, or caused the blood vessels to burst to prevent him seeing whatever had induced the terror?"

"Maybe. I'm not sure if such a thing could happen, but there's still so much about the human brain we've yet to learn."

"And yet, I saw nothing, David, did you?"

"No, nothing at all, apart from Forbes going into that terrible seizure of fear and the apparent changes in his facial appearance and of course, his eyes."

"Do you have any thoughts on the way his face seemed to change? Is that medically possible?"

"No, of course not. No-one can change their appearance like that. We are all born with our inherited physical characteristics, and apart from surgical intervention through plastic surgery, for example, we just can't go around changing our facial appearance at will."

"He looks pretty normal now," Kate asserted, looking closely at the sleeping man. "Could we both have hallucinated and imagined the change in his face?"

"What? Both of us at the same time? I doubt it. No, something very strange happened to him and to us, Kate. I don't mind admitting I'm pretty scared right now. I'm really and truly sorry I called you and got you caught up in all this."

"Oh, come now, David, dear boy. There's no need to apologise. This is the most interesting phenomenon I've ever had the opportunity to encounter and examine at close quarters. This could be the first time anyone has seen anything like this and just think what a report I'll be able to write at the conclusion of it all. I wouldn't have missed this for the world!"

"But, but what if we don't survive it, whatever it is?" I blurted out.

"David, calm down, please. I'll admit we've seen and heard some pretty scary things so far, but nothing that's taken place has appeared to put any of us in any immediate danger of harm has it?"

"What about Forbes?"

"I said a while ago that if whatever the thing is, the auras perhaps or something else, if it or they wanted to harm Forbes they've had every opportunity to do so, and yet, apart from using him as some kind of conduit they don't appear to want to harm him in any physical way."

"A conduit?"

"Yes, David. I've just been thinking, and I have the feeling that something is trying to use Forbes to communicate with us or with you perhaps, as you were the one who heard the music outside."

"But I only heard a few bars."

"Yes, but you heard something. I didn't, which makes me believe that whatever is going on here concerns you in some way as well as Forbes."

"But how can it? I'd never heard of Forbes until I received his phone call the other day, and I've certainly never been involved with the Jack Reid case and I'd sure as hell know if I was related to him, so, I say again, how can I be connected with this madness?"

"I wish I could tell you, David. For now, we must wait and see what happens when William awakes and also hope that Miles Prendergast can come up with some information that might assist us in our cause."

Kate was right of course. There was little we could do except monitor Forbes and hope that Prendergast could help by identifying something in Forbes's past that might link him with Jack the Ripper. As Forbes would sleep for at least another two to three hours thanks to the sedative I'd administered to him, and as Kate didn't expect any word from Prendergast for at least that length of time also, I suggested the two of us should try and blow the cobwebs from our minds by taking a walk outside. Kate readily agreed and a few minutes later we stepped from the chill atmosphere of the croft into a warmer than usual breeze carried from the south by a calm zephyr of a wind that gently pushed thin whispers of cloud across the sky, and gave the whole of my little island domain a warmth and freshness that had been sadly lacking in the previous two or three storm-ridden days. With each step that carried us further from the croft, I felt my mind clearing and the fog that had addled my brain slowly began to lift.

"It's like a different world out here," I said to Kate, who walked at my side, enjoying the fresh air and the breathtakingly beautiful scenery of Skerries Rock. Small it may have been, but the panoramic views it afforded to the visitor were without equal in the United Kingdom, I'd swear to it.

"It really is quite magnificent," she agreed. "It's a shame I've had to come see it under such circumstances. I could quite enjoy taking a few days break here, David, away from the hustle and bustle of civilisation."

"Then, as soon as all this is over, you must do just that, Kate, and I won't take no for an answer. First chance you get, you must come and spend a week, or two if you feel like it, and you can simply relax and enjoy my home as it was meant to be enjoyed."

"Thank you David. I'll be happy to take you up on your offer, but for now, we must try and solve the enigma that is William Forbes and his strange 'possession' for want of a better word."

The mere mention of Forbes snapped us both back to the reality of our current situation. As one, we turned and headed back towards the croft, Kate pausing just long enough to wave futilely to the unseen crew of a trawler that headed out towards the open ocean about a mile off the coast of Skerries Rock.

As we re-entered my home, we both felt that a subtle change had taken place. Neither of us could say exactly what had happened, but the atmosphere felt different somehow. As soon as we saw William Forbes, however, we could see a distinct change. He was in a sitting position on the sofa, his eyes wide open, slightly bloodshot, and unblinking. His mouth lay open, as though he'd stopped in the middle of speaking and been frozen in time. His whole body appeared rigid, unmoving, and only the steady rise and fall of his chest betrayed the presence of life within the statue-like figure.

"William," Kate said quietly. "Can you hear me?"

No answer.

"William," she tried again.

"William, it's me, David," I said, a little louder than Kate's words.

As we watched, Forbes slowly, inexorably began to turn his head to the left until his face looked directly at us. The whole movement of his head had taken place as though in ultra-slow motion and appeared more frightening because of it. His mouth remained wide open and then, terrifyingly, without so much as a single movement of his lips a voice that sounded nothing like that of the William Forbes we knew, emanated from deep within his throat.

"Release me."

Kate and I stared at each other. The voice that boomed from somewhere within William Forbes took us both by surprise.

"Release me," it repeated. "Release me now."

Deep and resonant, the voice sounded cultured, educated, but neither of us could escape the overwhelming 'edge' to that voice, a malevolence that pervaded each carefully spoken word. Kate was the first to react to it.

"Who are you?" she asked. "What do you want with William Forbes?"

"Release me!" the voice sounded impatient.

"I said who *are* you?" Kate snapped back.

Without warning, the body of William Forbes began to shake and tremble, his head returned to a face front position, and a screeching, tormented wave of sound erupted from his open mouth. The sound filled the room and Kate and I both covered our ears with our hands, such was the decibel level. The screams bounced off the walls and reverberated around the room, intensifying the sound level. Forbes continued to shake from head to toe, his body a seething mass of uncoordinated movement that appeared in danger of shaking the teeth from his mouth.

"What's happening," I shouted at Kate in order to make myself heard over the terrible keening that continued to assault our eardrums.

"I don't know, but look," she shouted back at me and I returned my gaze to the shaking man on the sofa.

From the mouth of William Forbes, a strange, mist-like vapour had begun to escape. The mist rose until it hung over the body of my house guest and began to take shape, taking a semblance of human form, and then just as it appeared to be taking a definite shape, in the blink of an eye it inexplicably vanished, literally into thin air. The screaming stopped just as abruptly, leaving an uneasy silence.

Where a second before the 'thing' had hovered in space above Forbes's head, there was nothing; there remained nothing in the room but Forbes, Kate and me, and the solid, rhythmic tick, tock, tick, tock of the grandfather clock.

Kate and I continued staring at the space the apparition had occupied, wondering what exactly we'd just witnessed, so the pair of us were thus totally taken by surprise when the voice of William Forbes, the voice we recognised as the 'real' Forbes, snapped us back to the present:

"Hello, you two," he said innocently. "What on earth's the

matter? You look terrible. Has something happened while I've been asleep?"

Neither of us spoke. We continued to stare at Forbes and now Kate and I were the ones who stood open-mouthed in amazement.

TWENTY-FIVE
WHO IS IT?

TEN MINUTES after Forbes had woken, the three of us were sipping hot tea, seated around the kitchen table. Although Kate and I would probably have benefited from another large shot of something stronger, I decided that Forbes would be best suited to tea, allowing time for the large dose of the sedative to dissipate from his bloodstream.

Incredibly, as his first words on waking had intimated, he had no recollection or knowledge of the terrible events that had occurred while he slept. As for the physical manifestations that he'd undergone, he expressed nothing but incredulity.

"You mean to say that I actually changed in appearance and spoke in a strange voice?" he asked after Kate and I had jointly given him a brief résumé of recent proceedings.

"I'm afraid so, William, though I don't think it was you that was speaking. Remember what we told you, your mouth was open but your lips never moved, yet the voice could be heard speaking quite clearly and succinctly," Kate replied, "but the most mysterious thing was the unearthly 'mist' that emanated from you right at the end, before simply disappearing into thin air."

"But if it wasn't me, then you're hinting that it really was Jack the Ripper, aren't you? You think I'm possessed by his spirit."

"William, I really don't know what to tell you. I've never encountered such a manifestation as this. The mist, the strange almost human shape it formed, makes me think we're dealing with a spirit of sorts, yes, but despite my profession, and I think I told you this earlier, I do not and never have believed in ghosts, per se. Whatever this is, it's something so powerful and so different from anything that I've thought possible that I'm having to look at it with a totally open mind, and must form my opinions as we go along."

"But, how could my face change? You both saw it didn't you? You said I looked like a different man."

"Which indeed you did," I answered. "I've never been so terrified in my life, to be honest. The sound of that voice coming from your mouth, the screaming and the demands it made were just unearthly, not of this world, there's no other way to describe it."

"But I didn't say much?"

"Just *'release me'* and *'release me now'*."

"But, if it wasn't the Ripper, then who could it be, and what did it mean by *'release me'*?"

"I don't know William," said Kate, "but it was just after it spoke those words that the mist, the fog, or whatever it was, emerged from within your body, your mouth to be precise. I'm wondering if it was commanding you, not us, to release it, and that somehow, you did just that."

"But, how could I?" asked Forbes. "You've just said I was virtually catatonic and the thing, whatever it was, appeared to be in total control of my body and my mind, which it must have been for me to have no recollection of the event."

"You were, and I don't know how you could have let this thing loose. Perhaps it gave the command and somehow your brain or your mind mentally released it, set it free from whatever held it inside you. I know, it all sounds far-fetched, I agree, but I have no rational explanation to provide at present. I'm sorry, William."

"You just said, 'whatever' was holding it inside William," I said. "You previously mentioned that you thought there might be two 'auras' surrounding him. Is it possible that one of those auras was in some way holding the other, malevolent one in check and that it has now been released to cause untold havoc on us?"

"You may well be correct, David. I need to try and think this through."

"You also said that all of this began as I listened to that tune from the dream, the Mary Kelly song," Forbes added, obviously anxious to try and find a solution to what must have been an even more frightening scenario for him than it was for us. "Why should a piece of Victorian music trigger such a reaction?"

"But it wasn't just any piece of Victorian music, was it William?" I said. "It was the very song that Mary Jane Kelly was heard singing shortly before her death. Surely it has some special significance to whatever's going on here."

Kate held her hand up, stalling me from saying anything further.

"Just hang on a minute," she said. "Maybe we've been looking at all of this from the wrong angle."

"How so?"

"David, from the start you and I have both been under the impression, perhaps understandably influenced by William's assumptions, that Jack the Ripper, or some incarnation of his soul or spirit, is behind all of this. That may still be correct, but remember the second aura? What if, and I know it's a big 'if', but what if that second aura is not another malevolence, but is in fact connected with one of the Ripper's victims?"

"I say, Kate, you think it's Mary Kelly, don't you?" Forbes exclaimed.

"I'm accepting it as a possibility, William. I've said all along that there are forces around us that we don't understand. I think we should be prepared to consider all the possibilities and scenarios that this mystery presents. You've assumed all along that Jack the Ripper was out to 'get' you. If we take that as a possibility, then why shouldn't we also examine the possibility that Mary Kelly is trying to stop him doing just that? The dream, the song, they all relate not just to the Ripper, but to the victims as well. You talked of the skeletal hands reaching out from the windows on that awful street. They could represent the Ripper's victims, and then the song only came to you when the figure of the Ripper appeared to block your path towards the light. Jack the Ripper didn't sing that song, William, but Mary Kelly did!"

"Kate, if what you're saying is true," I interrupted, "then who, if anyone, was asking for 'release' from within William? That sure as hell wasn't the voice of a young woman, so I'd find it difficult to believe that was the voice of Mary Kelly."

"David, you have to understand that we're dealing with some kind of supernatural phenomenon here. We can't assume anything. Who's to say that the voice we heard wasn't Mary Kelly, and that the fact that she is using William as a conduit is making the voice sound more masculine than feminine?"

"But the voice we heard was educated, cultured. Wasn't Mary Kelly supposed to be an illiterate Irish girl with little or no education?"

Forbes provided me with the answer to my question.

"There is in fact extraordinarily little in the way of solid fact known about Mary Kelly, David. No one can even be sure that Mary Kelly was her real name. She was also known as Marie Jeanette and probably one or two other names when she wanted to stay out of the local magistrates court. Some say she was Irish and came from a small farm in that country, others that she lived in Wales with her family before travelling to London where she supposedly worked respectably for a while before ending up in a brothel and finally ending upon the streets as a common prostitute. She may well have received an education of sorts, and as Kate says, we're dealing with the unknown here, so why should her spirit, if that's what it is, speak to us in her own human voice. She is dead after all, isn't she?"

"Well said, William," Kate smiled at him. "I think you're beginning to get the gist of all this."

"I'm trying," Forbes replied.

"Okay then," I re-joined the conversation. "So Mary Kelly is trying to stop Jack the Ripper from taking over William's body and mind, or at least from getting some kind of foothold on the reality of our world, is that it?"

"It's a possibility," said Kate.

I sighed, a long hard sigh.

"Kate, I know you won't commit to anything you're not sure of, but all you talk of is 'possibilities'. I don't mind a spot of speculation from time to time. We really don't have much to go on here, do we?"

"I'm sorry, David, really. I wish I could be more forthright about the whole affair but I'm almost as much in the dark as you are. All I have is a little more experience with these kinds of phenomena, and a little knowledge of 'things that go bump in the night' What I'd really like to find out right now is what, if anything, attempted to materialise in this room a while ago, and if something was indeed 'released' then where the heck is it now?"

"Yes, you're right of course, Kate. We should be making that a priority." I said, eager to do something to try and resolve the mystery that surrounded us and to alleviate my own fears that something terrible and extremely dangerous had been unleashed upon my island home.

William Forbes made as though to open his mouth to speak but the words froze on his lips as the three of us almost jumped out of our skins.

The telephone was ringing!

TWENTY-SIX
SOMETHING AND NOTHING

"Are you going to answer it or not?" Kate asked as the phone rang and rang as we all stared at the jangling instrument on the hall table. We'd all responded in shock to the sound of the phone as it stampeded into the middle of our conversation a few seconds earlier, so intensely had we immersed our thoughts in the eerie and quite terrifying subject under discussion.

Her words stung me into action, and I moved to answer the incessant ringing.

"Hello?" I spoke into the mouthpiece as I grabbed the phone from its cradle.

A stranger's voice replied, spoke a few words to me and I asked the caller to hold on a moment. I held the phone out to Kate.

"It's Miles Prendergast!"

Kate quickly took the phone from me and sat down on the stool beside the telephone table as she engaged in an animated conversation with her learned friend. Forbes and I were both anxious to hear what Prendergast had to say, but in the meantime, I thought it prudent to allow Kate some privacy, so I beckoned Forbes to follow me into the kitchen, where I made the two of us a pot of strong coffee.

A mere two minutes passed, we could hear the sound of Kate's voice, indistinct, as it carried through the croft, and both of us sat silently, sipping coffee and waiting for news from her friend, Miles Prendergast. A shadow fell across the room, and perhaps due to all that had recently occurred we both jumped at the sudden paling of the light. It was nothing, just the effect of a cloud formation blotting out the sunlight for a few seconds. We relaxed, slightly, enough to finish our drinks and, together, we carried on waiting. Forbes began drumming his fingers on the table. It rapidly became annoying and I asked him to desist.

"Sorry, David," he said apologetically.

"I'm sorry too. I know you're anxious for news of Prendergast's inquiries. I shouldn't have snapped like that."

"Please, don't apologise. We're all under enormous pressure, and I know you and Kate are doing all you can to help me. I just wish we could discover something concrete, some valid reason for all that's happened to me, and that now seems to be happening to you too."

"I must say, I'm mystified as to why I should have heard that music, William. Perhaps I really did imagine it; it could have just been the wind after all."

"But you recognised it, didn't you, when I hummed it to you, and when you heard the song on the internet? That can't have been your imagination."

"I know. I just can't figure any of it out. You came to me for help and somehow I appear to have become a part of the problem, rather than the solution."

"Whatever it is, it isn't your fault, David. You weren't to know that any of this would take place. If anyone should be apologising, it's me. I've brought all of this to your door after all."

"Look, William. I was mad as hell when I found out you'd held back the information about Jack Reid telling you my name and to find me in order to solve this mystery, but I have to admit, like Kate, that I'm totally committed to solving it now. Maybe somewhere along the line we'll even find out how and why Reid thought I was the man to help you."

The sound of Kate's muffled voice coming from the other room ceased, telling me that she'd completed her conversation with Prendergast. Sure enough, no more than five seconds passed before she appeared at the kitchen door.

"If you gentlemen would care to join me again, I've news from Miles that I think you'll find of interest."

Forbes and I certainly didn't need asking twice. The sound of chairs being pushed back, their legs scraping on the hard kitchen floor, preceded the two of us rushing through the door to follow Kate back into the sitting room where we quickly positioned ourselves in my comfortable armchairs once again and waited for her to fill us in on her conversation with Prendergast.

"Well, I have to say that Miles appears to have worked extremely hard on our behalf all morning. Let me say first of all that of course, as no-one knows who Jack the Ripper was, his investigation into your family tree, William, was purely to try and ascertain if we could find a connection between you and the Cavendish family. With the information you provided, Miles told me that he is pretty certain that no such connection exists. His search was made so much easier by the fact that the Cavendish family history has apparently already been researched on a number of occasions and therefore a comprehensive guide exists as far as they are concerned. Certainly, as far back as the opening years of the nineteenth century he could find no connection, however loose, between the Cavendishes and your own forbears. However, he did find out that there may be a small something that might muddy the waters a little. I gave Miles a great deal of peripheral information to work on as well, including the details Burton Cavendish noted in his own letters regarding the woman with whom he had the affair and who we have to accept as being the mother of Jack the Ripper. Cavendish of course, never mentioned her by name, only by a rough location. However, Miles noted that most of your own ancestors lived and worked in the same area as the woman mentioned by Cavendish. It is therefore possible, though not certain that you may have some tenuous link to the female line in respect of any bloodline of the Ripper, as of course, any illegitimate offspring that could be linked to your own family wouldn't necessarily have been officially listed as being as such in any official records."

"Oh, God," Forbes groaned. "So it is possible that I'm related to the monster somehow?"

"Anything is possible, William, without necessarily making it fact. I gave Miles some extremely wide parameters to work with, for obvious reasons, as I wasn't able to tell him exactly what we're seeking. He did discover, quite interestingly, that you did have a great, great uncle who was a country doctor in the very area Burton Cavendish referred to. He was married and had a son and two daughters, all of whom survived to maturity, so again, some intriguing possibilities exist there, wouldn't you say?"

"The more you go on, the more I'm becoming convinced that there is a connection between my family and the evil bloodline of the Ripper. What if one of those ancestors of mine was actually the father or mother of the Ripper, the woman Burton Cavendish had the affair with? After all, he never named her, so it could have been, couldn't it?"

And it could just as easily not have happened like that," I interrupted the flow of their conversation. To me, it was plain that whatever Miles Prendergast had discovered, it did little to prove anything one way or the other, and I said so to Kate, who, surprisingly agreed with me.

"You're quite right, David," she said. "Nothing that Miles told me proves that William is a descendant of Jack the Ripper, or even a relative of the Cavendish family."

Forbes looked extremely puzzled.

"So why," he asked, "have I been subjected to the dreams, or more specifically, the one recurring dream that Jack Reid also experienced, and why have all these terrible things been happening to me? If I'm not connected to the case in any way, surely I should not have been through all of this?"

"William, I have a feeling that your connection with the case is merely that of the part of a messenger," said Kate, her voice falling into a quiet and hushed tone.

"A messenger?"

"Yes. I think that Jack Reid used you, and don't ask me how he did it, to carry some kind of message out into the world. Whatever is going on, I believe you to have been possessed by whatever spirit previously resided within the mind and soul of Jack Reid. Somehow, he managed to pass that malevolence on to you, in order that it could escape the earthly bonds that held it in check within his own being. He, and I suspect the thing that dwelt within him, knowing he didn't have long to live, chose to pass on their 'essence' through an unwilling dupe. Anyone would probably have served their purpose, but you, being a solicitor would have been granted easy access to Reid and were allowed to spend time with him almost at will. Tell me, do you remember anything unusual at all happening while you were alone with him during any of your visits?"

Forbes's face suddenly assumed a look of horror as a terrible realisation dawned upon him.

"Yes, now that you mention it, something strange did

happen one day. I was listening to Reid as he recounted something of what happened to him during a hypnosis session that Ruth Truman had conducted with him. She'd attempted to reach into his mind and find out if his belief in possession by Jack the Ripper would show up in his childhood memories. She'd 'regressed' him as he put it, and I recall feeling very sleepy myself at the time, and the next thing I knew, Reid was shaking me by the shoulder, telling me that I must be very, very tired to have nodded off in such a way. I apologised, of course and professed to not knowing what had come over me. Reid said I must have been overworking and suggested I took a day or two off to recharge my batteries. As for the story he'd been relating to me, I remembered nothing of it, and though I asked him to tell me again, he said it didn't really matter, as nothing had come of it. I never did work out how or why I could simply fall into a deep sleep like that, even though it only lasted a couple of minutes, according to my watch.

Now at last, I believe I know what you're thinking, Kate. You believe he did something to me, or rather the thing inside him found a way to penetrate my mind and body and it's been using me ever since, is that it?"

"That's precisely what I believe," Kate replied.

"But why?"

"Because, William, the thing, the entity, or whatever it is, needed to find a way to communicate with its next host, if that's the correct word, but that host couldn't possibly be reached from within the walls of Ravenswood Special Hospital. It needed you, or someone like you, to act as a carrier, a means to find a way to that new host."

"But why come all the way up here to Skerries Rock?" I asked. "Why did the entity use Reid to instruct William to contact me? What the hell have I got to do with it?"

"Perhaps you are in some way another 'conduit' as Kate

called it earlier," Forbes replied. "Maybe it needs more than one of us in order to find its way to wherever and whoever it's seeking."

"Maybe you're right. Perhaps that's why I had that brief experience of hearing the Mary Kelly music. What do you think, Kate?"

Kate looked grave as she replied.

"I think that we must all be very, very, careful from now on. There are things happening here that are not of this world, of that I'm certain. I have a feeling that we're awfully close to discovering the real truth behind the mystery. If William and you are both part of the mystery then of course, it's equally possible that I am also included in the planned scenario."

"Planned scenario?" Forbes looked mystified.

"Oh yes, William. Whatever is taking place here is definitely not the result of some random phenomenon. Everything that has befallen you and David too, I believe, has been planned right from the beginning by someone or something with an extremely high degree of intelligence and forethought. Whether that intelligence is recognisably human of course, is another matter and I hope it won't be long before all is revealed."

"Bloody hell, Kate. That all sounds a bit grim and final."

"I know David, but believe me, I truly expect this whole affair to reach a conclusion before long. If this thing has a plan that involves us we can be sure it will not rest until that plan has been executed and I'm damn sure it doesn't include the entity remaining on Skerries Rock for any length of time."

"I'm not sure I follow your reasoning."

"Look, let's say that this thing really is Jack the Ripper in some non-corporeal form, do you really believe he's come back simply to stay trapped on a tiny little island off the coast of Scotland?"

"Oh, right, I kind of see what you mean."

"In other words," Forbes interrupted, "the thing intends to do something here and move on, perhaps to the mainland, where his new host is waiting for him?"

"Something like that, William," said Kate.

"But, what would it want here?" I asked again, pressing Kate for an answer.

"I don't know for sure," she replied, 'but something here is important to it."

"The page from the journal!" Forbes suddenly shouted. "It must have something to do with the journal."

Before Kate could reply, we were all interrupted once again by the sudden and

most unexpected sound of the telephone ringing. This time, I was quick to respond, and grabbed the phone from its cradle after only two rings.

It was Miles Prendergast. He had more to tell Kate. I passed the phone to her and once again beckoned Forbes to follow me to the kitchen. It was time to

replenish the coffee pot.

TWENTY-SEVEN

A GRIM REALISATION

Forbes and I finished our second cup of coffee. Kate remained closeted in the sitting room conversing on the phone with Prendergast. The two of us had sat in almost total silence all the while she spoke with him. There didn't seem much to say as we both appeared content to commune with our own thoughts until we heard Kate's latest news, if indeed Prendergast had provided her with anything else that might be of use to us. It had been a companionable silence, with neither Forbes nor I feeling the slightest bit uncomfortable at the lack of verbal communication. My house guest eventually broke the silence.

"She's been on the phone for ages."

I looked at my wristwatch.

"It's only been twenty minutes."

"Are you sure? It feels more like an hour."

"I suppose the fact that we're both anxious and waiting to hear what she has to say is making the seconds seem like minutes and the minutes like hours," I replied.

"Do you think Prendergast has found out something else, something that helps us?"

"We won't know that until Kate tells us, will we?"

"I wish she'd hurry up. What can be taking them so long?"

"We'll know soon enough, William. With all that's happened so far I think we can afford to be a little patient, if indeed Kate is finding some way to help you, and us, come to that."

"Yes, I know, you're right, of course. It's just that…"

Forbes never finished his sentence, as, just then, the door opened, and Kate strode into the room.

"Well, that was an interesting conversation," she said, almost cryptically.

"You've learned something haven't you?"

"Yes, William, or rather, Miles has learned something. When I spoke with him earlier I asked him to delve a little further into the Cavendish family history, to see if there may have been any previous examples of family members displaying murderous or violent tendencies. That would have fit in with my theory that this thing may go back even further than the time of Jack the Ripper."

Forbes looked a little confused and Kate remembered that the idea of a centuries old entity or intellect transferring from one host to another had been a matter we'd discussed while Forbes slept under the influence of the sedative. She quickly explained, and Forbes quickly came to terms with her theory.

"Ah, I understand, Kate. So you really do think that something could have been 'possessing' members of the Cavendish clan for hundreds of years?"

"I said before, William, anything is possible, and I asked Miles to do his best to conduct an in-depth search of his computer database for any strange or odd clusters of deaths that might fit the pattern we're looking for."

"And he's learned something?" I asked, as Forbes nodded his head, thoughtfully.

"He has, David, but please pour me a cup of coffee and we can all retire to the sitting room once more if you don't mind. I'd rather discuss this in comfort."

"Of course, Kate. I should have offered you one sooner."

"No need to apologise, just pour, David, please. My throat's positively parched after all that talking."

A minute later, armed with her cup of freshly made coffee, Kate sat down in the comfortable armchair by the fireside and Forbes and I waited for her to relate Prendergast's information to us.

"As a result of what Miles told me, I have no doubt that the Cavendish family has proved to be the conduit or receptacle for some kind of entity for far longer than we previously thought."

"You mean there've been others?"

"Yes, David, it would appear so. In 1704, during the reign of Queen Anne, a certain Hubert Cavendysh, spelled with a 'y' instead of an 'I', the 'I' not being used for nearly another hundred years, was hanged in Kent following a series of horrific murders which saw four women slaughtered in scenes apparently reminiscent of the Mary Kelly murder of 1888. Cavendysh, the local squire, admitted to the murders after a servant reported to the authorities that her master had developed the habit of going out late at night and returning in the early hours. She'd been unable to sleep one night and had witnessed his return to the house 'covered in blood from hand to foot' as she described it. The following day the body of the fourth unfortunate victim had been discovered in her home, gutted and butchered.

Going back even further, Martin deVilliers, another Cavendish ancestor, suffered execution by beheading during the time of Oliver Cromwell, in 1656 to be precise. There is little documentary evidence of his crimes, but a short note in the county records for that year listed him as being the 'inhuman monster' responsible for at least three motiveless murders, committed while employed on the service of the commonwealth. In other words, deVilliers had been one of Cromwell's men, possibly an officer in The New Model Army, as Cromwell's troops were known, who appeared to have taken advantage of his position in order to get close to his victims and perpetrate his crimes. The records do state that deVilliers died unrepentant and refused the presence of a minister of the church at his execution.

That's as much as Miles has been able to ascertain, I'm afraid to say. Comprehensive as the Cavendish family tree may be, he could find no other occurrences of multiple murder being committed by family members as the further back in time he went, the less information showed up, apart from the usual 'who married who' and what children they bore and so on."

"Even so, it's highly suggestive of a recurrent theme of violence running through the family bloodline," I said, and Forbes added;

"Yes, and the one who refused a priest could be indicative of some kind of aversion to anything religious, which might indicate a demonic possession perhaps?"

"Maybe," said Kate. "You'll be pleased to hear that no such connections could be found in your family tree William," she added.

"Ah, then it looks like you were correct in assuming that William is just some sort of link or conduit for this…whatever it is," I volunteered.

"Quite possibly, David. It does seem to me that the Cavendish family have, over the years, given birth to an inordinate number of murderers, and yet, the vast majority of the family appear to have followed quite noble professions. The last three generations for example have all been doctors, psychiatrists to be precise."

"Perhaps something in the family's genetic make-up has compensated for the odd bad egg by giving those blessed with freedom from that gene you mentioned the desire and the ability to help others, in some way giving them the need to expiate the crimes of their wicked and twisted relatives."

"That sounds plausible, David, but I doubt it's quite as simple as that. Even those 'bad eggs' as you call them would probably have led far more exemplary lives had they not been the targets of the malevolence of this entity. They probably couldn't help themselves."

"Which means that Jack Reid *was* telling the truth!" Forbes suddenly exclaimed. "If you really mean what you just said, Kate, then he had no way of ever stopping what happened to him. He had no more control over his actions than a runaway train would have of stopping at the next station."

"I believe you're right, there, William. We have to realise that something is among us, even now, and that Jack Reid was in some way trying to warn you, us, in advance that whatever this thing is, it has purpose and it has the ability to seek out and target its victims, hosts, or whatever you wish to call them. On reflection, I think Reid was in fact trying to warn the world!"

"Wait a minute, Kate. Are you saying that this, this...entity only infects or possesses members of the Cavendish family?" I asked

"I'm not entirely certain, but, even if it is restricted by some unearthly power to that one family we must remember that the female line of the Cavendishes has given birth to many offspring of differing surnames over the centuries. The list of potential hosts is therefore vast, far bigger than we could hope to track down and eliminate from our list of suspect hosts."

"Bloody Hell," said Forbes. "If this thing gets off the island it could end up anywhere."

"Potentially, yes," said Kate. "That's why we must try and ensure that it never leaves Skerries Rock."

"And just how do you suggest we do that, Kate?" I asked.

"Well, David. That's the thing you see. We can't touch it, feel it, or even see it properly. We don't even know what it is to be honest, so my answer to that one is an unequivocal, *I don't know*."

Forbes stared at Kate, that hunted look appearing in his eyes once more. He clearly felt the grip of fear as the atmosphere in the room appeared to chill with Kate's words. I admit I felt it too, and I realised that the next few hours might begin to become extremely uncomfortable for all of us if, as Kate suggested, we were about to go into battle against our unseen but very real enemy. I knew as well as she did that the entity, the spirit of the Ripper as we'd come to designate it, wasn't about to meekly give way and allow us to destroy it. Whatever powers it possessed were about to be unleashed and only Kate, Forbes and I stood between it and its future. In my mind, my island home on Skerries Rock had suddenly become a very lonely and impossibly isolated place.

TWENTY-EIGHT
SCREAMING WALLS

"He's here," said Forbes, his eyes darting around the room in much the way they had when he'd first arrived. His body tensed and my guest assumed the stance of a man ready to defend himself, but, against what?

"What makes you think so?" I asked. "Can you see something we can't?"

"No, but I can feel him. He's here, I know it."

"How do you know it's a *he*?" asked Kate.

"I don't know. It's just a feeling, can't you sense it too, David?"

I had to agree with Forbes. Something imperceptible had changed in the sitting room, though it would have been difficult for me to put an accurate description to it.

"It's certainly become very cold in here all of a sudden," I said. "In fact, it's as cold as the grave, and that doesn't feel right. The weather doesn't merit the house feeling like this. Look outside. The sun is shining and there's hardly any wind at all. For Skerries Rock, this is a mild day."

"There's no doubt it has grown colder in the last few

minutes, but I can't sense anything malevolent in the room, at least not yet." Kate added. "Perhaps you should light the fire, David?"

"Good idea," I said. The large brass scuttle that I used to keep a supply of logs ready for the fire stood empty on the hearth.

"William, would you mind coming and giving me a hand to bring some more logs in from the outhouse?"

"To be honest, I'll be glad to get out into the fresh air for a minute or two," Forbes replied.

"Will you be okay on your own, Kate?" I said, picking up the scuttle as Forbes and I walked towards the door.

"Of course I will, dear boy. Don't be silly. Go fetch the logs. I'll still be here when you get back."

As soon as Forbes and I stepped across the threshold into the fresh air, it became evident that we hadn't imagined the drop in room temperature in my home. The outside temperature felt at last five to ten degrees warmer. The warmth of the sun felt good on the back of my neck as we strolled across the yard to the outhouse that I utilised as my wood shed.

"There's definitely something evil in that room, David," said Forbes, as we began to gather a supply of pre-cut logs with which to fill the scuttle. The pile of firewood in the outhouse was growing depleted and I made a mental note to order a new supply from the emporium. Forbes went on. "I know you and Kate are oblivious to it, but trust me, I've felt it before and now it's in there with us, for sure."

"I'm not saying you're mistaken, William. In fact, you're probably correct, especially after what's happened so far. All I said was that I couldn't see or feel anything."

"Let's just be careful when we go back inside, David, please?"

"No problem, William. We'll all be on our guard, as Kate obviously thinks things are about to start happening anyway."

Five minutes later we returned to find Kate on her hands and knees, busily scraping out the remains of the previous night's fire from the grate, placing the ash and dead embers into a steel bucket she'd obtained from my kitchen. Hearing the front door open, she turned and smiled at us.

"Thought I'd keep myself busy while you boys were fetching and carrying."

"Thanks Kate. We'll soon have the fire set and the room'll feel a bit cheerier."

"What do you use to light it, David?" she asked.

I pointed to a small carved wooden box in the left-hand corner of the hearth.

"There's a supply of firelighters in there."

"Right then, you boys put those logs down and I'll see to the fire."

"Are you sure?" I asked.

"Of course. It's been ages since I had the chance to light a real old-fashioned log fire. You two go and make us a pot of tea or coffee, whatever you fancy."

Forbes and I dutifully left Kate at work on setting and lighting the fire and made our way to the kitchen. When we returned a few minutes later, armed with a pot of tea and one of coffee, Kate had already completed her task and we were met by the warming glow of the rising flames as the heat from the burning logs began to suffuse the room and bring some semblance of normality to the temperature in the croft.

"That's better, Kate," I said as Forbes and I placed the pots of hot drinks on the coffee table in the centre of the room. Forbes returned to the kitchen and came back a minute later with a supply of mugs, sugar, teaspoons and a plate of biscuits on a tray.

"A fire makes all the difference, don't you think? Makes everything seem less, well, less gloomy," said Kate as we sat together, the three of us, sipping tea and coffee and wondering what would happen next.

"It all seems a bit surreal, really," said Forbes. "I mean, you've convinced us that something terrible might be about to happen and yet here we are, drinking tea and coffee and sitting by a freshly made fire as though we're having a tea party."

"Yes, there's something terribly British about that, isn't there, William?" I asked. "No-one faces danger or the unknown quite like us, do they?"

"I don't think it's a really a matter for levity," Forbes went on. "My life, and yours and Kate's could be in real danger, David, don't you realise that?"

"I'm sure you're right, William, but in the meantime, we have to try and carry on as normal, don't you think so, Kate?"

"Of course, you're quite correct, David."

"So, what do we do next?" asked Forbes as we downed the last of our respective drinks.

"We wait, I suppose," I replied, and then looked up and waited to see if Kate would come up with anything contrary to my advice. Instead she nodded and said nothing. Her thoughts were obviously far from my sitting room at that moment. I didn't intrude on her private moment and instead sat looking into the dancing flames of the log fire, watching thin wisps of smoke rise from the tips of the flames and carry on their journey upwards through the chimney towards the clear blue sky that lay beyond the confines of my home. The logs themselves crackled satisfyingly as they burned, and the companionable sound of the grandfather clock, as it continued to tick in the corner of the room was the only other discernible sound in the room, until...

"What the hell is that?" asked Forbes, his face a mask of

terror and panic, as a loud and terrible screeching noise assaulted our senses.

"Bloody hell!" I shouted in response and such was the decibel level of that awful scream that I felt compelled to place my hands over my ears, though that manoeuvre had little effect in silencing the noise.

"Where's it coming from?" Forbes shouted above the din.

"It's everywhere, all around us!" I shouted back.

"Look there." Kate called out, pointing at the fireplace.

Incredibly, something appeared to be taking shape, born of the smoke and flames that continued to dance in the grate. The thing had little in the way of form at first, but, with each passing second, it began to assume something akin to human appearance, until, before our bewildered and unbelieving eyes, it completed its configuration. It hovered just above the hearth, a black and swirling mass that appeared to have no solid figure, and yet bore the unmistakable shape of a man, or could it have been a woman? It was difficult to decide, but one thing was certain. The shape, the thing, stood at least six feet tall, and possessed no discernible human features apart from its outline. It had no face, no head as such, just a shapeless bulge where one might have expected to find the head. The whole thing appeared to be swirling within a dense cloud of its own making, a shroud that held it cocooned, apart from the world in which we stood but yet allowing it to encroach into our time and space. Could this be the very entity that had possessed and cursed the Cavendish family for so long? I realised that Kate had so far done nothing in response to the manifestation. I looked across to where she stood. She appeared enthralled rather than afraid at the appearance of this strange unearthly apparition. Her face betrayed not a single hint of fear, and for a moment I imagined I saw a smile play across her lips as the thing continued to hover above the hearth, as the screaming continued all around us. At last, Kate shouted above the noise that filled the room.

"I don't think the noise is coming from that," she pointed at the amorphous hovering shape.

She was right. The wall of screeching terrifying sound that surrounded us felt as though it emanated from the very walls of the croft, and certainly not from the hovering shape that now rose almost majestically to a position just inches from the ceiling. The thing's 'head' appeared to bow as though it were looking down upon us and we stood transfixed as it began to move slowly but imperceptibly towards us. Frozen in place, not one of us dared move as it approached closer and closer until, with the screams continuing to reverberate around the room, it came to a stop, hovering just in front of, and above Kate. The three of us could do nothing but tremble against the shocking sound that filled our heads, threatening to send us over the edge into a madness born of terror, while at the same time unable to take our eyes from the strange and potentially evil manifestation that now began to visibly shrink as it drew closer to the motionless figure of Kate.

Then two things happened almost simultaneously. First, the figure that hung in the air began to throb as though it were being imbued with a life force of its own, drawn from some unknown and unseen source, and then, as suddenly as it had manifested itself, it dropped like a stone, enveloping Kate in a dark, fog-like shroud, and as she stood stock still, unable to resist the thing, whatever it was, it simply disappeared, or rather, I should say it dissipated, as a cloud of smoke might do, and appeared to fall to the floor around Kate's standing figure, until, within seconds, nothing at all remained. At the instant of its disappearance our ears were suddenly assaulted by the sound of silence. The horrible and terrifying wailing and screeching that had gone on for what seemed like hours but in fact must have been no more than a few minutes, died in an instant, leaving nothing behind but the solid ticking sound of the grandfather clock, the one constant in that room that had accompanied everything that had transpired over the last two days.

For a few seconds, no-one spoke or moved. Perhaps we all felt that to do so would invoke a repetition of what we'd just experienced. Forbes looked as though he'd just witnessed a vision of Hell itself. His face appeared deathly pale, his body shook and trembled from head to foot, but, perhaps most strikingly of all, if ever we required proof of the terror engendered by what had transpired, Forbes's hair provided it. Where before it had been light brown with tinges of grey at the edges, his head was now adorned in pure white! His lips trembled as though he wanted to speak but couldn't. I said nothing to him; he would speak when he felt the need.

I remained immobile, though I now felt no fear, no uncertainty. Something had happened to me during the long minutes of the screaming and the vision of the hovering apparition. I was no longer unsure of myself or the sequence of events that had visited itself upon my home.

I turned my attention to Kate, who appeared calm, unruffled and in complete control of herself, though she continued to stand, unmoving, as we looked at one another, exchanging knowing glances. At that moment, she and I seemed to connect in a way that our years of friendship had never allowed us to. We understood each other perfectly, and I think it was at that moment that we both knew exactly how this whole strange affair must end.

TWENTY-NINE

THE FIRES OF HELL?

A SHOCKED AND devastated William Forbes had locked himself in the bathroom, leaving Kate and I to talk in private for a few minutes.

"I've heard of people's hair turning white overnight, Kate, but I'd never have believed what just happened to Forbes if I hadn't seen it with my own eyes. How could his hair have literally turned white in the space of a few minutes?"

"Maybe it isn't *his* hair," Kate replied, cryptically.

"I'm not sure I follow you."

"David, we know that something is here with us. If I'm correct in my earlier assumption, there may be two separate entities at work here, both of them focussed in some way on William. They may have other intentions that we're not yet aware of but until we can rid ourselves of one or both of them, I believe that none of us are safe. As for William's hair, it may be he's changed again, as we witnessed before with his facial characteristics."

"Oh God, Kate. In other words, Forbes may have been

correct all along and the Ripper, if it is indeed the Ripper, is now within his body or his mind, or something?"

"That's just it, David, quite so. Remember that I felt the presence of two auras, both of them emanating from Forbes? They may now have been released and become 'active' in a real sense."

"So, are you saying that the 'auras' you talked of earlier are in fact these entities that are now attacking us?"

"I fear so, David."

"I must say, I was becoming pretty freaked when that thing that appeared from the fire appeared to hover over you and then exploded into nothingness all around you."

"I believe the same thing occurred with the earlier thing that appeared from within William. Somehow the first one managed to infiltrate itself into the house, which is why we now feel its presence by the drop in temperature and the odd feeling of being watched we've developed. As for the new one, I think it's done the same thing and is even now somewhere within the fabric of your home, I'm sad to say. I was just unlucky to be standing where I was when it dematerialised."

"That's a none too cheery prospect, I must say. How the hell can we fight what we can't see?"

"We must be on our guard, David, and I must ask you to keep a close watch on our friend, William."

"You really think he may be dangerous?"

"Let's just say we should be careful at all times, from now on."

Just then, Forbes reappeared, still looking shaken and with his shoulders drooped as though in resignation. He looked a beaten man, and despite Kate's warning I couldn't help but feel a degree of intense sympathy for him. Just a few short months earlier he'd been diligently pursuing his career in the law firm, and now here he stood, a man in fear of his life, with only two strangers standing between him and an as yet unknown fate.

"My hair," he almost sobbed. "How can this have happened?"

"Your own fear must have triggered an intense physical transformation, William," Kate offered by way of explanation. "The look on your face when all hell broke loose was one of abject terror. What went through your mind at that time, I dread to think."

"That's just it; I can't remember what I might have been thinking of. Those few minutes are simply a blank in my memory."

Kate gave me a knowing look. She was suggesting to me that Forbes had indeed been 'possessed' by something during those crazy few minutes and that he may still be harbouring some malevolent presence within him.

"I think we should all take things easy," I said, attempting to keep everyone on a clam and level-headed footing. "We're all agreed that something unearthly, supernatural perhaps, is taking place. We need to be vigilant and try and figure out a way to stop it once we ascertain what its purpose is."

"I agree," said Kate. "We need food, I think. We must keep our energy levels up and be prepared for anything in the next few hours, for I feel that events are building up towards something I don't yet comprehend."

I certainly didn't feel at all hungry, and neither did Forbes, but Kate's suggestion made sense, so we all made our way to the kitchen where I prepared a plate of corned beef sandwiches and a large bowl of salad which we all picked at without enthusiasm for the next twenty minutes.

With the sparse meal over and the dishes cleared away, we returned to the sitting room, where a chill had once again pervaded the room, despite the log fire continuing to burn brightly in the fireplace. As I walked towards the door to the hallway, intending to retrieve a thicker sweater from my bedroom, I tripped on the edge of the large rug that stood close to the door, and in attempting to stop myself from falling, I reached out for the wall, but instead my hand came into contact with the grandfather clock in the corner by the door. As I did so, a feeling of dizziness came over me and I staggered backwards away from the door and into the centre of the room. The clock rocked on its base, but its solidity and weight prevented it from falling and being damaged.

Seeing my apparent weakness, Forbes stepped forward and reached out a hand, taking me by the arm to steady me.

"Are you okay?" he asked.

"Yes, David, what on earth's the matter?" Kate added.

I stood silently for a moment, with my eyes closed until the dizzy spell passed, and it was only when I opened them once again that a realization came over me. For some reason, a further degree of understanding of our situation had formed in my mind during those few moments of dizziness, as though my mind had opened up to receive the input of certain information to which it had previously been closed.

"I'm fine, thank you," I replied in response to their concerns. "I just felt dizzy for a few seconds. I'm okay now. This whole affair must be having a greater effect on me than I imagined. I'm beginning to act like a neurotic old lady."

"Not at all, David," said Forbes. "We're all in much the same state. I admit I'm terrified, and I don't mind admitting it."

"He's right, David," said Kate. "Perhaps you should sit down for a while, take the weight off your feet and maybe try to sleep for an hour or so."

"I don't think that would be a very good idea, Kate, do you?" I said, looking at her in a way I don't think I'd ever looked at Kate before.

Something was going on, something I didn't yet understand, but a sudden sense of something being not quite right had entered my head. Was it the result of the dizzy spell? Could I be imagining things, hallucinating perhaps? Kate and Forbes both looked quite different to me, the same and yet not quite the same as they had a few seconds previously. Their features appeared slightly blurred and indistinct. I shook my head, trying to clear it, thinking that my eyes had been affected by the dizziness. It didn't work. They remained just out of focus. I couldn't say why at the time, but I took the decision to say nothing to either of them and kept silent as I sat and allowed myself a few moments grace to try and recover my equilibrium.

"David, I said, are you alright?"

Kate's voice suddenly broke through into my head.

"Of course I am. Why, what's wrong?" I asked as I saw the worried look on her face.

"You've been sitting there in a trance-like state for the last ten minutes. Your eyes were open but you just seemed to ignore William and I when we spoke to you."

"Yes, we were beginning to worry about you," Forbes added.

I couldn't understand it. As far as I was aware, I'd just sat down on the sofa to clear my head. It appeared however that I'd just lost ten minutes of my life, if the others could be believed. I decided to bluff my way through things, not let on that I was worried myself about the occurrence, though indeed I most certainly was.

"I'm fine, really," I said. "I must have been daydreaming or something. I'm so sorry if I appeared rude. I think recent events are catching up with me. I suddenly feel very, very tired."

"That's understandable," said Forbes. "I'd say we're all pretty much worn out, eh, Kate?"

"Definitely," Kate replied.

"You're sure you're okay, David?" Forbes asked again, and I nodded.

"Let's get back to trying to solve this mystery we've got ourselves caught up in, shall we? If we're in danger, we must find a way to fight it."

"Bravo, David. That's the spirit," said Forbes. "Listen, why can't we simply make a run for it? You know, grab your boat and leave the island, head for the mainland. If those things are here, trapped in the croft perhaps, they may not be able to follow us over water. What d'you think?"

I looked at Kate. She appeared to hesitate for a few seconds and then replied to William's suggestion.

"It sounds a remarkably simple way of doing things, but you may have a point, William. You would have to understand though, David, that if we abandon your home and leave it to these entities, you could never return, for they would still be here, waiting to snare the unwary visitor and the whole thing might begin all over again. You'd have to place your island completely off-limits to visitors."

"Yes, something like the government did when they infected Gruinard Island with Anthrax back in the nineteen-forties," Forbes added.

"Er, that's all very well, but I don't have the power of the government to keep people away."

"No, David, but I'm sure we could think of some story that would satisfy people and maybe even convince the authorities to place Skerries Rock out of bounds to visitors."

"But, Kate, this is my home. Everything I own is here. This island is my living dream, and now you want me to simply abandon it and run away."

"Yes, I do, before your living dream becomes your own personal living hell!"

I had to admit she'd got a point.

"What about we try and get away, but come back better armed with experts who can maybe help us eradicate these 'entities?" I asked, eager to find a compromise solution.

"Look, I just want to get away, as fast and as far as possible," said Forbes, who now appeared totally absorbed by his own suggestion of a getaway from Skerries Rock. "Please, can't we at least try?"

Another ten minutes passed as the three of us argued the point until I agreed at last to attempt a return to the mainland later that afternoon. The others agreed to leave the future of Skerries Rock in my hands for the time being, after I agreed to consider their suggestion of a blanket ban on any and all visitors. I'd seen the sense of at least trying to prove to ourselves that we could indeed leave without carrying the entities with us. I'd asked Kate what we'd do if they did indeed manage to attach themselves to us or the boat, but she remained steadfastly in Forbes's corner, saying that we'd be no worse off than we now were, which I found a little odd, and more than a little suspicious. After all, hadn't we all previously agreed that we must not let these things, whatever they were, reach the mainland?

Ten minutes later, William Forbes and I made our way down to my boathouse, where we began fuelling up my boat. Forbes appeared relieved to be out of the house and in the open air, and I couldn't say that I blamed him. The problem, as far as I was concerned, was that something now seemed very wrong about the current situation. We were actively engaged in a plan that could well see the entity or entities currently plaguing us being unleashed on the unsuspecting population on the mainland. It appeared obvious to me that the unseen and evil malevolent force had but one goal, and that remained to inhabit the mind and body of a suitable host in order that it might continue its seemingly eternal killing crusade. The biggest mystery in my mind remained the fact that Kate's friend, Miles Prendergast, had asserted that Forbes was in no way related to the Cavendish family unless a tenuous link existed, extending perhaps from the family of the woman who'd given birth to the original Jack the Ripper, and whose name remained a mystery to us all. If Forbes was as Kate suggested, a conduit or means for the entity to reach the outside world, why direct him to visit me on the pretext of helping him to solve the mystery of his dreams and the apparent power contained within the page of the Ripper's journal? What the hell had I got to do with it all?

As the last of the required fuel dribbled into the boat's tank, a sudden wave of nausea swept over me. With the nausea, I experienced a light-headedness that made me begin to sway, and I must have appeared to Forbes much as a drunken man would.

"I say, are you okay, David?" he asked as my legs almost gave way and only a supreme effort on my behalf prevented me falling from the low boat dock into the cold dark seawater.

As suddenly at it had appeared, the nausea and dizziness left me and an odd sensation ran through my entire body. In those few moments a clarity of thought that had little do with my own thought processes gave me a sudden and very clear picture of everything that had taken place so far. An understanding that could only have come from another's mind coursed through me as a sense of all-pervading danger and imminent disaster took hold of me.

I turned to Forbes, about to shout a warning, but it came too late. He'd jumped into the boat, doing his best to help and hurry things along by disconnecting the fuel line from the engine inlet. It was the final act of his life.

The blinding flash that erupted from the engine compartment of the boat engulfed Forbes in one single horrifying sheet of flame. There was no explosion, just a sudden rush of sound followed by the glare of the flash and the awful sound of Forbes's agony as the angry flames consumed him where he stood. I ran to the wall of the boathouse where a fire extinguisher stood in its cradle, ready for use. Although it only took a matter of seconds for me to return to the boat with the extinguisher, the screams of the man in the boat seemed to go on for ever and ever. Such was the searing heat that emanated from the burning figure in front of me that my eyes felt as though they too were on fire. His clothes were gone, quickly eaten away by the angry tongues of flame. Forbes twisted and flailed as his flesh literally began to melt before my eyes. My nostrils filled with the sickening stench of burning flesh. I gagged at the smell. The screaming stopped as his throat filled with the flames that now grew in intensity, his bones cracking and shattering as they were consumed by the awesome power of the conflagration. As the burning wreck of what a few seconds before had been a living, breathing human being collapsed into nothing more than a pile of smoking ash on the deck of the boat I suddenly realised that not a single scorch mark, not a piece of equipment on the boat itself, or the deck where he'd stood had been affected by the fire. The only thing that had burned or been affected in any way was William Forbes.

I stood staring at the small pile of human ash that lay on the boat deck. Everything that Forbes had feared had come to pass in a few horrifying seconds. I felt a passing sense of guilt, though I now knew that there had been little I could have done to prevent the eventual demise of the man. He'd been exactly what Kate had said he was, a conduit, a vessel that had unwittingly allowed a fearful and terrible presence to enter the world once again. His job done, Forbes had been expendable. Why keep him alive when he filled no useful purpose as far as the entity was concerned?

I said a silent prayer for the departed soul of William Forbes. At least he was now at peace. He could no longer be harmed by any being, human or otherwise. His suffering had ended in a few terrible, pain wracked seconds. The boat remained in perfect working order, as the thing that had murdered Forbes intended. I now knew the truth, and it was time to put all my faith in the knowledge I'd gained. Within my heart, and deep inside my soul, the presence that had entered my mind during the two dizzy spells I'd experienced now filled me with hope. No longer an 'entity' as Kate might have called it, but a part of my inner core, I knew that together we had one more battle to fight. If we won, the terror would be over. If not, there was little hope for the immortal soul of Kate Goddard, or for mine!

THIRTY
REQUIEM

STUNNED by having witnessed the terrible and agonising death of William Forbes, though no longer surprised by what had taken place, I checked the boat was secure and then made my way back up to the path towards the croft. My jaw had set with a grim resolution to end the terror that had visited itself upon my home once and for all. In addition I knew that it would be my task, and that of the 'being' that had become my inner self, to rid the world of a creature that had terrorised generations.

The sky shone a clear light blue, in contrast to the deep blue-green of the ocean that met with it on the distant horizon. The day felt warmer than many in quite some time and the sunshine gave a false air of good cheer and bonhomie to the overall vista of Skerries Rock. There'd been nothing cheery however about the fate of poor Forbes.

Three-quarters of the way along the path, with the croft in clear view, I saw Kate, standing in the doorway, waving to me. I waved back. In a few seconds, I covered most of the short distance between us and Kate turned her back and walked ahead of me into the living room. I closed the door behind me as soon as I crossed the threshold. The atmosphere within the croft had again turned cold as the grave. In the hearth, the log fire burned brightly, its warmth somehow dissipating into nothingness, obliterated by the all-pervading chill. Kate stood in front of the grandfather clock, showing no sign that she felt the cold, as I expected. I wasted no time on pleasantries. The time had arrived to end this, once and for all.

"Why did you kill poor Forbes, Kate?"

She looked surprised for a second, and then her face adopted a look of total composure as she replied.

"You know?"

"I know enough."

"But how?"

"The second entity, the one you've been running from, or at least the thing inside you's been running from."

A wave of anger mixed with bewilderment spread across her face.

"The thing was in Forbes. I was sure of it."

"So if you'd known it was in me, you'd have killed me?"

"Of course."

"Who are you, really? I know you're still you, Kate, but what or who is that thing that's taken control of you?"

"You can call it Jack the Ripper if you like, David, but it's really been around so much longer. I tried to tell you earlier. It's an elemental being, a force we don't really understand. It's been here on Earth for centuries, trapped by the gravitational pull of our atmosphere. It would rather not be here but has no choice. It feeds on what we'd call negative emotions. The stronger the emotion, the longer it sustains itself. It's like a snake that can survive a whole year on one large meal, but in this case, it inhabits a new host every now and again and uses its human host to carry out a series of killings that enable it to feed off the fear, the terror and of course, the sport of the kill itself."

"That's bloody evil, through and through," I replied, though I already knew the truth of what she'd told me from the second entity that had lodged its essence within my mind.

"Of course, you'd think that, which is why that puny thing within you is trying to destroy me, thinking that if I'm gone, the entity within me will die too. It won't work, David. I warn you. It's stronger than all of us and can't be destroyed by any force here on Earth."

"You seem to be forgetting, Kate, that the second entity is not of this world either."

"I forget nothing, David. The thing housed within your body is a so-called 'Guardian', an elemental charged with tracking down and liquidating beings that have transgressed the inter-dimensional plain, and passed into worlds they should never have inhabited. It can never be as powerful as the soul of the 'Ripper' who now resides within me. He is too strong, too clever, and will not allow himself to be destroyed."

So, everything the entity that had entered my body during the first of my dizzy spells had implanted in my conscious mind had proved true. I'd doubted it at first, but had slowly grown to trust what it told me. Its telepathic power enabled it to speak to me without words, as thoughts implanted in my mind, so that it felt as if I was thinking its thoughts as it read mine. It provided me with a vision of the vast boundaries of space and time, a swirling mass of gaseous and half-real ephemera where beings devoid of corporal being resided in the vastness that stretched to infinity, far beyond human understanding. Such is that vastness that it had taken those in charge of protecting lesser species such as we on Earth over four hundred of our years to track the rogue being to Earth, yet even that was comparable to no more than a millisecond in their concept of time. At last, however, this guardian had found its quarry and had decided to use me, rather than Forbes, as the conduit for its destruction.

Forbes's mind had been too weak to carry within it the awesome mental power of the guardian. In so doing, it proved to me that Jack Reid had been an innocent bystander, no longer in control of his own mind and body, and the same must apply to Mark Cavendish and, God Forbid, to the original Jack the Ripper and those of his ancestors who'd also been chosen as hosts by this terrible being. I now knew that the thing within Forbes had been benevolent all along, though its various manifestations had scared the life out of us mere mortals as it struggled to gain release into our world in order to carry out its task. I still didn't know, however why the evil force that now resided within the Kate thing had come to choose the Cavendish family as its perennial hosts in the first place. The evil elemental had, all along, been contained within the pages of the journal, its last refuge after the death of its Victorian host and from there it had struck out at each of its new hosts over the last century. Even when the journal had been all but destroyed during Mark Cavendish's fateful trip to Poland enough remained for the being to remain hidden within that last page. It explained the eerie warmth that people had felt when they'd handled the page. It was, as some had thought, very much alive.

"So, 'Jack the Ripper' was as innocent as Jack Reid, and so many others. The thing you call an elemental controlled them all, and they had no way of stopping it?"

"Precisely. The first Cavendish to be controlled by the elemental was simply available at the time, and, after finding itself trapped on Earth, the being found it convenient to continue to use the future progeny of the family. They were easy to locate and control. They also possessed a certain gene structure that meant the being could inhabit their bodies for a long period of time without causing total mental and bodily breakdown of the host, as often happens when it comes into contact with humans."

"But Jack the Ripper was different, wasn't he? He tried to resist."

"Very clever, David. Yes, he did. He felt the presence of the being within him and tried all he knew to fight against it. His Victorian mind saw it as 'The Voices' He even turned to his pathetic natural father, Burton Cavendish for help. All Cavendish did was provide drugs to dull the man's brain, and they made it easier in reality for the being to maintain its hold on the weak-minded fool. Far from being the monster that history has painted him as, he did all he could to resist the mind control of the elemental and in fact could almost be described as doing all he personally could to stop the Ripper murders by fighting to retain his own mind, unsuccessfully of course."

A series of images and thoughts suddenly lanced into my mind. The guardian, whoever or whatever it was, communicated with me again and I saw the next avenue of the solution opening up before me. I knew I must be careful though. The thing within my friend Kate was undoubtedly clever, resourceful and had lived too long to be taken lightly.

"Why you, Kate? Why has it chosen you this time? You're not a male, or a Cavendish."

I was leading her and the thing on. I already knew what her answer would be, thanks to my new found source of intelligence.

"Oh, but I am, David, dear boy. The mother of the Ripper had other relatives of course and I'm simply the descendant of one the offshoots of that family. Miles Prendergast expressed surprised when he discovered my roots and I've sworn him to secrecy for the time being. I told him it's important, historically, for me to check certain facts, before he enters the relationship into his genealogical records. He'll never have chance to do so, of course. I'm afraid that Miles must meet with an unfortunate 'accident' soon after I leave Skerries Rock."

"Then of course, I can't allow you to leave."

"Bravely spoken, David, but you and that thing within you must know that you don't have the power to destroy me, or it."

"Ah, poor Kate. You also forget that the guardian in me is well aware of the one frailty in your new found 'friend'. I know about water, Kate."

For the very first time since my return to the croft, Kate's face bore a worried, uncertain look.

"What do you mean, water?"

"That thing within you has no body of its own. It also has an aversion to water. It can't simply fly over the sea back to the mainland. There is no water in the vast tracts of space these beings originate from, as you should know, Kate. Their life essence is only able to traverse bodies of water if they are contained within the corporeal body of their host. Burton Cavendish almost destroyed it when he threw his son's body into the Thames, but he was too late. The essence, guessing Cavendish's intentions, had already left the Ripper and implanted itself in the journal pages. All I have to do to stop it is to kill you!"

Kate screamed, her face a mask of contorted anger as the realisation of what I'd learned dawned upon her and on the thing within her. She flew at me in a rage that belied her age, though of course she now existed under the control of the evil malevolence that controlled her body and mind. Sadly for her, I stood ready for just such an onslaught. Pulling my hand from my pocket in less than a second, where it had rested throughout our conversation, I drew out and fired the small calibre pistol that I usually kept stored in the boat house. Even Kate and the thing inside her had no previous knowledge of it. The bullet struck her right in the heart, and she pitched forward, falling into my arms. I stepped back as her weight carried her onward and downwards and I gently laid her inert body on the floor. There'd been no time for sad goodbyes, or apologies. I released my hold on her and stepped back to look down at the lifeless body of my friend. I knew that deep within her, the malevolent and evil thing that had lived and cursed the Cavendish family for centuries would even now be trying to find a way to escape from her body and transfer itself to mine, but I had the protection of the guardian to shield me, and without a second's hesitation, I turned, and walked to the door of the croft, pausing only long enough to strike a match and set light to the heavy door curtain. The flames that quickly lanced up from the material would soon consume the room and anything within it.

I ran as fast as my legs would carry me towards the boathouse, tripping a couple of times along the way, but always managing to remain upright and on the move. The boat stood at the boathouse dock where I'd left it, the pile of ash that had once been William Forbes still lying where he'd been consumed by those awful flames. I soon had the engine running, and as I left my island home, I looked back just once to see the flames from my burning home stretching out their orange fingers towards the afternoon sky. Within two hours I'd tied the boat up beside the dock at Balnakiel and set foot once again on the mainland. I made straight for old Sandy McMurdo's place and found him, as usual, behind the counter of the emporium.

The look on his face as I rushed through the door of his establishment quickly told me that I must have presented a terrible sight.

"My God, Doctor Hemswell. What on earth has happened to you? You look terrible!"

"Thank God you're here, Sandy. Just call the police will you, please? They're dead, all dead," I blurted out, before collapsing from what I later learned had been deemed shock and exhaustion, right there, upon the floor of McMurdo's Emporium.

I woke up some time later, in the local hospital, with a police officer positioned in a plastic chair at the side of my bed. As soon as the man realised my eyes were open, he immediately rose from his chair, walked to the door of the room, opened it and called for assistance. A doctor and nurse quickly came in response to his call and I was soon being examined by the white-coated physician, who rapidly pronounced me to be relatively fit and healthy as far as he could ascertain. It was then that the police officer spoke into the radio mike attached to his uniform collar and a minute later two plain-clothes detectives entered the room.

After asking me to confirm my identity and as the doctor and nurse departed from the room the older and more senior of the two men spoke.

"Doctor Hemswell, it is my duty to place you under arrest for the wilful murders of William Forbes and Katherine Goddard."

As a look of total shock and disbelief spread across my face the detective continued by issuing the standard police caution and as soon as they could arrange it I was allowed to dress and soon found myself in the back of a police car being driven to an unknown destination for questioning. It was while I was sitting in the back of the car, my hands firmly cuffed to prevent any attempt at escape, that I realised the guardian had gone. I was alone in my own mind once again. Obviously his job done, he'd left me and departed for…for where? I knew I'd have a hard time explaining everything that had transpired since the arrival of William Forbes on Skerries Rock, but they'd have to believe me, wouldn't they? At least, I thought they would. I couldn't get that damn tune out of my head though. It stuck there all the time, playing over and over in my brain.

EPILOGUE

RAVENSWOOD SPECIAL HOSPITAL, JUNE 16TH. THE DIARY OF DOCTOR RUTH TRUMAN

I<small>T IS</small> an odd coincidence that placed David Hemswell in my care. After treating the notorious serial killer Jack Reid on both of the occasions he found himself here at Ravenswood, I now find myself as the physician in charge of treating the man who killed Reid's own legal representative and also one his own best friends in a strange and perplexing case that still has the police somewhat baffled. At his trial, Hemswell stuck to his outlandish story of elemental beings, demonic possession and some strange 'guardian' who helped him dispose of an evil being that had taken over the mind and body of his friend, Kate Goddard, after she, in turn, had murdered the unfortunate William Forbes by instigating some form of spontaneous human combustion to devour the poor man. Not one shred of evidence could be found to substantiate any part of his story. Hemswell insisted the police speak to Miles Prendergast, and a woman named Christine Westerman who he said could provide evidence that would support his tale. Prendergast was able to confirm only that Kate Goddard had contacted him on some genealogical maters and Christine Westerman confirmed that Goddard had approached her in an attempt to identify a piece of music that appeared to be connected to one of the victims of Jack the Ripper, but, apart from that, the notion that elemental beings from some undefined location in the emptiness of space remained just too fanciful to be taken seriously.

The result of the trial had an air of inevitability about it and it came as no surprise to anyone concerned with the case when Hemswell was committed to Ravenswood 'At Her majesty's Pleasure'. In other words, he received a mandatory life sentence behind the walls of this, the country's most secure psychiatric hospital. Only if he is one day considered cured of his illness and no longer a danger to society will David Hemswell be considered for release.

After nine months in my care here at Ravenswood, Hemswell continues to surprise me by refusing to accept responsibility for his crimes. I find it hard to accept that a man once regarded as one of the country's leading criminal psychologists sticks so rigidly to his unbelievable story and makes no attempt to rationalise his actions. Until he does, there appears little hope of me making much progress in his treatment.

Instead, David Hemswell continues to delude himself that he has in some way destroyed the being that was at one time Jack the Ripper, and at other times in history a killer just as bloody as the Whitechapel Murderer himself, and tells me often that he is satisfied with what he has achieved in his life, and that no one else now needs to suffer as others have over the centuries. He often sits in his room for hours on end, whistling to himself. He always whistles the same tune, an irritating little ditty that he describes, when asked, simply as the 'Requiem for the Ripper'. At present, I see little hope for Hemswell's future rehabilitation.

He receives an occasional visitor, who I have come to now quite well. Sandy McMurdo is the proprietor of the local store in the village of Balnakiel, where David Hemswell formerly bought most of the provisions for his home on his island home on Skerries Rock. At Hemswell's request, McMurdo has been legally appointed as his representative for all matters relating to Skerries Rock which he still owns of course. At Hemswell's request, Skerries Rock has been placed off-limits to all visitors with only McMurdo and his son allowed to set foot on the tiny island and then only to do whatever is necessary to keep Hemswell's home maintained in a habitable condition, ready for the day when my patient might be declared cured of his affliction and declared sane enough to go home. Signs have been erected around the little island, warning potential visitors that visitors are strictly prohibited, due to danger of poisoning. Barbed wire fencing reinforces the signs, and McMurdo and his son are diligent in their duties on behalf of their friend. According to Sandy McMurdo, at Hemswell's request he even keeps David's old grandfather clock wound and fully working during his weekly visits to the island. He jokes that the pendulum is the only thing that moves on the island. Sometimes, according to Sandy, by his own admission, he feels as though, somehow the old clock has a life of its own, and it's watching him...

Dear reader,

We hope you enjoyed reading *Requiem For The Ripper*. Please take a moment to leave a review, even if it's a short one. Your opinion is important to us.

Discover more books by Brian L Porter at https://www.nextchapter.pub/authors/brian-porter-mystery-author-liverpool-united-kingdom

Want to know when one of our books is free or discounted? Join the newsletter at http://eepurl.com/bqqB3H

Best regards,
  Brian L Porter and the Next Chapter Team

ABOUT THE AUTHOR

Brian L Porter is an award-winning author and dog rescuer whose books have also regularly topped the Amazon Best Selling charts, twenty-two of which have to date been Amazon bestsellers. The third book in his Mersey Mystery series, *A Mersey Maiden* was voted The Best Book We've Read All Year, 2018, by the organisers and readers of Readfree.ly.

Last Train to Lime Street was voted Top Crime novel in the Top 50 Best Indie Books, 2018. *A Mersey Mariner* was voted the Top Crime Novel in the Top 50 Best Indie Books, 2017 awards, and The Mersey Monastery Murders was also the Top Crime Novel in the Top 50 Best Indie Books, 2019 Awards. Meanwhile *Sasha, Sheba: From Hell to Happiness, Cassie's Tale* and *Remembering Dexter* have all won Best Nonfiction awards. Writing as Brian, he has won a Best Author Award, a Poet of the Year Award, and his thrillers have picked up Best Thriller and Best Mystery Awards.

His short story collection *After Armageddon* is an international bestseller and his moving collection of remembrance poetry, *Lest We Forget*, is also an Amazon best seller.

Rescue Dogs are Bestsellers!

In a recent departure from his usual thriller writing, Brian has written six bestselling books about the family of rescued dogs who share his home, with more to follow.

Sasha, A Very Special Dog Tale of a Very Special Epi-Dog is now an international #1 bestseller and winner of the Preditors & Editors Best Nonfiction Book, 2016, and was placed 7th in The Best Indie Books of 2016, and *Sheba: From Hell to Happiness* is also now an international #1 bestseller, and award winner as detailed above. Released in 2018, *Cassie's Tale* instantly became the best-selling new release in its category on Amazon in the USA, and subsequently a #1 bestseller in the UK. Most recently the fourth book in the series, *Penny the Railway Pup*, has topped the bestseller charts in the UK and USA. The fifth book in the series, the bestselling *Remembering Dexter* won the Readfree.ly Best Book of the Year 2019. The most recent addition to the series is *Dylan the Flying Bedlington*, already a #1 bestseller.

If you love dogs, you'll love these six illustrated offerings which will soon be followed by book 7 in the series, *Muffin, Digby, and Petal: Together Forever*

Writing as Harry Porter his children's books, *Wolf,* (Young adult) *Alistair the Alligator* and *Charlie the Caterpillar,* (Early readers) have achieved three bestselling rankings on Amazon in the USA and UK.

In addition, his third incarnation as romantic poet Juan Pablo Jalisco has brought international recognition with his collected works, *Of Aztecs and Conquistadors* topping the bestselling charts in the USA, UK, and Canada.

Many of his books are now available in audio book editions and various translations are available.

Brian lives with his wife, Juliet and a wonderful pack of nine rescued dogs.

His blog is at https://sashaandharry.blogspot.co.uk/

FROM INTERNATIONAL BESTSELLING
AUTHOR BRIAN L. PORTER

The Mersey Mysteries

A Mersey Killing

All Saints, Murder on the Mersey

A Mersey Maiden

A Mersey Mariner

A Very Mersey Murder

Last Train to Lime Street

The Mersey Monastery Murders

A Liverpool Lullaby

The Mersey Ferry Murders (Coming soon)

Thrillers by Brian L Porter

A Study in Red - The Secret Journal of Jack the Ripper

Legacy of the Ripper

Requiem for the Ripper

Pestilence

Glastonbury

Purple Death

Behind Closed Doors

Avenue of the Dead

The Nemesis Cell

Kiss of Life

Dog Rescue (Family of Rescue Dogs)

Sasha

Sheba: From Hell to Happiness

Cassie's Tale

Penny the Railway Pup

Remembering Dexter

Dylan the Flying Bedlington

Short Story Collection

After Armageddon

Remembrance Poetry

Lest We Forget

Children's books as Harry Porter

Wolf

Alistair the Alligator, (Illustrated by Sharon Lewis)

Charlie the Caterpillar (Illustrated by Bonnie Pelton)

As Juan Pablo Jalisco

Of Aztecs and Conquistadors

Many of Brian's books have also been released in translated versions, in Spanish, Italian and Portuguese editions.

Made in the USA
Monee, IL
22 July 2022